Murder Backstage

A *Murder, She Wrote* Mystery

OTHER BOOKS IN THE *Murder, She Wrote* SERIES

Manhattans & Murder

Rum & Razors

Brandy & Bullets

Martinis & Mayhem

A Deadly Judgment

A Palette for Murder

The Highland Fling Murders

Murder on the QE2

Murder in Moscow

A Little Yuletide Murder

Murder at the Powderhorn Ranch

Knock 'Em Dead

Gin & Daggers

Trick or Treachery

Blood on the Vine

Murder in a Minor Key

Provence—To Die For

You Bet Your Life

Majoring in Murder

Destination Murder

Dying to Retire

A Vote for Murder

The Maine Mutiny

Margaritas & Murder

A Question of Murder

Coffee, Tea, or Murder?

Three Strikes and You're Dead

Panning for Murder

Murder on Parade

A Slaying in Savannah

Madison Avenue Shoot

A Fatal Feast

Nashville Noir

The Queen's Jewels

Skating on Thin Ice

The Fine Art of Murder

Trouble at High Tide

Domestic Malice

Prescription for Murder

Close-up on Murder

Aloha Betrayed

Death of a Blue Blood

Killer in the Kitchen

The Ghost and Mrs. Fletcher

Design for Murder

Hook, Line, and Murder

A Date with Murder

Manuscript for Murder

Murder in Red

A Time for Murder

The Murder of Twelve

Murder in Season

Killing in a Koi Pond

Debonair in Death

Killer on the Court

Death on the Emerald Isle

Fit for Murder

Murder Backstage

A *Murder, She Wrote* Mystery

A NOVEL BY JESSICA FLETCHER & TERRIE FARLEY MORAN

Based on the Universal television series created by
Peter S. Fischer, Richard Levinson & William Link

BERKLEY PRIME CRIME
New York

BERKLEY PRIME CRIME
Published by Berkley
An imprint of Penguin Random House LLC
penguinrandomhouse.com

Library of Congress Cataloging-in-Publication Data

Names: Fletcher, Jessica, author. | Moran, Terrie Farley, author.
Title: Murder backstage / a novel by Jessica Fletcher & Terrie Farley Moran.
Description: New York : Berkley Prime Crime, 2024. |
Series: A Murder, She Wrote mystery |
"Based on the Universal television series created by
Peter S. Fischer, Richard Levinson & William Link."
Identifiers: LCCN 2023044552 (print) | LCCN 2023044553 (ebook) |
ISBN 9780593640753 (trade paperback) | ISBN 9780593640777 (ebook)
Subjects: LCSH: Fletcher, Jessica--Fiction. |
LCGFT: Detective and mystery fiction. | Novels.
Classification: LCC PS3552.A376 M84 2024 (print) |
LCC PS3552.A376 (ebook) | DDC 813/.54--dc23/eng/20231016
LC record available at https://lccn.loc.gov/2023044552
LC ebook record available at https://lccn.loc.gov/2023044553

Printed in the United States of America
1st Printing

Emelia, Billy, Katie, Madeline, Abby, Shane, and Juliet
Best grandchildren ever

Murder Backstage

A *Murder, She Wrote* Mystery

Chapter One

I was in the midst of writing a pivotal scene in my latest book, *When Margot Was Murdered*, so I simply ignored my ringing telephone. The book's protagonist, Luisa, Margot's best friend, over the course of the last two paragraphs had her "aha" moment and realized who the killer must be. She was about to devise a plan to trap the murderer when the phone's jangle brought me back to the dining room of my home in Cabot Cove, Maine, far from the book's location of Northwestern University in Evanston, Illinois.

I was able to ignore the ringing until the answering machine kicked in and I heard an unmistakable British accent with just a hint of London cockney calling my name. I dashed to the telephone and picked up the receiver before my favorite cousin, Emma Macgill, could complete her message and hang up.

"Hello, Emma. I'm here," I said.

"Jessica, is that you? I was about to ring off. I haven't called too early in the morning or too late in the evening, have I? You know I never can keep the time difference between our two countries straight." The words tumbled out fast and furious, a true reflection of Emma's animated personality. When we were children, at every family gathering Emma was always the one who led the rest of us in raucous games of Sheriff of Nottingham, Capture the Flag, and a few others that she invented on the spot.

"Emma, it's been such a long while, and your timing is perfect; it's nearly seven in the evening here, so I am guessing that it's close to midnight in London. You are in London?" Knowing that Emma's career as an actress had her traveling all over the globe, I could never be sure.

"Oh yes, dearie, I am. I was asked to fill in for Glory Adams when she, well . . . I am not sure how to make the truth sound believable, but I will give it a go. Everyone knows we actors wish one another good luck by saying 'Break a leg.' Well, Glory had the misfortune to break hers right on the stage of the Apollo Victoria Theatre in the middle of act two of that lovely new musical by Carlton Craig." Emma's slight giggle let me know that there was some better news to follow.

"I can tell you I was proper chuffed when Carlton himself called and asked me to take on the role. With less than a week's rehearsal, I took over from the understudy, who I thought was doing rather a nice job but the producers didn't agree, so here I am." Emma sounded as proud as she rightfully should. Carlton Craig was the most highly acclaimed composer and lyricist in London's West End, which, in turn, was the most celebrated theater district in all of Europe.

"That sounds like quite an honor, and I am certain you are a smashing success," I said.

Emma surprised me with her reply. "The audiences seem to think so. Their response has been extraordinarily kind at every performance. The past eight weeks have been grand, but . . . let's just say I wasn't entirely comfortable playing a role that wasn't actually mine, so it was somewhat of a relief when Glory called Carlton to tell him that her surgeon and her physical therapist have both pronounced her fit to return to the stage. She will take back the role next week." Emma sounded quite relieved.

"How nice that she has healed so quickly," I said. "Is it possible that you will have some free time on your hands? If so, I hope you are thinking of coming to Cabot Cove for a bit of rest and recuperation. We haven't seen each other in ages, and I am very close to finishing my latest book. We would have plenty of time to catch up. And I can assure you that Seth Hazlitt and my other friends would be delighted to see you again."

"Close enough. I am flying across the Atlantic, and I have high hopes we can organize a get-together even though I won't be landing anywhere near Cabot Cove, worst luck. Wait until you hear my latest news. You'd have to have been living under a rock for decades and decades if you've never heard of Derek Braverman," Emma said, but there was still a touch of uncertainty in her voice.

"Heard of him? Emma, of course I have. Who on earth hasn't? Derek Braverman has been a major entertainer for at least forty years. He acts, he sings, he dances, and he has won numerous awards for his work in theater, movies, and television. Not to mention he's achieved great notoriety for his off-camera escapades. And he appeared to enjoy every moment of those antics." I truly hoped that Emma hadn't gotten involved in any escapades, so I stopped there, curious to hear whatever news she had that involved Derek Braverman.

"Well, Derek has just celebrated his eightieth birthday and has decided to retire, but before he does, he wants to star in a good old-fashioned revue, because it was in musical revues that he got his start in the industry. You'll remember the type of stage show I mean—lots of singing and dancing, with skits aplenty, not to mention a magician and a comic or two. I believe in bygone America, shows similar to our revues were called vaudeville. He's arranged for two months of performances at the Northern Alberta Jubilee Auditorium in his hometown of Edmonton, which is the capital of Canada's province of Alberta. I can tell you that I was absolutely gobsmacked when he invited me to costar."

"Emma, that is marvelous. If he wants his final show to be memorable, he certainly made a wise choice in selecting you." Knowing her as I did, I was sure my cousin would add the pizzazz that the aging lothario would need in order to wow the audience with a lively show.

"Jessica, it is all turning up roses. With Glory coming back to take her rightful place here in London, I will have time to take a few days' holiday in sunny Spain, and when I get home, Alan Hughes, who has long been Derek's favorite director, will be sending scripts around for us to preview and make a suggestion or two. Alan is pushing to have rehearsals start in a jiffy." Emma paused for a breath.

"Oh, Emma, this all sounds very exciting. Do you think you will have time to stop by Cabot Cove so we could have a short visit on your way to or from Canada?" I asked.

"I have a much better plan, Jessica. Since Maine is so close to Canada, why don't you come to Edmonton toward the end of rehearsals and stay through opening night? Bring a friend or two if you like. I've been told a local hotel has a block of rooms for the cast and our guests. The Hugheses are far too miserly to pay for your rooms, but I promise you will get the best rate possible."

"The Hugheses? You mentioned Alan, the director, and . . . ?"

"And his wife, Rosalie, who, as the major investor in the show, wears the title of producer like a crown. What do you say, Jessica? Do you want to slip over the border to Edmonton, and we can have a proper visit with a bit of fun thrown in?"

"It does sound delightful, but from here on Maine's Atlantic coast, 'slipping over the border' is likely to be a three-hundred-mile car ride to Quebec. Edmonton is so far west that traveling there would add a couple of thousand miles to the trip, which would have to be by airplane." I sounded hesitant even to my own ears.

"Jessica, once I am in Edmonton, I'll be closer to you than I am right now, and we'll be on the same continent. It would be a shame not to take advantage. And I will be there for a good while, so if the days I suggest don't work for you, we can choose some others." Emma's enthusiasm was fast becoming contagious. "Besides, you did say you are nearly done writing your latest mystery."

Well, she had me there. "When did you say you would be arriving in Edmonton?"

She mentioned a date and said, "If you could come about two weeks later, I would make sure to have some free time, and you could enjoy the glamour of attending Derek Braverman's final opening night. And I wouldn't mind if you asked your doctor friend, Seth Hazlitt, to join us. I haven't seen him in ever so long. In fact, invite whoever you like. 'The more the merrier' has always been my motto."

I laughed. "Emma, you make this get-together sound utterly doable. Give me a day or so to check with my editor and my publicist to make sure my schedule is clear. And I will definitely talk to Seth."

"As soon as I ring off this call, I will email you all the details. Do try. It's been ages and ages since we had a good laugh about old times."

"You mean like the time you crept into Uncle Gerard's bedroom and put a frog under his pillow?" I laughed at the memory of our fastidious uncle standing in the upstairs hallway, bellowing, "Whichever child put this slimy toad in my room will be made to cook it and eat it. Come stand here, all of you, until the guilty one confesses."

"Poor old Gerard. Always such an easy target. Now, you go finish whatever it is you are working on so that we can have our chats in person ever so soon," Emma said, and disconnected the call.

I was so looking forward to the possibility of a vacation that would involve spending time with dear Emma and seeing her on the stage once again that the following morning the first thing I did was email my agent and the appropriate personnel at my publisher's to verify that my professional schedule would be clear for a nice leisurely trip to western Canada.

It was a lovely crisp morning, which seemed to promise a cloudless day ahead, so I took my bicycle out of the shed and pedaled over to the wharf, where I planned to meet Seth for breakfast at Mara's Luncheonette. I couldn't wait to tell him that we'd received an invitation to visit with my cousin Emma and see Edmonton, a place I'd never visited although I'd long heard it was a vibrant, entertaining city.

I slid my bicycle into the nearly full bike rack. At this hour, I knew that meant Mara's would be crowded with locals enjoying coffee and conversation. Sure enough, when I opened the door, the aroma of fresh-brewed coffee and the crackle of sizzling bacon was nearly overshadowed by lively conversations bouncing off all four corners of the dining room.

Mara, who was at the register making change for a couple of fishermen, gave me a brief wave and pointed toward the middle of the room, where I saw my friends were chatting away while feasting on Mara's award-winning blueberry pancakes. Cabot Cove's favorite doctor and my longtime friend, Seth Hazlitt, was sharing a table with two of my other good friends, our town sheriff, Mort Metzger, and Dan Andrews, the editor of the *Cabot Cove Gazette*. There was an empty chair waiting for me.

Chapter Two

"Ayuh, good morning, Jess. Is the book you are working on finally finished?" Seth asked as he pulled the chair away from the table and I sat down.

"It's not quite finished, but I made a breakthrough yesterday, and I am confident that I will be able to send it to my publisher with time to spare." I nodded to Mara, who'd come to the table, coffeepot in hand.

While she filled my cup and topped off Mort's, Dan said, "That must be a great 'mission accomplished' kind of feeling."

"No more so than the feeling you must have when you finish an excellent story that gets the *Gazette* readers all stirred up. For example, just the other day when I was having my hair cut at Loretta's Beauty Parlor, your article about the state highway commission reviewing plans to update that interchange on Route 130 was all anyone could talk about. Eve Simpson is terribly excited and thinks it would be a great opportunity for her to sell off that land the Meyers family lets lie fallow just north of the highway."

Dan turned slightly pink and said, "On the other hand . . . and I know there is always an 'other hand.'"

I laughed. "On the other hand, Ideal Molloy said she is sick and tired of all this construction of roads and buildings. She would like Cabot Cove and the surrounding area left just as they are."

"And there you have the difference between your writing and mine," Dan said. "Your readers want your hero or heroine to find the culprit and ensure that justice is served, while my readers have varying opinions as to what is right and what is wrong. And no matter how straightforward I make my presentation of the facts, there is always someone writing a letter to the editor accusing me of bias."

"That hokum and bunkum goes with every job. If I had a nickel for every time I had to listen to a citizen berate me because one of my deputies gave them a speeding ticket that the citizen thinks wasn't justified because there was no traffic or some such nonsense, I could've retired a long time ago." Mort Metzger laughed.

Mara, who had stood patiently by during our banter, coffeepot in hand, said, "My line of work is much easier. I simply say, 'If you don't like the food, I suggest you don't bother coming back.'"

We all laughed. And I said, "Mara, I can't imagine any person not liking whatever comes out of your kitchen. Speaking of food, could I have one blueberry pancake and one boiled egg?"

"No short stack of pancakes for you today, Jessica?" Mara asked, sounding more curious than miffed.

"Unfortunately, I know I am going to be glued to my computer chair for the next few days, so I have to be careful about what I eat. Hopefully it will be no time at all until I can rejoin the short-stack crowd."

Mara refilled coffee cups all around and then said she'd be back in a flash with my breakfast.

"Well, Jess, I must say you look extremely chipper for a writer who is heading down the path to deadline. Ofttimes this close to submitting a book, you are more than slightly worn, but today you seem downright perky. Is your editor going on vacation? Or did you get an extension of some sort?" Seth asked.

"I received a phone call from one of my cousins last night that buoyed my spirits. I have some really exciting news to share."

Three sets of eyes turned toward me expectantly.

"My cousin Emma, who is an English actress," I explained for Dan's sake, since I knew he'd never met her and he might never have heard me speak of her, "called last night to let me know she will be flying over to North America quite soon . . ."

Seth interrupted. "Mort, you remember Emma, don't you? She's the cousin who could be Jessica's twin except that Emma has bright red hair and a funny British accent that I find highly entertaining. And some of the phrases she uses! If you say something she doesn't believe, Emma will never hesitate to tell you, 'That's a load of tosh.'"

Mort nodded and began to answer, but I cut him off. I didn't mind if he agreed with Seth about Emma's language, which I admit is quite colorful, but I was determined to immediately squash any twin talk.

"Oh, Seth, I admit there is certainly a family likeness, but I think 'twins' is carrying it a bit too far," I protested.

"That's because the two of you see each other, while the rest of us look at the two of you sitting or standing side by side. The first time I met Emma, I found the resemblance downright jarring until I got used to it." Seth was not at all subtle about correcting me, and once he did so, he changed the subject. "So, tell me, when can we expect Emma to visit us here in Cabot Cove?"

As soon as I said, "Unfortunately, Cabot Cove is not on her agenda," Seth dropped his head a few inches to hide his frown.

I knew I could cheer him instantly. "Seth, don't look so dejected. You have a personal invitation from Emma to join me in visiting her in Edmonton, Alberta, Canada, where she will be performing with Derek Braverman in a musical revue. She told me he claims to be retiring and wants his final stage performance to be an old-fashioned song-and-dance revue in a theater in his hometown. He telephoned Emma and invited her to be his co-star," I said.

"Derek Braverman! Remember *The Red Lagoon*? He played some sort of avenging angel, spent half the movie singing about justice and the rest of the movie slicing villains to pieces with seventeenth-century swords." Mort thrashed the air with an imaginary sword. "I must have watched it a hundred times when I was a kid."

Dan Andrews laughed. "In my neighborhood, most of the boys wanted to be Braverman. During mock battles, we drove the opposition crazy by drowning out their Superman chants with a chant of our own: 'It's a blade; it's a grenade; it's Braverman.' And then we'd charge across the playground, with toy guns and plastic swords at the ready."

"What was the name of that sandy-colored palomino Braverman rode when he starred in the television show *Settle the West*?

I always insisted that a stuntman did all that trick riding and fence jumping, but my brother was Braverman all the way." Seth rubbed his neck and got that faraway look that I frequently noticed when he talked about his childhood.

"Golden Boy. Man, that horse was a beauty," Mort said. "I am on your side about the stuntman, Doc. No way an actor could have pulled off all those tricks. It would take a trained rodeo rider to get a horse to do all that swimming across rivers, kneeling to pick up Braverman when he was hurt, not to mention those fancy cliff jumps. Now that I think about it, I bet Golden Boy had a stunt double too."

"Wouldn't surprise me, valuable horse like that," Seth said.

"And does anyone recall Braverman's real name?" Dan asked.

"Derek Braverman is his real name," Mort said.

"Are you sure? I seem to remember two boys a couple of grades ahead of me in school having a battle behind the gymnasium because one kept insisting that Derek Braverman's real name was so stupid that he made up the name Braverman because he wanted to sound 'way cool.' When he said it for the third time, the other boy swung a fist at him and the fight was on, at least until Sister Deirdre grabbed each of them by the neck and hustled them into the principal's office," Dan said.

"And they were never seen again. The dreaded principal's office. I was there more than a time or two. It never ended well." Mort gave an exaggerated shudder, causing us all to laugh.

I hadn't noticed Mara standing by. She set my plate in front of me and signaled an offer of refills with the coffeepot in her other hand. "Sheriff, it's a good thing that principal knew her business and moved you to the right side of the law, or else think where you might be today. More coffee, anyone?" Mort and I both held up our cups, and when she filled mine, Mara said, "So I guess you'll soon be off on another adventure. As I recall, that cousin of yours is a spunky one—always an eye toward fun and filled with energy."

Obviously, she had been listening to our conversation for a good few minutes. "That describes Emma to a tee," I said.

"And she was great for business. I remember one time the two of you were having lunch here when Isabella Batson's little boy, Tommy, barely more than a toddler at the time, had a complete meltdown right over at that table." She pointed off to our left. "Totally embarrassed, Isabella was doing her best to gather up her son and head for the door, but your cousin intervened."

"Yes, she did. I remember it well. Emma sang 'London Bridge' and pantomimed the falling bridge. Then she did an exaggerated curtsy when she sang the last three words, 'my fair lady.' Tommy giggled and said, 'Again.' Emma replied, 'Only if you help out,' and Tommy surprised us all by doing just that. After their duet was over, Tommy went back to his grilled-cheese sandwich as if he hadn't been mid-tantrum a bare ten minutes earlier." I laughed at the memory.

"That's right, and everyone in the place clapped and cheered. It was the talk of the lunch crowd for the next few weeks. Plenty of customers came in and asked me what time the next show started or did they miss the curtain call, everyone with a grin. Like I said, having your cousin here was good for business." And as if the word "business" reminded her that we, too, were customers, Mara asked if we wanted anything else, and when no one did, she left our checks on the table and moved along with her coffeepot.

"If you're going to meet your cousin Emma, it sounds like

you'll have an enjoyable time," Dan said. "So exactly when are you leaving?"

"Well, I have to finish my book and Emma has to get her schedule nailed down, but I am going to stop by to see Susan Shevlin on my way home to get some information on traveling from here to Edmonton. I am sure there will be multiple flight transfers involved."

"Ayuh, *we* can expect a long day of travel." Seth gave me a wink and a nod. "But seeing Emma again will be worth it."

Delighted that Seth had agreed to come along to Edmonton without my having to listen to all his usual hemming and hawing before he made a decision, I left Mara's and biked over to Susan Shevlin's office. Not only was she a good friend and the wife of Cabot Cove's mayor, Jim Shevlin; Susan was an excellent travel agent, who'd rescued me more than once when my travel plans unraveled at the last minute. No matter what happened to trample my schedule, no matter where in the world I was, Susan could always orchestrate a change of route that suited my needs.

When I walked into her office, Susan was on the phone, but she waved me to come and sit by her desk. She hung up the phone and raised a finger in the universal "give me a minute" signal before tapping a few words on her computer keyboard. Then she leaned back in her chair, closed her eyes, and said, "Sorry about that, Jessica, but it has turned out to be an extremely busy day, and, as you can see, I am all alone. Nancy had a dental emergency, something about a cap loosening during dinner last night. Every time she takes a day off, it reminds me how valuable her assistance is when she is here. Now"—she opened her eyes, moved forward, and folded her hands on the desktop—"how can I help you today?"

I opened my purse and pulled out a copy of the email Emma sent me after our phone conversation, passed it to Susan, and explained that Seth and I were planning on joining Emma in Canada, but we didn't have travel dates certain as yet.

"That is definitely not a problem. Look at this. Your cousin has included airport and hotel information, as well as car service provided by the hotel. There is also a list of tourist attractions and restaurants. She really wants you to visit! And as soon as we have definite dates, I will make that visit a reality. In the meantime, I will call Mary Jo Simard—who, according to your cousin, is the hospitality liaison at the hotel—and get a feel for what I am sure will be a fun and exciting vacation for you and Seth. Speaking of, do you want adjoining rooms?"

"That's not necessary, but rooms on the same floor would be convenient. I'll let you get back to work, and as soon as I get any concrete information from Emma regarding dates, I will be sure to let you know." I stood. "And please tell Nancy I hope her dental problems were easily solved."

As I rode my bicycle into my backyard, I could hear my telephone ringing. I hurried inside but was too late to answer. Mort's vivacious wife, Maureen, left a message asking me to call back when convenient because she had some questions about my trip to Canada. Never let it be said that news doesn't travel fast in Cabot Cove. I put the kettle on the stove, fixed myself a cup of tea, and settled down at the kitchen table, telephone in hand. Judging by the excitement in Maureen's voice, I had a feeling that once I spoke to her, one of us would have to call Susan Shevlin.

Chapter Three

Maureen answered on the first ring. "Jessica, you are a speedy one. I barely hung up the phone, and here you are calling me back."

"Well, I have been so busy trying to wrap up my latest book, I am afraid that I have been neglecting my friends, so when I got your message, I thought it best to return your call at once."

Maureen was so lively and cheerful that even when I am in that "all is hopeless" malaise that seems to affect every author at one or more points in the writing process, just the sound of her voice could make me smile.

"Here is the thing, Jess, and believe me I won't be mad if you say no, but well, I happened to call Mort earlier, and he mentioned that you had finally come out of your writer cave for a group breakfast at Mara's. Believe me, he sounded mega-excited when he told me about your trip to Canada to visit your cousin who is starring with Derek Braverman. He kept saying, 'And just think, besides seeing him live onstage, Jessica and Seth will actually get to meet him in person.' I can tell you that Mort's been over the moon about Derek Braverman since childhood."

"I certainly got that impression. Mort, Dan, and even Seth had a grand time dredging up memories of swords and horses, while I confess, I am more likely to reminisce about his song-and-dance movies. My favorite was *The Happiest Springtime*, closely followed by *Sing the Day Away*."

"Oh, those musicals were perfect entertainment. I swooned when, in *The Happiest Springtime*, Derek slid off his horse, miraculously landed on one knee in front of his pretty blond costar, whipped a ring box from his pocket, and proposed, all while singing a love ballad. What was that song? Oh, I remember; it was the one about wanting to sprinkle diamonds in her hair." Maureen sighed. "So romantic."

"It was that and more," I agreed. "Derek has had quite a career, and according to my cousin Emma, he is planning on ending it with a grand flourish."

"That's why I called. I have been pushing Mort to take a vacation. You know, Jessica, he works so hard. And when he started talking about your trip, it got me wondering if we could tag along . . ."

"Say no more," I answered. "I think that is a grand idea. I am not sure why I didn't think to invite you."

"Probably because you don't live with Mort. Lately I have been watching him come home exhausted every night. And whenever he has an extremely tough case, he winds up tossing and turning sleeplessly in bed. I need to get him away from crime and criminals for a while."

I couldn't help but laugh. "I am just finishing months of

writing a murder mystery, so I know exactly what you mean. Why don't you call Susan Shevlin and have her add you to our travel plans."

"I will. But first I better tell Mort. He'll go into shock, stammer about how he can't take time off just now, but you and I both know he will," Maureen said, followed by her signature giggle; then she went on. "Thanks for letting us impose, Jessica. You are a great friend."

"It's no imposition at all. I am sure that, as my cousin Emma would loudly declare, all of us together will have a cracking good time," I said right before I hung up. I made a note to check in with Susan in a day or so to be sure she'd added the Metzgers to my travel plans, and I went right to my computer to work on the loose ends of my manuscript.

Three weeks later on a cloudy gray morning, Demetri, co-owner of our local taxi service, pulled up to my front gate in a shiny blue Subaru Forester, with Seth sitting directly behind him. As Demetri was putting my luggage neatly in the trunk beside Seth's over-large suitcase, Maeve O'Bannon, my neighbor, pushed through her front gate and came over to give me a brief hug.

"Now you go and enjoy your trip to the far reaches of Canada. Edmonton, is it? I will take care of everything hereabouts. You needn't worry at all. I have things well under control. And I will be free of wondering what you are up to, because you're traveling with our best doctor should you stub your toe or get bitten by a bug. And with the good sheriff and his wife along, I don't have to worry about your getting up to any sort of mischief, do I?" Maeve chuckled, waved to Seth, then turned and disappeared back into her own yard.

Seth gave me a broad smile as I climbed into the seat next to him and fastened my seat belt. "Here we go, Jess. I can't remember when I have felt this good about taking a little time for myself. I am looking forward to seeing western Canada, to spending time with Emma—she is always great company—and, most of all . . ."

"Most of all, meeting Derek Braverman," I said, finishing his sentence.

Seth laughed. "Well, I intended to say 'having a relaxing time with you and Mort without a dead body in sight,' but, I admit, meeting Derek Braverman is going to add spice to our adventure."

In the front seat, Demetri was talking over the radio to his business partner and cousin, Nick. When he hung the radio back on its receiver, he said, "We are right on time. Nick has the sheriff and his wife in his cab, so we should all arrive at Cabot Cove airport with time to spare."

We pulled into the airport parking lot directly behind Nick's car. I was barely out of Demetri's Subaru when Maureen rushed toward me with open arms and swept me into a hug. "Jessica, I can't thank you enough for allowing us to join you on this vacation of a lifetime. Why, Mort is so excited, I actually caught him in front of a mirror last night practicing saying hello to Derek Braverman."

Maureen didn't realize Mort had come up behind her. "And I'm not embarrassed to admit it. Good morning, Mrs. F. Where's . . . oh, there he is. Hey, Doc, I'm sure you feel as skittish as I do."

Seth surprised me by saying, "Skittish as a newborn calf." As he and Mort shook hands, they started, as they'd done at Mara's a few weeks before, to recount their Derek Braverman fanboy stories.

Nick and Demetri piled our suitcases onto a luggage cart while I gave the tall young porter, whose badge said his name was Clancy, our flight information.

He smiled. "Yes, ma'am. You must be the group heading off to Canada to meet Derek Braverman. Jed Richardson told us all about it during the morning travel briefing. Any chance you could bring back autographed pictures?"

Although the thought of asking the famous actor for an autograph had never entered my head, I replied, "We'll do our best."

As he handed me my luggage receipt, Clancy said, "And you are flying in style today. Jed recently bought himself a brand-spanking-new Beechcraft Bonanza G36—it is the queen of the air when it comes to six-seaters. You'll be having a true luxury ride down to Boston. And I am proud to say that you all are the first passengers Jed is flying in his new beauty."

Seth had come up beside me and shook his head vigorously. "I can't say I like that. I'd rather ride in a plane that's been in the air for a while. Made other trips. Known to be safe."

Clancy laughed. "You needn't worry. Besides the fact that Jed is a top-rated pilot, he's taken the plane for cargo trips as far as Ontario and back, so he knows how to handle it. And after seeing today's weather report, I can promise you a smooth, safe ride."

The interior of Jed's new plane was elegant blue and gray with touches of red. And Jed beamed when we all complimented him on how roomy and comfortable the seats were.

In no time at all we were in Boston and hurrying to our Air

Canada flight that would take us to Toronto Pearson Airport for a layover before our final flight to Edmonton.

Toronto Pearson was a spotless modern airport, and bright sunshine flooded through the high, wide windows of Terminal One. There were a number of restaurants to choose from, and we decided on a not overly crowded café with a modern look.

A pert brunette hostess dressed in navy blue pants and a light blue shirt, which seemed to be the uniform of the restaurant's staff, greeted us at the door. "*Bonjour.* Good day." And when we replied in English, she continued. "Party of four. Would you like a table by the window?"

Mort and Seth answered simultaneously, "Yes, we would."

Seth followed with, "Can we see the planes take off and land?"

The hostess nodded. "Yes, you can, although not so many this time of day. Still, I am sure you will see quite a few."

As she led us toward the windows, she picked up a bright blue bowl filled with odd-colored potato chips. I thought they must be barbecue, not my favorite, but if everyone else was as hungry as I was, I suspected the bowl would be emptied rather quickly.

The hostess ushered us into a silver-gray booth and placed the bowl of chips in the center of the table with a flourish as she said, "Enjoy."

Mort pulled a couple of chips from the blue bowl and said, "I'll be the taste tester. Mmm. That's good, but I am not exactly sure . . ."

"Those are Toronto's own specialty, ketchup chips, and I am Jacques, your server this afternoon." A sandy-haired young man, dressed in the same blue uniform as the hostess, flashed us a bright smile and handed us each blue-covered menus. "May I ask if you are visiting Toronto?"

Seth shook his head. "Perhaps another time. Today we are heading to Edmonton and are fortunate enough to have time between planes for a decent meal."

"Ah, then I must point out that ketchup chips are not the only dish that makes Toronto the foodie capital of Canada." Jacques was clearly in his glory as he prepared to introduce visitors to his favorite cuisine. "Let me introduce you to *nourriture délicieuse* that, while you may find it elsewhere, will never satisfy as it does here in Toronto."

"You mean like poutine? We have that back home in Maine. One of my deputies eats it all the time," Mort said.

"Even so, nowhere will you find any with the flavor you will find here. We enjoy vinegar in our gravy," Jacques said with great authority. "There are several local specialties that I highly recommend, particularly the peameal bacon sandwich, or a hearty tourtière."

Jacques grinned at the blank looks on our faces. "Peameal bacon is what you as Americans call Canadian bacon, dredged in cornmeal and fried. You may enjoy the sandwich any way you like, but I recommend you order it all dressed, which includes peameal bacon, mayonnaise, cheese, lettuce and tomato on a hearty bun, your choice of sourdough, whole wheat, or plain."

Mort rubbed his hands together and said, "That sounds terrific, but what was that other dish you mentioned?"

"Tourtière is a tasty French Canadian dish. Spiced meat, potato, and onion wrapped and baked in a pastry crust. You will love the combination of clove, nutmeg, and cinnamon that together give the meat pie a glorious aroma to match its delicious flavor," Jacques said. "But please take a moment to look at your menus. And I will be happy to answer any questions you may have."

He busied himself filling our water glasses.

My palate was intrigued by the idea of the spices combined with meat and vegetables in the tourtière, and nothing on the menu tempted me to change my mind. Seth joined me, while, as I thought he might, Mort opted for the peameal bacon sandwich. And Maureen surprised us all by ordering a smoked-meat sandwich from the menu after Jacques assured her it was made with prime brisket.

As Jacques set off for the kitchen with our orders, a plane came in for a landing just outside our window, attracting everyone else's attention while mine was captured by a small white placard in the center of the table with the heading *Lester B. "Mike" Pearson.* It explained that the airport was named for Pearson, a native of Montreal, who became the fourteenth prime minister of Canada. He also won the Nobel Peace Prize when he organized the United Nations Emergency Force in response to the Suez Canal Crisis.

I passed the card to Seth, who was always interested in local history wherever he traveled, and by the time Jacques came back with our food, Seth was using his cell phone to search Mike Pearson and regaling us with snippets of Canadian history.

Chapter Four

Our flight from Pearson to Edmonton lasted just over four hours and was a fairly smooth ride, although a few minutes of turbulence about halfway through briefly jarred Seth from his post-meal nap.

Since Mort and Maureen were seated a few rows in front of us, I was happy to use the quiet time to read a Mary Higgins Clark book that had been waiting for me to finally send *When Margo Was Murdered* to my editor. As always when I read her books, by the time I reached the story's end I was convinced that I still had much to learn about writing mysteries.

The pilot's announcement that we should buckle up, as the plane was about to descend, woke Seth, who immediately began to tell me he hadn't slept at all; he'd merely been resting his eyes. Once the plane was on the ground, we gathered our things and thanked the flight attendants before we deplaned. Mort and

Maureen were waiting for us at the bottom of the Jetway, but a woman stepped in front of them and thrust a pen at me.

I was puzzled for a moment until she said, "J. B. Fletcher. You are J. B. Fletcher, the mystery writer, aren't you?"

I nodded. I'd learned not long after my third book, *A Faded Rose Beside Her*, was published that readers do, in fact, pay attention to the author's picture on the book cover, and they show up asking for signatures at the oddest times and in the oddest places. "I am Jessica Fletcher. May I help you?"

She opened a book she had under her arm—it was a copy of *Yours Truly, Damian Sinclair*—and asked, "Would you mind terribly?"

I took her pen, and for a moment I was tempted to write *Yours Truly, Damian Sinclair*; instead, I wrote *Enjoy* and signed my name.

She thanked me and went on her way.

As the four of us followed the signs to the baggage carousels, Maureen said, "Wow. Does being approached out of the blue like that ever get annoying?"

I thought for a moment. "She bought the book and she recognized me. In my profession, that deserves a signature."

As it turned out, we didn't need to remember that our luggage would eventually be circling on carousel two because as soon as we entered the baggage area, I heard my name shouted in a broad English accent. My cousin Emma was waving three small brightly colored national flags, one for England, one for Canada, and the Stars and Stripes for the United States.

She rushed toward us, and when she flung her arms around me, the flags nearly poked Seth. Fortunately, he ducked out of the way. Then Emma slipped her arm through mine and began to sing, "The Macgill cousins are arm in arm" to the tune of "Happy Days Are Here Again." Then she gave me a kiss. "Oh, Jessica, we are going to have such a grand time."

A second later she turned to Seth. "And there you are, Doctor, handsome as ever. Isn't it a lucky girl who gets to have you come flying across a continent for a visit? Do us a favor, deary. Round up the baggage tickets and give them to Wyatt so he can get everything to the car." She pointed to the porter standing by patiently.

Before Seth had a chance to respond, Emma had moved on. "Do I recall seeing this man in a dashing uniform, wearing a gun and a badge? I suppose the appropriate greeting is 'Howdy, Sheriff.'" She reached to shake Mort's hand. "And here we have another redhead, although I see you are a bit more coppery than I am. Well, I suppose I can take the competition if you can." And Emma reached in to kiss Maureen on the cheek.

Since it felt like we'd been traveling from dawn to dusk, I was surprised to see the sun still in the sky as we walked out of the airport, until I remembered we'd flown from the eastern time zone, through the central time zone, and into the mountain time zone. As is my habit when traveling, I always keep my wristwatch on Cabot Cove time. It gives me the cozy feeling that home is waiting for my return. I only needed to remember to subtract two hours each time I looked at it.

Emma slid her arm through mine as we walked. "It is such a treat to have you here. I can't wait for us to have a proper cuppa and an ever-so-long chin-wag. I still have rehearsals, and that silly director, Alan Hughes, is being an absolute annoyance, running the same scenes over and over again with minor script changes, but I promise we'll have plenty of time for fun. And here's Rob Langford. You'd all best introduce yourselves, as he will be available to drive you around Edmonton during your stay."

Rob, a middle-aged man with a neatly trimmed white chin-strap beard, stood by a silver-gray limousine and touched his cap in a light salute as he held the passenger door open.

Rob and Wyatt, who'd followed along behind us, settled the luggage in the trunk after we'd all piled into the spacious interior of the limo. The seats were gray plush, and I noticed Maureen rubbed her hand along her armrest and said, almost to herself, "So luxurious."

Once we were all comfortably seated, Rob verified with Emma that we were going directly to the hotel. After he climbed behind the steering wheel, he reminded her that there was a compartment of drinks and snacks, and then he must have pushed a button somewhere because a privacy window rose from the seat behind him and tucked into the limo's ceiling.

"Would you look at that," Seth said. "Now that we are in our own isolation booth, do any of you have scandalous secrets you'd like to share?"

"Oh, Seth, don't be silly." I flapped my hand at him and turned to Emma. "I can't thank you enough for not only inviting us to Edmonton but for putting Susan Shevlin in touch with a woman named Mary Jo, who is in charge of hospitality for the hotel. Together they have provided us with an excellent list of attractions that will be sure to keep us busy when preparing for the show keeps you otherwise occupied. I understand we have a lot of exciting adventures ahead of us."

Mort said with a slight hesitation in his voice, "By any chance,

Emma, do you have any idea when or even if we might meet Derek Braverman?"

"As it happens, you are in luck. Derek owns a large ranch out by McFadden Lake, where he spends much of his free time when he is in Canada, but for his own convenience he is staying at the hotel during rehearsals and performances."

"Our hotel?" Mort's eyes widened as if he must have misunderstood.

"The very same." Emma gave me a wink to let me know that there was more news coming. "And if you are not too worn out from your day's travels, you are invited to dinner tonight with Derek, Alan and Rosalie Hughes, and any of the cast members who may be hanging about the hotel."

I'd rarely seen Mort Metzger at a loss for words, but I would always remember this moment as one of those times.

Emma opened the snack compartment and offered us our choice of cold drinks, fresh fruit, and an assortment of cookies. I was grateful for a can of seltzer, which had a tangy citrus flavor.

Emma passed around a package of cookies and insisted we each have one. "Leclerc Célébration butter cookies with milk chocolate are the best biscuits I have ever tasted. Try one, and I guarantee you will be tossing away your clothes so that you have room in your baggage to bring boxes of them home with you."

I suspected that each one of us was thinking of our personal favorite cookies, but it only took a bite or two for us all to agree that the cookies Emma offered were extraordinarily delicious.

When we reached the hotel, Rob opened the car door and assured us he would take care of the luggage. We walked into the hotel lobby, and a tall, curvaceous woman who was probably in her early thirties greeted us effusively and a bit louder than I thought was necessary.

"Dear Emma, thank you for escorting our American guests from the airport. Hello, everyone. I'm Mary Jo Simard, and I promise to ensure that your stay will be as comfortable and exciting as possible."

She began to shake hands first with Mort, followed by Maureen and then Seth. When she reached her hand toward me, her voice went up several octaves. "Who have we here? Can it be? Why, yes, it is: world-famous mystery author J. B. Fletcher."

She looked around and, satisfied that she had the attention of any number of people in the lobby, continued. "We are so delighted that you are here . . ."

She was interrupted by two elderly ladies who had been sitting nearby and were now crowding in between us.

The taller one, whose dark black hair had close to an inch of gray roots, said, "Is it true? Are you J. B. Fletcher?"

"Well, yes, but . . ."

She grabbed my hand with more strength than I would have expected and began to shake it vigorously. "This is a great honor. I am Iris Crenshaw, and this is my sister-in-law, Vivian Zhang. We are your biggest admirers, aren't we, Vivian? The two of us belong to multiple book clubs just to be sure we never miss an opportunity to discuss one of your baffling mysteries."

"That's very nice . . ." I tried to cut her off but to no avail.

The shorter woman had a softer voice that matched her snow-white hair, but she was no less irksome. "Are you going to do a reading in the gift shop? They have a number of your books on display. I saw them this very morning. We can't wait to hear you read."

Mary Jo Simard clapped her hands gleefully, as if the senior citizens had given her a brilliant idea.

"Ms. Zhang is right, of course. You absolutely must do a presentation in the gift shop, a short reading, followed by a question-and-answer session. Why, we have dozens of books for you to sign, and our guests will be thrilled to meet a writer of your stature. I will arrange it with the shop manager and let you know when you are scheduled to speak and sign."

"Really, I must insist," I began, stopped, and started again. "I am here on vacation with friends. I am not on tour. This is not a professional visit. My time is completely reserved for my cousin Emma and my friends."

"Oh, I am sure you can make some accommodation," Mary Jo said airily.

"Mary Jo, girl, calm yourself down," Emma intruded. "Let my cousin have a bit of time to unpack and rest. We can talk about this later."

Recognizing that she was outnumbered, Mary Jo raised her arm and waved her hand, and in a split second, a man who had been hovering near the reception desk was by her side.

"Now here is our bell captain, Panuk. He will escort you to your rooms and, if you like, collect your passports, which will remain securely in our hotel safe for the duration of your visit."

I nodded and immediately handed over my passport. Seth and the Metzgers did the same.

Mort teased, "Well, at least we will know exactly where our passports are if we have to get back across the border in a hurry."

Panuk wore a perfectly pressed green uniform trimmed with gold buttons, and I thought perhaps that his gold lapels signified his rank. He appeared quite warmhearted. As he accepted our passports, his welcoming smile reached right up to his lovely amber-colored eyes.

"Ladies, gentlemen, this way please." He ushered us toward the elevators. "My associates have delivered your luggage to your rooms, but I wish to confirm for myself that everything is to the satisfaction of each of you, our very special guests."

Emma blew me a kiss. "I'll see you in a while, luv." And she turned and walked in the opposite direction.

As we rode to the fifth floor, Seth teased, "Well, J. B. Fletcher, that was quite a show Miss Mary Jo put on, discovering a famous author in our midst. Do you think a little birdie by the name of Susan Shevlin might have given away your secret identity?"

"Oh, I am sure of it, but no matter," I said as the elevator doors opened and we followed Panuk to our rooms. "I have no intention of interrupting this vacation for anything even vaguely related to work. Why, I sent my latest manuscript to my editor a mere five days ago. I plan to rest and enjoy my time with Emma and all of you. I promise you that no one, not even those two kindly older ladies, will be allowed to interfere."

Adamant as I may have felt at the time, I couldn't possibly foresee that, within a few short days, our vacation would be seriously disrupted by a calamity that would cause difficulty for us all.

Chapter Five

We walked halfway down the corridor. Panuk unlocked a door, saying, "This is your suite, Mrs. Fletcher. Dr. Hazlitt, you will be right across the hall. Mr. and Mrs. Metzger, you are next to Mrs. Fletcher in suite 509 just down this hallway. Please follow me."

While Panuk escorted my friends to their rooms, I walked around the tastefully decorated suite, which, I was happy to see, included a tiny kitchenette. Both the living room and the bedroom were decorated with vases containing a profusion of live flowers. When Panuk returned to ask if I required any further assistance, I had only one question.

I pointed to one exquisite crystal vase overflowing with sprightly pink flowers. "These flowers are gorgeous. I've never seen them before. Do you happen to know what they are called?"

"Of course, madam. They are called wild rose, and they are the emblem of our wonderful province of Alberta. I am glad that you appreciate their beauty. Flowers are meant to be enjoyed. Each province has a flower that represents it. I am Inuit, born in the Northwest Territories, where our flower emblem is the lovely white mountain avens, which blooms for a short time each spring. As you can imagine, the winters farther north are very long, so spring flowers are always welcome."

"I expect so," I said. "Thank you for taking the time to explain. I appreciate learning about the places I visit. You are fortunate to have beautiful flowers as your emblems. Back in my home state of Maine, our state flower is actually the white pine cone, chosen, I suppose, in response to our being known as the Pine Tree State. I have always thought it would be better to have an actual flower as our symbol the way the other forty-nine states do." I shrugged. Selecting and naming the Maine state flower was definitely out of my control.

Panuk nodded in sympathy and, clearly eager to move on to his next responsibility, asked if I required anything else. I'm sure he was pleased when I said, "No, thank you."

I was nearly done unpacking when I heard someone knock on my door. I expected it to be Emma and that she would be raring to go on some escapade or another and clamoring for company, but when I opened the door, I found Maureen Metzger standing there with the same look on her face that usually indicates one of her new recipes turned out to be a spectacular failure.

"Maureen? What on earth? Come in and sit down." I pointed to the love seat by the bay window that overlooked much of Edmonton. She clearly wasn't ready to talk quite yet, so I offered her my tried-and-true cure-all, a cup of tea, and she bobbed her head slightly, which I took as a yes.

I found tea bags and an electric kettle in the kitchenette, and by the time I brought two cups of tea into the living room, Maureen was standing, looking out the window. "It is a beautiful city."

She took a teacup and moved back to the love seat. I sat in a nearby chair and sipped my tea, waiting until Maureen was ready. Finally, she put her cup on the coffee table. "Mort says I am being plain silly and said if I don't believe him, I should talk to you. I mean, I knew that we would be visiting your cousin and that she and her actor friends are all famous. But . . ."

I waited for a second or two, and when she remained silent, I encouraged, "Yes, go on."

"When those two women pounced on you in the lobby, I realized that you have a fan base wherever you go. Seth is a doctor. Mort is a sheriff. Both positions of standing. Then there is me. I have no status at all. I don't want to embarrass you by being the friend you brought along who doesn't fit in with the high-powered people we are going to meet."

"Maureen, you are a kind, humorous, and cheerful person who adds joy to everything we have ever done together, be it a quiet dinner at my house, working on a charity event for the middle school, or relaxing on a fishing trip or a long bicycle ride. I am positive you will add to the quality and sense of adventure of this visit, and I am sure everyone will enjoy your company. Now go back to your room and get dressed for dinner with the stars. I guarantee you will outshine them all."

Maureen giggled—a sound I knew well and a guarantee she was feeling better—and said, "Well, as long as you're sure I won't be embarrassing you, then I have no reason to worry. I am sorry that I bothered you with this silliness."

She stood, gave me a spontaneous hug, and I heard her signature giggle once again as she said, "Now I better make sure Mort showers and changes for dinner. I am starving. I hope they call us soon."

I opened the door, and we found Emma walking along the hall. "Aye, there you are. I was looking for your room. I hope they treated you nicely."

Maureen gave Emma a smile and a brief hello and then headed back to her room, a much happier person than when she arrived at my door. Much as I loved my cousin, I was hoping that Emma's visit would be a short one. I desperately wanted to relax for a while before dinner, and I knew we'd have days and days to catch up.

As if she'd read my mind, Emma said, "Jessica, luv, I can't stay, but I wanted you to know that our dinner tonight is downstairs in the Victoria Room. Cocktails in an hour, dinner served half an hour after. It is a private dining room, very posh. Mary Jo is ringing your friends, but I wanted to tell you myself because"— she pulled a mock sad face—"I hope the doctor and the sheriff won't be disappointed, but Derek messaged a few minutes ago that he will not be joining us. Mind you, not that I care as long as he foots the bill, but I am hoping the men will not be too disappointed. Still, they are old enough to know that tomorrow is another day."

She turned to leave and then turned back to give me a kiss on the cheek. "Whenever I see you, which is not nearly often enough, I feel like I am twelve again. Promise me that once we've both gone home, it won't be so long until our next get-together."

I was more than happy to make that promise, and with a broad smile, Emma tapped her heart, waved to me, and left.

I kicked off my shoes, sat on the love seat for a few minutes, then decided to call both Seth and the Metzgers. We agreed to meet at the elevator in an hour. I took a quick shower, did a few stretches, and dressed for dinner.

As it turned out, the Metzgers opened their door at the same moment I did, so the three of us walked down the hallway together. Seth was standing by the bank of elevators, tapping his foot impatiently. As soon as he saw us, he pushed a button to summon the elevator.

"My, don't you ladies look festive this evening. I can't hold a candle to you in my tweed jacket and black slacks." Seth gave us a big grin.

Maureen and I thanked him for the compliment. Then Maureen chucked Mort under the chin, saying that we were pleased to be escorted by such dapper-looking men. Mort gave a half smile, apparently the best he could do.

"Oh, honey," Maureen said, "we are going to be in Edmonton for a good long while, and I promise you will have plenty of opportunities to meet Derek Braverman."

Mort gave a halfhearted nod. "Exactly what that Mary Jo woman told me on the phone, but it is still a big disappointment. I have been looking forward to meeting him from the minute you told me Jessica had invited us to come along on this trip."

I raised an eyebrow at Maureen, who winked in return. It seemed that her asking to tag along would remain our little secret.

The elevator moved swiftly without stopping until we reached the lobby. When the doors opened, Mary Jo Simard was standing in front of us.

"I hope you all managed to get a brief rest after your long day of travel. Let me show you to the Victoria Room. It is unfortunate that Mr. Braverman can't be with us tonight, but he has decreed that our appetizer will be mushroom fondue with wild boar, which he considers a Canadian delicacy. Naturally, you will be able to pick your own entrée. Dessert also will be up to you, but I strongly recommend the flapper pie. It is a prized staple here in the province of Alberta. We compete with our neighbors in Saskatchewan as to where it is tastiest."

She stopped in front of gray plush double doors, one decorated with what appeared to be a diamond crown and the other emblazed with a sovereign's scepter and orb. THE VICTORIA ROOM was written in gold letters above the doorway.

Mary Jo pulled one door open with such a flourish that I half expected her to shout, "Ta-da!" but as it happened, we walked into an empty, silent room.

Mary Jo was flabbergasted. "Well, the table is set, so I am sure your servers will be here any moment." She looked to the far end of the room. "Oh, Quint, thank goodness."

A handsome dark-haired man with just a touch of gray edging his sideburns and a well-groomed mustache stepped out from behind a floor-to-ceiling royal blue drapery. Since he was dressed in black slacks and a white Eton jacket, I presumed he was a server who'd come through from the kitchen entrance. He moved behind the bar, casually threw a towel over his arm, and, with a purposefully careless smile, announced the bar was open.

Mort and Seth headed to the bar and peppered the bartender with questions about Canadian whisky.

"First thing you need to know is that there is no *e* when we spell it. In Canada it's *w-h-i-s-k-y*. Now if you want the best we have in stock this evening, I can offer you J. P. Wiser's. It's a blend of grains that you are guaranteed to savor. I have a bottle on the bar tonight because we were expecting Mr. Braverman, and good old Wiser's is his favorite. Care to try it?" Quint asked.

Mort and Seth didn't have to confer for even a second. They both nodded their heads eagerly.

Maureen whispered to me, "As if either of them would choose something other than Braverman's favorite."

A shrill voice coming from the doorway prevented me from answering.

"Alan, I told you. Didn't I tell you? Without Derek, we needed to be *early*. Can't you see we have guests?" A sallow-faced woman wearing too much makeup and a gauzy pink dress with wide sleeves and an irregular hem was finger stabbing the gawkish man with oversized eyeglasses and pinched lips standing by her side. As soon as she saw me watching, she lowered her tone and turned her attention to me.

"Oh my, of course, you must be Emma's sister. You look exactly like her. Well, except for the hair." She tottered toward me, wobbling on heels that were much too high. "And why isn't she here to greet you?"

"Because I met some special people in the lobby, and I was sure it would impress my *cousin* and her friends to no end if I waltzed through the door with Frederick the Great and Gracelyn Lapointe, who are only the most famous magic act in all of Canada and in Australia, too, the way I hear it." Emma took over the room immediately, as she usually did, handling the introductions with great aplomb. I was especially pleased when she introduced Maureen not as Mort's wife but as a society leader of the highest caliber. "There's no one like her in all of Cabot Cove. A regular star, she is."

Having never met Maureen before this afternoon and without asking me any particulars about her, Emma simply improvised and was as on target as she'd been in an improv show I'd seen her do in London several years ago. Naturally, Maureen was beaming, and I was sure she would no longer feel insecure about being amid the company we would be keeping for the next few days.

Two servers dressed in white shirts and royal blue bow ties entered and began placing appetizers on the table. Mary Jo quickly encouraged us to find our place cards. I was pleased to be sitting next to Frederick the Great. What could be more fun than dinner conversation with a magician?

I noticed that Maureen Metzger was seated between Rosalie Hughes and an empty chair. I suspected that Rosalie wouldn't be the most pleasant conversationalist, so I hoped, for Maureen's sake, that the empty chair would be occupied by someone chatty and fun.

Rosalie commanded, "Mary Jo, do sit down. Now, where is Dennis? He knows I cannot abide when guests arrive late to a dinner party."

Just then a man wearing a sport shirt and slacks walked into the room, bent his shaved head down to kiss Rosalie on the cheek, and murmured an octave above a whisper, "Sorry I am tardy, Madame Producer, but I was on long distance with New York."

Rosalie simpered and patted his cheek. "I am sure it was an interesting call. You can tell me all about it later. Now please be seated so dinner can begin."

He obediently took the chair on the other side of Maureen, and I heard him introduce himself to her as Dennis Oliver, the assistant director. I did notice that he placed his phone next to his plate. How important did an assistant director think he was? The director's phone was nowhere to be seen. I could only think that he was trying to impress Alan with his work ethic—always on call or something like that.

While Frederick was telling me a charming but extremely long-winded story about a show he'd done in Perth, the finale of a series of shows he'd done in Melbourne and Sydney, Australia, I kept one ear on Maureen and her dinner companions. When she wasn't giving orders to Mary Jo about the meals and the service, Rosalie chatted across the table with Seth, asking him about Cabot Cove as if she were truly interested, although she seemed not to remember that Maureen was from the same town.

I was relieved when Dennis turned to Maureen and asked if this was her first trip to Canada. When she replied in the affirmative, he confessed it was his first as well just as Quint the bartender leaned in to take their drink orders.

"Really, sir?" Quint looked at Dennis full on; then his eyes fell to Dennis's cell phone. "I could have sworn we met someplace before. In fact, Calgary comes to mind."

"Bartender, you are wrong," Dennis said loudly enough to draw everyone's attention while he quickly placed his hand atop his phone. "Unless you visited California or New York City, I assure you, we have never met."

Rosalie leaned across Maureen and reached over to touch his

arm. "Dennis, please? We are at a civilized dinner, not some common, noisy gathering."

I was shocked that Rosalie took such a sharp tone, so I glanced around the table to see how the others reacted. Everyone was focused intently on their fondue except for Alan Hughes, who had a panicked look on his face as he stared directly at Quint, the bartender. I wondered what that look could possibly mean.

Chapter Six

The next morning when I stepped off the elevator, Seth was sitting in one of the plush leather chairs in the lobby. He waved the newspaper he held in his hand.

"How'd you sleep, Jess? I'm afraid the time change had me up with the chickens, but the good news is that I found stacks of this tourist newspaper over there by the free coffee. Care for a cup?" He waved toward a distant wall.

I shook my head. "I got up a bit earlier than I needed to, but it gave me time to do my hotel room exercises, so I feel invigorated. I'll wait for breakfast. Was there anything to learn from the paper? Anything we tourists need to know?"

"Well, for one thing, I can tell you that the traditional name of Edmonton is Amiskwaciy Waskahikan. It means Beaver Hill House, so I'm guessing that trapping beavers for pelts was important around these parts once upon a time.

"And," he continued, "there is a handy crossword puzzle that contains information about the sights to see in and around town. 'Galaxyland' nearly stumped me. I had the *g* and the 'land,' but I couldn't make it work until I got 'onyx' in seven down and the *x* gave me the brainstorm I needed."

The Metzgers came out of the elevator, apologizing for being a few minutes late, and we all went into the Victoria Room. This morning several smaller tables, each with four chairs, indicated that our breakfast would be less formal than last night's dinner. Two servers were waiting and immediately presented coffee and menus.

Maureen and I opted for eggs Benedict, while Seth ordered fried eggs with a side of pork sausage. Mort surprised us by considering the pancakes, but he decided they couldn't compare to Mara's prizewinners, so he chose French toast with back bacon.

"Here you all are, bright as rays of sunshine bouncing off the Tower Bridge. I rang Jessica's room, but when she didn't answer, I hoped I'd find you here." Emma was accompanied by a pretty young woman whom she introduced as her understudy, Eileen McCarthy.

"Worse luck for us that Alan is insisting Eileen do a complete run-through of my songs and skits this morning. I'm going to tag along so we can all agree on the little things that make a show— if I always take ten steps stage left, Eileen has to do the same, or it will confuse the other players in the scene. Can't have that, now, can we, Eileen?"

Eileen shook her head, blond curls bouncing on her shoulders, then said to us all, "I am so honored to have the opportunity to work with Emma. I am learning so much."

Emma blushed slightly and said, "Eileen is a talented girl who will do fine on her own. She need not bend nor bow to anyone."

I seemed to be the only one puzzled by the comment. I suppose my tablemates took it as theater talk. I was wondering who wanted Eileen to bend to their will.

Emma went on to promise she would be free to explore with us after lunch. "But with Rob as your driver and Mary Jo as your guide, I am sure you'll have a fine morning. Does anyone have any idea what local sights you might want to see first?"

Seth picked up his newspaper and said, "Doesn't have to be this morning, but I marked off a few things in this tourist guide—the Royal Alberta Museum, Elk Island National Park, and some others. I suppose I should have numbered them to indicate my priority. Now I'll have to read the descriptions all over again." He slapped the breast pocket of his shirt and then reached behind him to search the pockets of the jacket he'd hung on the back of his chair.

I could see he was getting more bothered by the minute. "Seth, what are you hunting for?"

"My pen. I had it the whole time I was waiting for you all to come down for breakfast. I marked tourist attractions and filled in the crossword. I must have left it on the end table by my chair." He bolted to the door and disappeared into the lobby.

"I don't know, Jessica. Seth seems awfully upset over this pen. I hope he finds it," Emma said, and something clicked for me.

"Oh no. Last year, Seth won an award from the Maine Medical Association for his work on a special project for children's health. The society gave him a plaque that now hangs in his office and a sterling silver pen that he treasures. I hope that's not the one he is missing. The pocket clip is a caduceus, the two snakes wound around a staff. It is exquisite."

Seth's face was so morose when he walked back into the room that I didn't need to ask. The pen was still missing. He slouched in his chair, and I decided not to ask him for any more ideas for our morning jaunt.

Emma and Eileen left for their rehearsal, and we ate in silence for a few minutes until Seth pushed his chair back. "I'm going to see if anyone turned my pen in at the desk."

Mort tagged along. When they were gone, Maureen said, "Oh, I hope he finds it. I have never seen Doc Hazlitt so distraught."

Before I could answer, Mary Jo Simard, dressed in a trim beige pantsuit, came into the room clapping her hands, as if she were a camp counselor and we were twelve-year-old campers. She stopped in mid-clap when she saw Maureen and I were alone.

"Where are the men?" she demanded. "I told Rob we would be ready to leave in ten minutes."

For the life of me, I couldn't see what the hurry was, and I said so. "Mary Jo, this is meant to be our free morning. We are all looking forward to learning about your wonderful city, but in a leisurely way."

"Oh, I am sorry. Alan Hughes asked that we set up this room for a one o'clock lunch for four. I assumed you were the four and that he wanted you here at that specific time." Mary Jo looked perplexed; then her frown cleared and she said, "Well, if you're not planning on being back here for a one o'clock luncheon, I am going to suggest we do some poking around town and then have a nice meal at the Canada Clubhouse. It's a lovely day, and if the weather holds, we can eat outdoors. I will wait outside with Rob, but please don't take too long. Lots to do."

As soon as Mary Jo left the room, Maureen and I exchanged a look and then laughed.

"Don't you think Mary Jo would have made an excellent drill sergeant?" Maureen said.

"I couldn't agree more." I folded my napkin on top of my plate. "Let's find Seth and Mort before Sergeant Mary Jo makes us do push-ups because we are running late."

"Or gives us kitchen duty as punishment for our tardiness," Maureen said as we headed to the lobby.

Seth and Mort were at the reception desk. When we approached, Seth looked much happier than when he'd discovered his pen was missing, but when I asked if his pen was in the lost and found, he shook his head.

"Not yet. But Armand"—Seth pointed to the desk clerk—"told me that the cleaning crew finds dozens of lost items every day, and he is confident my pen will turn up. Nothing for me to do but wait."

"And in the meantime, Mary Jo has commanded that we meet her and Rob in the driveway for a day of adventure," I said.

Mort offered Maureen his arm. "Are we ready to go?"

We all agreed that we were.

Rob asked about our plans for the morning, and Seth pulled out his tourist newspaper and said he hoped we'd all be interested in Elk Island National Park.

We agreed that a national park sounded like a great place to get a feel for Canada. Rob was delighted. "I always say Jasper and Banff are bigger, but Elk Island is better, cozier if you will, and a lot less crowded, since most tourists are not as clever as you are, Dr. Hazlitt. You'll get a 'close enough to touch' view of the most magnificent animals: mule deer and white-tailed deer aplenty, along with wood bison and the plains bison. Of course, it's best not to try to actually touch any of the animals. And it's Canada, so we're sure to spot moose and elk along the way. You can bet I know all the best roads."

I had put on my sturdiest shoes in preparation for the usual tourist activities that required a lot of walking, but I was not the least disappointed to ride in the comfort of the limo and be greeted by a herd of bison as Rob drove along what he called Yellowhead Highway. We were also surrounded by so many elk that Maureen commented that she understood how the park came by its name.

Since he was plainly a nature lover, Rob was an excellent tour guide, describing the history of many of the plants and small animals we saw along the way. That left Mary Jo with little to do other than look slightly bored and scroll through her phone constantly, so I wasn't the least bit surprised when she interrupted Rob in mid-description and directed him to drive to the Art Gallery of Alberta so we could browse the current exhibit before we stopped at the Canada Clubhouse for lunch.

"You will enjoy the art gallery. Why, the building itself is an unusual work of art, wrapped as it is in a steel ribbon. And there are several exhibits of modern art, including some by Canada's finest Indigenous artists. Oh, excuse me," Mary Jo said as her phone softly emitted a classical tune I couldn't quite identify. After saying hello, Mary Jo was silent until she said, "Of course," and hung up.

"Well, isn't that lovely? The Hugheses have invited us to their suite for predinner cocktails, and according to Rosalie, Derek Braverman is looking forward to meeting Emma's family and friends." She smiled as proudly as if she'd personally made the arrangements and seemed confident that she had elevated our excitement level to a thousand. She wasn't far wrong.

Mort let out a whoop that came close to shattering our ear-drums, and he and Seth started both talking at once, so their conversation was somewhat garbled but filled with anticipation.

Happy as we were to see them so excited, Maureen and I both rolled our eyes at their childish behavior.

The construction of the museum building was indeed re-markable. I couldn't imagine how the architect, whose name I learned from a brochure was Randall Stout, could have conceived of, much less designed, it. The next page of the brochure solved that mystery for me. Mr. Stout drew inspiration from the shape of the North Saskatchewan River and the aurora borealis, both of which have a profound impact on Alberta.

I think everyone was enjoying the museum exhibits as much as I was when Mary Jo announced it was time for lunch and be-gan directing us to the limousine.

It wasn't long before Rob turned into the parking lot of an el-egant restaurant situated on the edge of a large lake. Our table was next to a floor-to-ceiling window that allowed us an unob-structed view of the lake and its surroundings.

As our waiter distributed menus, Mary Jo said, "Lunch today will be courtesy of Mr. Braverman."

That set Mort and Seth into high fives and fist bumps all over again. After we placed our orders, Seth asked Mary Jo what she thought of Braverman.

I don't think any of us expected her snide response.

"You know these show-business types. They are all the same, self-absorbed and demanding." Mary Jo flicked her wrist as if dismissing an entire industry. "Take that Eileen McCarthy, the one Emma brought along to meet you this morning. Wait until you get to know her—basically a stand-in who fancies herself a star. Gets everything she wants, that one. I hope that I am around to see it when she gets what she deserves."

Apparently, I was not the only person at the table who couldn't think of any kind of response. We began studying our menus to avoid eye contact with one another and especially with Mary Jo.

At long last, Mort broke the silence. "This is probably a good time for me to order Canadian poutine. That way I can report back to Mara that it couldn't hold a candle to hers."

The Cabot Cove crew all laughed, which seemed to snap Mary Jo out of her reverie. She asked what she had missed.

I told her that we were talking about our hometown luncheonette, and she nodded, picked up her phone, and began scrolling, just as she had been doing in the car. I noticed that Rob was sitting at a small table by himself, reading a newspaper and drinking what looked like a cola.

I said to no one in particular that I thought we should invite him to join us. Seth had started to slide his chair back to do just that when Mary Jo held up her hand. "Please don't. He is an employee of the hotel, not a guest. I am sure Mr. Braverman would not appreciate having Rob's meal added to the lunch tab."

She was still speaking when our waiter set a mouthwatering salad piled high with vegetables, blue cheese, and chicken breast in front of her. Mary Jo thanked him and spread her napkin on her lap, apparently unaware that she, too, was an employee of the hotel. One might even call her a stand-in.

Chapter Seven

W e arrived back at the hotel with plenty of time to spare before we were to meet for cocktails. I went to my room, planning to do a full set of my travel exercises, but since I always prefer fresh air when I do my routine, I was disappointed that our very modern hotel had windows that did not open. Still, I took a few deep breaths and marched in place to get my heart pumping, then did some squats and side bends. I followed that with a dozen wide arm circles and a dozen small ones. I was about to shake all over, loosening every muscle, when I heard a tap at my door.

I opened the door and Emma said, "Cheers, luv. How'd you enjoy your touring?"

"Come sit down. I'll make us a cuppa. Actually, we had a wonderful day, including a national park, an art gallery, and a lovely lunch right on the water of what I now know is called Big Lake."

"Well, I am glad you had a better time than I did." Emma sat on the love seat, slipped off her shoes, and put her feet on the coffee table. "I am not sure what has gotten into Alan Hughes. He has always been a fussbudget, but this morning he was completely brassed off. Drove that sweet Eileen McCarthy to tears more than once, I can tell you. And for what? He's pushing her as if I were about to disappear. Really, Jess, it's not like I ever miss a performance."

I stood over her with a teacup in each hand and motioned with the right.

Emma looked at me, clearly not understanding until I said, "Your tootsies."

"Oh, sorry." She dropped her feet to the floor and took a teacup from my hand. "It was just a tiresome, worrisome day. If Alan keeps getting all shirty with her like that, what are we to do if she walks out on the production? You know, if she did, that would be the exact moment I would happen to catch the flu or break a bone, and I'd need an understudy and have none to be found."

I gave myself time to order my thoughts by first sitting in the chair and then sipping my tea. In due time I asked my questions. "What exactly do you know about Eileen? Have you worked with her before?"

"Never seen her in my life until I got here and she was one of a dozen or so girls who answered Alan's call for understudies. He narrowed it down to three before I arrived. Of the three, Alan and I agreed that Eileen's range—for the musical numbers, you know—was closest to mine, and when he made the offer, she took the job. But all this unnecessary work. I don't understand."

"Well, Alan is the director. It may well be that he wants all performers to be of excellent quality. What about Derek Braverman's understudy? Is Alan treating him the same way?"

"Oh Lordy, no. Derek doesn't even know he has a true understudy. Jorge Escarra is an old Canadian friend of Derek's. Alan hired him as a member of the ensemble with a private agreement that if an understudy was needed to go on for Derek at any performance, Jorge would do it. It is all very hush-hush because Derek has been insisting since he first decided to do this farewell tour that if he couldn't go on for any reason, the performance would be canceled. I can hear Derek bellowing, 'This is my show, and it is me that the audience paid good money to see.'

"Anyway, the Hugheses have too large a wad invested in this show to let it be closed because Derek has to have his appendix removed. Show business. When it comes down to it, it's a business like any other."

"Oh, as a writer, I well understand that, but it seems odd to me that, just today, Mary Jo Simard was talking about Eileen McCarthy as though they were mortal enemies, and now you tell me that Alan is treating her badly. I wonder . . ."

"Oh, no need to wonder, deary. I can chalk Alan's behavior up to preopening night jitters, and I can certainly explain that Mary Jo had a man she fancied as a possible beau, and it might have come to that until Eileen McCarthy came on the scene."

"Now that makes sense. Do you know who the man might be?" I leaned forward and rested my teacup on the table, not wanting to miss a word.

"Believe me, Jessica; there are no secrets in a theater troupe. Do you remember our first dinner? The night that Derek begged off?"

"Yes, of course."

"And do you remember the dishy young barman? Quinton Chabot is his name, and Mary Jo took a fancy to him, working here at the same hotel and all. Well, as it turns out, our costumer, Lene Gadue—she lives here in Edmonton but stayed at the hotel for the first couple of days we were in town—said she needed to see us at will since her work starts with her doing drawings and the like. Anyway, she was having trouble sleeping one night and decided to go for a walk, and she saw 'the new girl,' as she calls Eileen, at the end of the driveway with a man who'd served Lene a drink in the bar earlier that night. Eileen was sniffling and crying, and the man had an arm around her. Lene took it as a lover's tiff. Two days later, Alan Hughes introduced the man to us as a new part-time stagehand."

"You think Eileen got the bartender—what's his name, Quint—a job. Why would Alan Hughes do such a favor for Eileen and then proceed to be consistently tough on her at rehearsal?"

"Now, there's a question I haven't been able to answer even in my own mind." Emma set her teacup on the table and stood. "Well, I wanted to stop for a bit of a chin-wag, but now it's nearing time for us to all show up and admire the one, the only Derek Braverman. I'd best go put my glad rags on."

I locked the door behind Emma and glanced at my watch. She was right. It was past time to get changed and join the festivities.

I'd just finished putting on my lipstick when I heard a knock on my door that was so loud I assumed it had to be Seth or Mort, either one of them raring to get to the cocktail hour and meet Derek Braverman. When I opened the door, they were both in the hallway. Seth was about to knock on my door again, and Mort was holding the door to his suite open, saying, "Come on, Maureen; we don't want to be late now, do we?"

I held up a hand to Seth and said, "Just let me get my purse," and in the short time it took me to do so, Seth and Mort were already at the elevator, and Maureen was a few steps in front of me.

She stopped to give me a chance to catch up and whispered, "Honestly, they are behaving like children."

I nodded. "Don't begrudge them reliving childhood memories. It will keep them young. Much better that than grumpy old men."

Maureen giggled, and when we reached the elevator, she said in her most grown-up voice, "Well, boys, I hope you and Derek Braverman have a wonderful time tonight."

The door to the party suite was open, and a crowd was gathering. Emma was in the midst of a group, telling a story that ended with everyone laughing. No surprise there. She waved us over and introduced us to Nicholas Dufond, the stage manager for the theater. He said a few words of greeting and then excused himself to get a drink. As I watched him move to the bar, I noticed that the "dishy" young bartender, Quinton Chabot, was nowhere to be seen. An older, white-haired gentleman was deftly filling glasses with ice and pouring drinks.

Rosalie Hughes joined our little group. "Oh, thank goodness, real people. I can't listen to Alan another minute. He is so busy planning and replanning the show; every face he sees reminds him of something he wants done. He just spent ten minutes 'directing' that stagehand"—she pointed to a middle-aged man in jeans and a denim jacket—"how to move a chair offstage quickly. For pity's sake, that is the man's job. I'm sure he well knows how to move a chair."

She drained her wineglass and walked away, sloping first to her left and then to her right as she headed to the bar.

"Someone's a little tipsy. And that's not a bit unusual, I might say." Emma turned and called to a striking dark-haired man dressed in strict business attire: a navy blue suit, white shirt, and blue-and-beige striped tie. "Jorge, come meet the family."

She introduced each of us, and while we were shaking hands, Emma told us that Jorge Escarra was the finest baritone in all of Canada.

Jorge laughed and kissed her cheek. "As much as I appreciate the compliment, you mustn't let Derek hear you say that or we will be two songbirds out of a job."

Emma laughed and said, "Well, why don't we sing a song or two and show the room what we've got?"

Jorge looked around. "The acoustics here would be awful." He smiled directly at a spot somewhere between Seth's and Mort's shoulders. "At the right time and place, I promise you all a lovely serenade, but in the meantime, I believe I see the man of the evening in the doorway, sizing up his audience."

Like a group of synchronized swimmers, we turned our heads toward the door, and there stood Derek Braverman, looking much taller than he appeared on television and movie screens until I realized the cowboy hat and boots he was wearing added a few inches.

Alan Hughes appeared from wherever he'd been socializing and immediately latched onto Braverman's arm. "Derek, every member of the cast and crew is delighted you could join us. Shall we say hello to the stagehands? You remember Spencer and Red."

And where, I wondered, was stagehand Quint? And then I

gave a quick look around the room and realized that Eileen Mc-Carthy was among the missing as well.

Derek Braverman allowed Alan to lead him around for small chitchat sessions until he reached us. Then Braverman broke away from the script and embraced Jorge, giving him several friendly pats on the back.

"Jorge, mi amigo. ¿Estás pasando bien?"

The two men separated, and Jorge replied, "How could I not be having a good time? I am surrounded by beautiful women. Emma, please introduce—"

Derek cut him off and searched until his eyes met mine. "This is the charming lady I have been waiting to meet. Jessica—may I call you Jessica?—you have no idea how many of my lonely nights in hotel rooms have been made less unbearable by your wonderful books. And, of course, your gracious picture on the back cover added to my delight."

He lifted my hand to his lips just as Seth said, "Actually, most people think Emma and Jessica could be twins except for the hair color."

Derek never took his eyes off me and said, "That may be so, but I don't see it."

I was starting to feel uncomfortable, so I pulled my hand away as gently as I could and murmured how glad I was that he enjoyed my books. Then I quickly introduced Seth, Mort, and Maureen.

Derek's hellos were perfunctory, and he managed during those few minutes to move closer to me. "Jessica, I understand you will be signing books in the gift shop before you go home. I promise to be the first reader in line. Dare I hope for a personalized signature?"

If Mary Jo Simard had been within my reach, I would have strangled her then and there. I needed to stop the idea of a book signing in its tracks. "Mr. Braverman, there has been a misunderstanding. I do not intend—"

"While you are in town, please stop by rehearsals anytime and bring your friends. 'We should spend together what time we can.' Don't you like that sentiment? It's from a show I was in ages ago. The more meaningful lines never quite go away." Derek's smile was beginning to look more like a leer.

Before I could answer, Alan Hughes, who'd been standing quietly by, said, "Er, actually we are quite busy preparing for the show. It might not be the best idea to have visitors wandering around the theater."

"Nonsense. How about tomorrow afternoon? That's it! Tomorrow afternoon. Good old Nick will take care of the details. Where are you, Nick?" Derek boomed. "Ah, here he is. Nicholas Dufond, our stage manager, will see to all the details. Emma, darling, you will arrange with Nick to provide a backstage tour for Jessica and her friends, won't you?"

"I'd be delighted." Emma gave a sweeping curtsy as though she were onstage and playing the role of an obedient parlormaid.

By the glint in her eye, I could tell she was enjoying Alan's discomfort at having his schedule disrupted, so I was sure tomorrow was going to be an exciting day for us all. And as it turned out, tomorrow would end with the kind of dreadful excitement that not one of us could have foreseen.

Chapter Eight

The next morning, Seth and I were on our second cup of coffee when Mort came into the Victoria Room.

"Good morning, Doc, Mrs. F." He looked at the empty, untouched tables and said, "Quite a party last night. I suppose some folks are sleeping in this morning."

"And I see your wife is among the missing." Seth pointed out the obvious.

"Maureen went to the gift shop. Somewhere along the way yesterday her sunglasses went missing. She searched everywhere she could think of and finally decided to buy a replacement pair—and that reminds me, Doc, did your pen ever turn up?"

"Not so far as I know," Seth replied. "I'll check at the front desk before we go wandering today. Have either of you heard what plans have been made for us? Are we still going to tour the theater? I haven't seen that Mary Jo woman all morning. I hope she conferred with Emma and Nick from the theater. I'd find a backstage tour interesting, especially since the Cabot Cove Players put on their shows in the auditorium of the community center. Not a lot of nooks and crannies there, I can tell you."

Before we had a chance to reply, Maureen came into the room, and I could see she was rattled.

Mort stood and pulled out the vacant chair, but when he got a look at her flushed face, he asked, "What is the matter, honey? Was the shop out of sunglasses?"

"No, no." She held up a pair of tortoise-rimmed eyeglasses with dark lenses. "But, Jessica, I think . . . well, maybe you should see it for yourself."

She tapped my arm and headed for the door. Mort and I exchanged looks and followed behind her while Seth said something about holding down our table, as if there were a long line of hungry people waiting for breakfast in the Victoria Room.

As soon as we reached the hallway leading to the gift shop, I stopped in my tracks. There was a large sign with my picture square in the middle and an announcement: COME MEET EVERYONE'S FAVOURITE MYSTERY WRITER, J. B. FLETCHER. DATE TO BE ANNOUNCED.

A bright blue arrow pointed to the gift shop.

"Oh no," I said. "I will put a stop to this."

I marched resolutely into the gift shop, with Mort and Maureen at my heels. A young woman wearing a pink-checkered apron and a name tag that said GLORIA was stacking copies of several of my books on a table next to the doorway.

She began to ask if she could help us; then she recognized me. "J. B. Fletcher! Oh my goodness." She wiped her hand on the side of her apron and extended it to shake mine. "Welcome. I can't tell you how excited we are . . ."

"Please," I interrupted as gently as I could. "I'd like you to take down the sign in the hallway. I am not on tour; I'm on vacation."

Gloria looked confused for a few seconds and said, "There must be some kind of communication mix-up. Mary Jo said . . ."

"Exactly who do you think got things mixed up?" Mort demanded in his strongest sheriff voice. "Mary Jo or J. B. Fletcher?"

Behind us, just inside the doorway, someone interrupted our conversation. "Mrs. Fletcher! We didn't realize the book signing would be happening today! We would have been so very sad to have missed it, wouldn't we, Iris?"

I turned to see Vivian Zhang tuck a straggling white curl behind her ear.

Iris was quick to reply, "Oh yes. If I missed having you sign my books, it would simply break my heart." And she looked at me with sad puppy-dog eyes.

The pro-signing people were closing in on me, and I was in a quandary about how to respond politely. Fortunately, Mort was well entrenched in sheriff mode. He raised his arm and began gently guiding the two elderly women toward a display of dish towels embroidered with *Edmonton* across the top and a large bison in the center. "Sorry, ladies, but Mrs. Fletcher is here to see the gift shop. The book signing hasn't been scheduled yet."

"That's good news." Vivian gave a sigh of relief. "Iris, we haven't missed a thing."

"You'll let us know when to bring down our books for the signing, won't you, sir?" Iris turned the puppy-dog eyes on Mort.

"Sure will. There'll be plenty of notice." Then he turned to me as if we had someplace to be and said, "Come along, Mrs. F.; we're falling behind schedule."

As Maureen and I followed Mort out of the gift shop, we heard one of the ladies say, "He calls her Mrs. F. Isn't that the cutest thing? Do you think she would mind if we called her Mrs. F. when we come back to get our books signed?"

Maureen started to giggle, and I couldn't help but join in. The entire episode was so far-fetched that I am sure if I'd written it in one of my books, my editor would have questioned my sanity.

Poor Gloria—I was sure we left her completely baffled. One minute I was insisting there would not be a book signing, and the next minute I was being escorted out of the store by what appeared to be my entourage—and, from Mort's conversation with Iris and Vivian, Gloria would definitely think the book signing was going to happen shortly. We would have to take the time to straighten that out later, and I was positive the key person responsible for this nonsense was Mary Jo, not Gloria.

As we came along the hallway, Seth was walking across the lobby toward us, hands stuffed in his pockets, looking rather glum.

"I'm guessing that the cleaning crew didn't find his pen," Mort said under his breath.

Seth confirmed that as soon as he joined us; then he asked what was so important in the gift shop.

Since he was already gloomy, I decided to let the book-signing story wait for another time, so I changed the topic by asking if he'd seen Emma or Mary Jo this morning.

"Nope. Not a single person came into the breakfast room after you left. With only the servers to keep me company, I decided to check at the desk for my pen and then come looking for you."

Maureen pointed behind a pillar at the far end of the lobby. "There's Mary Jo, and she seems to be arguing with that man."

I stepped closer to Maureen to get a better view. Although

they were well hidden from most people in the lobby, from our vantage point it was evident that Mary Jo was indeed involved in what appeared to be a heated argument with Quint Chabot. When she began shaking her finger in his face, Quint pushed her hand away and strode down a back hallway.

Mary Jo swiveled her head as if deciding where to go or what to do, but when she saw us looking straight at her, she made an instant switch into professional mode. Pulling a tissue from her pocket, she patted her eyes and cheeks. While walking toward us, she forced a tight smile.

"Good morning, everyone. How was breakfast? I can assure you we are in for an exciting day today. We'll be having lots of adventures. Be sure to have your cameras at the ready." I am sure she would have continued babbling to prevent us from asking about her argument with Quint, but she was interrupted by Emma yoo-hooing at us from the elevator bank.

She began talking before we had a chance to wish her good morning. "Sorry to say, I will miss touring with you. The long and the tall of it is that our crabby taskmaster, Alan Hughes, has decided that the dance routine I have been working on for the past however long is not what he had in mind. So it's up to the Hugheses' suite I go to learn and practice a new dance routine with our poor put-upon choreographer."

I was incredulous. "In his hotel suite? Won't Rosalie find that terribly inconvenient?"

Emma threw me a questioning look. "How would it inconvenience Rosalie? Oh, I take your meaning. Not to worry, we won't be working in the Hugheses' living quarters. Before we arrived, Alan booked our rooms and arranged for what he calls 'the company suite.' It's where the party was held last evening. We also use it as a rehearsal suite. Alan wants the choreographer to change something to do with the timing. I'll be blasted if I know what or why. As it stands, I will miss exploring with you this morning, but I can promise I'll be ready to take you for your theater tour after lunch. Never you worry; I made that crystal clear to Alan."

Mary Jo chimed in. "Emma, I have a spectacular morning planned for your friends. I promise to text you when we arrive back here so you can join us for a buffet lunch in the Victoria Room. Afterward you can accompany us to the theater."

"Then I will see you all for lunch. Alan Hughes will get quite an earful if he tries to stand in my way." Heading off to the elevators, Emma waved and said, "Cheerio."

Mary Jo clapped her hands, which was a habit I, for one, wished she would lose, and began steering us through the lobby to the main entrance. As we walked, I gently reminded her that I had no intention of doing a book signing while I was on vacation with friends. She merely nodded and began to discuss the day's activities.

"This morning we are going to visit Fort Edmonton Park. I am quite sure you've never seen anything like it."

Seth objected. "We spent yesterday morning in Elk Island National Park. Isn't one park much like another? Lots of flora, lots of fauna."

Mary Jo replied, "Not in this case."

And as the day went by, even Seth had to admit she was right.

During the drive to Fort Edmonton Park, Rob explained to us that the park was a history lesson we would view by a walk through time. The wide-open space was divided into areas where we could see replicas of the community during its varied history, beginning with the Indigenous Peoples Experience, moving through the Settlement Era, and gradually changing into more modern times.

As soon as we entered the park, I could see that the great joy was that we could wander through the exhibits on our own time, and of course that meant we occasionally drifted apart from one another. I was not at all surprised when Seth was drawn to the Fur Trading Era, which was displayed through the interactive 1846 Fort. Mort was fascinated by the 1919 Baldwin steam engine that rode on a track from one end of the park to the other. I was sure he would have ridden it all day if there hadn't been so much else to see.

Every one of us was extremely interested in the history of the First Nations and Métis people who lived on the land for centuries and provide culture and wisdom to this very day.

When Mary Jo rounded us up for lunch, we were all disappointed not to have more time at the park, but Mort and Seth perked right up when they remembered we were going to spend the afternoon at the theater.

Mort looked like a little boy hoping that Santa would come early this year when he asked Mary Jo if she thought Derek Braverman would be at the theater while we were there.

"Who knows?" She dismissed the question with a flap of her hand. "These theater people don't care about anyone but themselves. So why care about them?"

I was amazed that she continued to be downright rude anytime she was questioned about the troupe that was bringing quite a bit of income to the hotel that employed her. I would have thought she would be more outwardly gracious, no matter her personal feelings.

I imagine we all felt the same, as there was complete silence as she herded us to the parking lot, where Rob snapped open the limo door and ushered us inside. He left the privacy window open and began a lively conversation by asking our impressions of the exhibits and attractions. He frequently interrupted to tell us entertaining stories of his own visits to Fort Edmonton Park with family or friends. The atmosphere in the car was so relaxed and entertaining that Mary Jo's rudeness was instantly forgotten.

When we got back to the hotel, Emma was waiting for us in the Victoria Room, and when Maureen asked for her opinion of show folk in general and her fellow performers in particular, Emma had plenty to say, including hilarious anecdotes about forgotten lines, costumes that mysteriously ripped while the actor was onstage, and so on.

"Of course, we've all had a time when we've gone to shambles, but unless you are working with someone who is a bit dodgy, anyone who is onstage will give you a rescue if they possibly can. Even a stagehand will try to provide help from the wings. Why, I once fumbled my lines, not once but twice in the same scene. Turns out I was coming down with the flu, but a stagehand heard my dilemma and stood in the wings, cool as can be, and, checking the cue cards, he whispered my lines just loud enough for me to hear and repeat. That's the kind of people that work in my business, dearies."

After spending our lunchtime listening to Emma provide an insider's view of the cast and crew, we headed off to the theater, a place where, as Emma assured us, comedy and drama were always on tap. Little did we know how right she was. Especially when she mentioned drama.

Chapter Nine

As we approached the Northern Alberta Jubilee Auditorium, it was easy to see why Emma was excited to be featured in a show there. The building was massive and very modern, with high, wide windows covering the entire second and third levels over the main entrance.

As Rob pulled into a space at the edge of the parking lot, he said, "This is the Northern Jubilee, or Jube, as we call it. Its twin down in Calgary is called the Southern Jubilee. They were built to celebrate Alberta's fiftieth anniversary as a province. Much as it's an honor to have Mr. Braverman perform his swan song here, he should feel grateful to be playing in one of the finest venues in Canada, especially since Edmonton is his hometown."

I was surprised and pleased when, before we left the hotel, Emma very nicely but firmly told Mary Jo that she would not have to accompany us to the theater. "You've gone above and beyond in escorting my cousin and her friends. Why don't you kick off your shoes and take a break? I've got it from here."

Mary Jo objected, but Emma wouldn't hear of it, so we were sure to have a relaxing afternoon with no hand clapping to move us along.

Nicholas Dufond was waiting for us in the lobby, flanked by the two stagehands who attended the party last evening. The older one, who I judged was nearer to sixty than fifty, had red hair even brighter than Emma's, so it was no surprise when Nicholas introduced him as Red Pompey. The younger man, Spencer Smith, was certainly no more than forty. He gave us all a cheerful smile that reached right up to his brown eyes, which were a perfect match with the color of his hair. Both men were wearing green coveralls with *Jubilee* embroidered over the left breast pocket.

All three men seemed delighted to have the opportunity to show off the theater that would shortly be home to what Nicholas called *Derek Braverman's Old-Time Revue*.

Emma shrugged her shoulders. "I told Derek and Alan that it sounds like we are putting on a funeral, not a show, but Derek was having none of it. He's determined and Alan won't go against him, so there was no sense in my flogging a dead horse, as it were."

I could tell Nicholas was clearly unsettled by Emma's flamboyance, because he quickly changed the topic to our visit. "I have a grand surprise for you. Frederick the Great and his lovely assistant, Gracelyn, are downstairs in one of our rehearsal rooms, and they have graciously agreed to show you a trick or two. Red will show you the way. After your backstage tour, we will meet again because I have another treat for you in the auditorium."

Red certainly knew his way around the theater. He guided us through doorways and down staircases as he told us stories about the history of the theater and the many famous entertainers who'd brought great joy to audiences through the years.

"Of all the gismos and gadgets in any theater, this is my favorite. We are now under the stage." He walked about ten yards away from us, stepped onto a wide black platform, and pointed up toward the ceiling. "Now watch." He pushed a lever, and a square hole opened in the ceiling. "I am standing on a lift that can bring the orchestra right to floor level in front of the stage. It's very dramatic and audiences love it. I've done it thousands of times and never lost so much as one fiddle player. Still, there is always a first time." He laughed, pulled the lever, and we watched the ceiling close.

"Now when you are at a show and the lights dim and you hear a few strains of music, which gets louder as the roof of the lift opens and the orchestra rises, you will know that I am down here, pulling on that rusty old lever." His laugh was a bit more manic, and he turned back the way we'd come and signaled us to follow along behind him.

We walked past what Red called the costume shop, and through the open door we could see three sewing machines lined up along the back wall and about a dozen racks with outfits neatly hung. I would have enjoyed a closer look, but Red hurried along.

"Here we go." Red knocked on a door.

Gracelyn opened it a few inches and murmured, "Password, please."

"*Wizardry!*" Red boomed.

The door opened wide and we entered the room, which was so dark it was impossible to see clearly.

Gracelyn lit a candle and pointed it to her left where a cloud of smoke was rising from the floor; when it cleared, Frederick the Great, wrapped in a gray spangled cape, was standing in front of us.

"Welcome to you all," Frederick said in a deep, gravelly tone. "I am preparing for my part in Braverman's show, and I am happy to have an audience. You, sir." He pointed to Mort. "Please step up to the table."

Mort hesitated for no more than a second when Maureen gave him a gentle push.

"You are a sheriff, are you not?"

"I am."

"Then I will trust you to assist me with a simple card trick." Frederick shuffled a deck of blue-backed cards and spread them faceup so we could see that they were a normal deck. He then picked up two blank cards with pink backing, wrote something on each card, and turned them facedown so we couldn't see what he had written.

"Now, Sheriff, I ask you to spread the deck until you find a place for one of my pink cards."

Mort did so, and after Frederick slid the card into the deck, he asked Mort to find a place for the other pink card. After Mort complied, Frederick spread the deck on the table and pulled out the two pink cards and the blue cards immediately to the right of them.

The blue cards were the queen of diamonds and the four of clubs. And on the pink cards we could see that before Mort had made his choices, Frederick had plainly written the names of the two cards.

We cheered and clapped, and Red said, "Aw, that's nothing. You should see him do the ring trick."

"Well, the ring trick will have to wait for opening night, dear friends. Frederick the Great needs to rehearse," Gracelyn said as she led us to the door.

"Wasn't that something to see?" Emma said. "Red, I wonder what else you have in store for us."

"Right this way." Red led us down a long hallway and showed us thick ropes hanging with weights attached from the ceiling several stories above us. "These ropes are the ones that raise and lower the curtains, and we stagehands have to make sure the curtains move exactly on the correct minute." He puffed out his chest with pride. "Can't have the curtain come down while the actors are still speaking or singing. That wouldn't be right."

"You don't have to tell me how important that is," Emma said, and we all laughed.

Red opened the door to what looked like the main workroom of a major factory, with all sorts of saws and machines along with paint and paste. "And this is where the scenery comes to life. Sets are built, and then sets are struck down to be reused. You see that wall, the one with the window halfway up? By the time we use it again, the window will be gone, and the wall will look like brick or some such. Gotta love the talent of the set designers. Use and reuse is their motto."

We walked along the passageway, and when Red opened the next door, all I could think was that the large room was a cross between Toyland and a furniture store.

"This is our prop room. Does anyone know the difference between scenery and props? Anyone but Miss Emma, that is?" Red gave us a few seconds to think. "No guesses, eh? Well, I'll tell you. Scenery stays put. A wall is a wall, but props can be carried or moved, so from the audience you may see an actor carry an umbrella or move a small chair."

"I never thought about it," Maureen said, "all the work that goes into the preparation for every scene."

"And with as many scenery changes as Mr. Braverman's revue has, we stagehands have to be on our toes. For example, you see this cane? Derek brought it in from some old movie he starred in because he wants to use it again. Now let's get up to the auditorium for the big finale."

As we left the prop room, Mort expressed surprise that it was left unlocked.

"Who'd want this old junk?" Red asked as he led us back the way we'd come and stopped by the orchestra lift. "Okay, ladies and gents, we are going to take a shortcut. Please move to the center of the lift."

"You are not serious," Seth blustered.

"Never more so." Red grinned. "This lift can hold a twenty-person orchestra and all their instruments. It will have no trouble raising our puny little group."

I felt a little uneasy, but I stepped onto the lift along with the others, and we all moved slowly to the center. The ceiling above us opened and in no time at all, the lift stopped and we were on the main floor of the auditorium, directly in front of the stage. Clearly this was all prearranged, because Spencer, the stagehand we'd met earlier, was waiting for us. He guided us to seats in the fifth row center and asked if we were comfortable, which of course we were, and excused himself.

"Imagine if we could snag these seats for opening night," Mort said.

"I don't know. What do you think, Emma? Isn't it more likely that we'll be up there?" Seth pointed to the second balcony just as a spotlight lit the center of the stage and Jorge Escarra stepped out in front of the curtain.

Spontaneously we all began to clap.

"Thank you, thank you so very much. I apologize that last night I was unable to perform for you, because the acoustics in the hotel suite, well, it would not do justice to any song and especially not this one."

And he began to sing the Canadian national anthem, "O Canada," in his strong, clear baritone voice.

Every one of us stood immediately.

After he finished, Jorge asked us to be seated. "Now if I may, I will share with you one of my favorite folk songs. I hope you will enjoy 'Land of the Silver Birch.'"

It was a rousing song that spoke to much of what we'd seen of Canada on our tours: gorgeous countryside, lakes, beaver, and moose. The chorus, made up largely of "booms," had us clapping and stamping our feet.

Jorge looked at his wristwatch, and when we were quiet, he asked, "Now, before we adjourn for the day, do you have any questions about, well, just about anything at all?"

Mort's hand shot up in the air. "From what I could tell from last night's party, you and Derek Braverman are longtime friends."

Jorge preened. "Yes, we are. You could say lifelong."

"Then you'd be able to tell us his real name." Mort was so

satisfied that the mystery was finally going to be solved that he signaled a thumbs-up to Seth, who returned it with a confident smile.

Jorge Escarra blanched. Clearly Mort's question made him downright uncomfortable. He clenched and unclenched his hands and stammered slightly as he answered. "Um, um, er, I don't understand the question. Of course Derek Braverman is his real name. Why would anyone think differently?" Then Jorge shouted, "Red! Spencer! Isn't it past time to escort our guests to the lobby?"

Then he disappeared behind the curtain, reminding me of the Wizard of Oz.

"Well, that was daft," Emma said. "One minute we are all best chums; then the sheriff's question turned Jorge all bonkers. If it is any help, as far as I know, Derek Braverman has always been Derek Braverman, so I can't for the life of me figure why the question rattled Jorge."

If Red or Spencer noticed anything odd about Jorge's sudden disappearance, they didn't show any sign.

"Loved the 'Silver Birch' song, now, didn't you?" Spencer said. "Those booms can always get the blood pumping. Come along; we have one more surprise for you."

He and Red led us up the long aisle to the theater lobby, and as we walked through the door, Derek Braverman was waiting for us. "You didn't think we'd let you stop over without a small celebration, now did you?" He turned to a well-lit bar set up off to one corner, and on cue, Quint Chabot, wearing his bartender's uniform, hoisted a bottle of champagne and proceeded to pop the cork.

"Please, everyone, let this afternoon be the beginning of many weeks of festivities acknowledging my retirement from show business." Braverman took a glass from Quint, held it up in the air, and then drained it dry. I was somewhat surprised he didn't smash it on the floor.

Jorge Escarra joined us, and after Derek had us all praise Jorge's singing, I noticed the two had moved off to a quiet part of the lobby and were having a hushed tête-à-tête. At the same time, Red Pompey was leaning on the bar, and he and Quint Chabot were speaking through clenched teeth. I was not close enough to hear what they were saying, but Emma was pretending to study a poster on the wall near the bar, so I was sure she caught the gist of their argument and we would surely gossip about it later.

Mort and Seth were hovering not too distantly from Jorge and Derek. I suspected they were waiting for a chance to talk to Braverman one-on-one.

Just as Spencer Smith offered to get Maureen and me another glass of champagne, the front door opened and Dennis Oliver entered the lobby. He came to a full stop, clearly taken aback by our presence.

"Hello, all; don't let me interrupt." He looked around, waved to Derek, and headed to a side door, but as he passed the bar, Quint stepped in front of him and offered him a glass of champagne.

"I'm here to work, not to play," Dennis said as he tried to brush past Quint, who responded, "Well, you don't have to be so cross about it."

Dennis stood stock-still for a moment, glaring at Quint, then said, "Watch your mouth," and stormed out of the lobby.

Before we could recover from that odd scene, Derek rather

loudly told Spencer to go out and ask Rob to bring the car around to the front door. That was the signal that our visit was coming to an end. I looked around, and Emma was nowhere to be seen. And that would be far from the most mysterious thing to happen in the theater before the evening's end.

Chapter Ten

Rob pulled the limo directly in front of the wide glass doors at the exact moment Derek realized that Emma was not in the lobby. He ordered Red to find her, and a couple of minutes later, we were all surprised to hear Red's voice over a loudspeaker reverberating throughout the building. He requested that Emma return to the lobby because her party was ready to leave.

Instead of being pleased, Derek was apoplectic. "I could have done that. Anyone can bellow. I wanted him to find her and bring her back immediately so that you people could leave."

He began pacing back and forth, and when Mort and Seth walked over to him, he must have assumed that they were about to question him, so he spoke first. "I know. I know. You've heard the old rumors about my name not being my name. Well, I am sorry to disappoint, but my birth certificate clearly says Sebastian Derek Braverman, and since the eighteen letters of Sebastian

Braverman would be an awkward fit on a movie marquee, I went with my middle name. There is no secret about it, but since you both seemed awfully interested in my name, I thought I would explain why you may occasionally hear that Derek Braverman is my stage name."

Mort turned red faced and began to apologize, going so far as to mention the rumors Dan Andrews heard in the schoolyard all those years ago.

Braverman cut Mort off when Emma came through the auditorium door. "My dear Emma, this place is too big for you to go wandering off alone. You've no idea the number of ghosts that could be hovering, looking for souls to steal."

Emma brushed him off with a laugh. "This theater is far too new to have many ghosts of past actors floating about, trying to find new bodies so that they can take to the stage once more. Besides, I only went to my dressing room to pick up a pair of earrings I left behind when the rehearsal of our song-and-dance set last Thursday went long into the night. I found my way there and back without the least bit of trouble."

"Your chariot awaits, as do your companions," Derek said lightly, and walked to the bar so Quint could refill his glass. "I will see you at dinner in the Victoria Room."

The car ride back to the hotel was subdued, probably because we were all tired after such a long, exciting day. I was feeling stiff and decided to use what free time I could find before dinner to get some exercise.

Rob clearly understood our mood, because after he asked a question or two about our theater tour and got halfhearted answers, he put some soft music on and closed the privacy window for the duration of the ride back to our hotel.

When he pulled the car into the driveway, I suppose I should not have been surprised to see Mary Jo waiting for us in the entryway. As soon as we exited the car, Mary Jo was filled with questions, clearly wanting reassurance that we had enjoyed our day, but when she saw how lackadaisical we were, she said she had an announcement and switched to hand-clapping mode as if to liven us up, but the only person who responded was my cousin Emma, whose energy was always boundless.

"Whatever you have in mind, Mary Jo, I guarantee we are up for it," Emma said.

I was just as sure that Emma's enthusiastic answer made at least one or two of us groan internally.

"I am so glad to hear it," Mary Jo said. "Mr. Braverman is sponsoring another private dinner for you in the Victoria Room to be followed by hosting you all in the Beaver Bar to watch an exhibition game featuring the Edmonton Oilers hockey team. The game is raising money for Food Banks Canada, and Mr. Braverman is one of the financial supporters." Mary Jo smiled as though she was ready to accept accolades for arranging the evening. Instead, she received perfunctory thanks, and we made our way into the hotel lobby.

It was just my luck that Iris and Vivian were sitting on a love seat not far from the front door. Vivian was knitting something multicolored, while Iris was people watching. As soon as she spotted me, Iris called out, "Give a wave, Vivian; there is J. B. Fletcher. Never fear, we will be at your book signing, Mrs. F."

Rather than telling them I had no plans to do a signing, I smiled in their direction and, along with my friends, kept on walking to the elevators. As we rode to the fifth floor, I announced that I was going to change my clothes and find the hotel gym. Maureen asked if she could come along.

"To tell you the truth, Jessica, as much fun as we've been having, I feel like I've been neglecting my exercise routine. Anyone else want to join us?"

Emma said she was going off in search of the choreographer because being at the theater had given her a few ideas for changes in her dance routine but that she would knock on my door before dinner. Seth and Mort both opted for naps.

Maureen and I agreed to meet back by the elevators in twenty minutes, and we all went our separate ways.

The hotel gym was large, clean, and brightly lit. As soon as we walked in, we were surrounded by energetic music. To my left was a row of treadmills, with an equal number of exercise bicycles just opposite. Other than two gentlemen pumping hand weights in front of the mirrors along the far wall, the gym was empty.

"Oh, this is heaven." Maureen sighed. "It's a treadmill for me. What's your choice?"

I climbed on the nearest bicycle. "I think I will pretend I am pedaling my way through Fort Edmonton Park."

While she walked and I biked, Maureen and I talked about all the wonderful things we had seen since arriving in Edmonton.

We'd nearly finished the half hour we'd agreed upon when the door opened and a middle-aged woman dressed in a tan sweatshirt and jeans came into the gym.

"I hate to bother you, but I seem to have lost my compact.

Perhaps you've seen it? It is round, silver with the monogram *MG* on the top."

Neither Maureen nor I had seen it, but we stopped exercising in order to help the woman search. It quickly became evident that the compact was not in the gym.

Before she left, the woman introduced herself as Margaret Gallagher. "I was in the lobby while I waited for my husband to take a business call on one of the house phones, and I took the compact out of my pocket to 'powder my nose,' as they say. Then Barney, my husband, needed to do some work on his laptop, so I came up here to walk on the treadmill until he was done. It wasn't long before he came looking for me, and we went out for the afternoon. In the car, while Barney was driving to the Royal Alberta Museum, I decided to do another touch-up and, well, my compact was missing."

We suggested that she check with the front desk, not that either Seth or Maureen had any success finding their lost items through the lobby cleaners' efforts, but we hoped she'd have better luck.

She thanked us, and after she left, I said to Maureen, "Isn't it odd that so many visitors to this hotel seem to lose their belongings?"

"It might seem that way to an experienced traveler like you, Jessica, but as someone who needs to live by the 'a place for everything and everything in its place' rule or my life is in absolute shambles, I am amazed that I have lost *only* my sunglasses. Of course, we will be here a while longer, so there is a strong possibility I may lose something else." Maureen giggled, and she glanced at the wall clock. "Well, time's up. We'll be expected in the Victoria Room for dinner before you know it."

So, laughing and talking about the caprices of hotel life, we headed to the elevators.

Emma knocked on my door a few minutes before dinner, and we went down to the Victoria Room together. Mort and Maureen were already seated at the long table. Seth came in so quickly that I thought he must have been in the elevator right behind ours.

He looked around and said, "Ayuh, I thought I was running late, but this table is still rather empty, so I must be on time."

Mary Jo came in right behind him and stood at the head of the table. "Derek Braverman sent his excuses and said he would meet you later in the Beaver Bar. Not to worry, he will be here in plenty of time for the hockey game."

Then she looked at the empty places and said, "I have no idea where the Hugheses or Dennis Oliver are, but we certainly don't want you to be late for the game, so dinner service had better get started."

She wiggled her fingers at the servers who were standing next to the bar, and they disappeared behind the curtain, only to come back immediately carrying plates of salad.

"I'm sorry; I have hotel business to attend to. Please let the servers know if you have any difficulties." And Mary Jo slipped out of the room.

Emma said exactly what we were all thinking. "Well, this is a dinner I am looking forward to—not one person at this table is likely to get all shirty about some unimportant thing and ruin the evening for the rest of us."

"Shirty?" Mort asked.

"Cranky, ill-tempered," I said as I took a bite of the sliced bell pepper that edged my salad.

Maureen said, "True. I remember Rosalie getting 'all shirty' because Dennis Oliver was two minutes late for dinner. I was afraid we wouldn't be allowed to eat at all if he didn't show up. And was I a happy one when Dennis Oliver planted himself in the vacant chair. Dinner could begin."

We all laughed, and the tone of the evening was set, at least until Panuk came in very discreetly just as the dessert dishes were being cleared.

He whispered, "I am sorry for the intrusion," and handed Emma a note.

She unfolded it and said, "Worse luck. I am sorry to let you all down, but it seems I've been ordered to work this evening. You will have to enjoy the hockey game without me."

"Don't be so quick to run off," Seth said. "If by work you mean you are going to be singing and dancing, I for one would enjoy coming along to watch."

Emma chuckled. "Sorry, Doctor, but you are talking about the fun part of my job. There's lots of drudgery too. And don't forget spontaneous orders from the director. Alan sent this note because he needs me to go back to the theater to meet with the costumer."

"When? Now? Whatever for?" Seth asked.

Emma took out her cell phone. "Ah, the answer will be here. I turned the ringer to silent when we were at the theater, and it seems I never bothered to turn it on again. And I've two text messages from Lene Gadue. She's the costumer." She tapped the phone.

"Fittings. Lene is ready to do fittings. Jess, why don't you come along? I'd value your opinion about the costumes, and on the way you can tell me the latest news about Grady, Donna, and young Frank. I expect he is six feet tall by now."

"Not quite, but he is taller every time I see him. And I wouldn't mind learning how a professional costumer gussies up a famous star," I teased.

"Oh, go on with you." Emma laughed. "And here is the fine gentleman who will be our driver."

Although I expected to see Rob, Spencer Smith was standing in the doorway.

"Good evening, Ms. Macgill. Mr. Hughes asked me to drive you to the theater to meet Ms. Gadue. I am to unlock the doors and stay in the theater until you are ready for me to drive you back here." Spencer outlined his duties with careful precision.

Always gracious, Emma promised my fellow Cabot Covers that we wouldn't be gone for long and that we would join them in the Beaver Bar very shortly.

Emma and I spent the ride catching up on new family doings and reminiscing about long-ago antics. It seemed like only a minute had gone by when Spencer parked his midnight-black Jeep Compass at the Jubilee Auditorium and pointed to a woman sitting on a bench with a super-large rolling suitcase in front of her. "There's Ms. Gadue. I hope she wasn't waiting long."

He had no reason to fret. Lene Gadue, a young, statuesque blonde, was cheerful and completely professional. She thanked Emma for taking time from her evening to accommodate the fittings and thanked Spencer for agreeing to open the building. "I was so pleased when Mr. Hughes assured me that you would stay in the building for as long as we needed and act as our body-guard."

Spencer flushed at the compliment. We entered the building, and he asked us to stand in the lobby while he went to turn on the building lights. Emma introduced me to Lene, who said she was delighted to meet Emma's mystery-writer cousin. In a few minutes, Spencer came back and escorted us to the costume shop. Once he unlocked the door, he told us he had some pullies to check, but he would be quite nearby. "Just give a shout, and I'll come running."

Lene got right down to business; she placed a large art pad on an easel. "Here is the drawing for the powder-blue velveteen ball gown for the duet of romance songs you and Derek will sing as the opener for act two. And this"—Lene reached into her suitcase—"is the mock-up for you to try on so we can get the measurements absolutely perfect."

She was scooping a voluminous amount of muslin out of the suitcase when the three of us heard Spencer shriek. "Get an ambulance! I think . . . I think he's dead."

Chapter Eleven

Lene dropped the muslin on the floor, nearly tripping herself in the process, and we three raced out into the hallway. Following the sound of Spencer's repeated calls for help, we got to the orchestra lift where we saw Spencer kneeling next to a man's motionless body sprawled on the lift floor. Although his head was bloodied, Quint, the bartender and sometime stagehand, was easily recognizable.

Since I wasn't positive that the emergency number in Canada was the same 911 that we used in America, I was grateful Lene pulled out her cell, tapped in three digits, and quickly described the situation. She listened briefly and then said, "Yes, of course. We will. Thank you.

"The 911 operator has asked that someone meet the responders at the front door to direct them this way and that at least two of us stay here with . . ."

Emma immediately leaned down next to Spencer and lightly touched his shoulder. "What do you say, luv? You and I will let the helpers in, shall we?"

He nodded and touched the key ring on his belt. Then, as if relieved to have a purpose, Spencer stood straight, and he and Emma made their way to the lobby.

I moved as close as I dared to the body. Quint was no longer wearing his bartender clothes. Instead, he had on work boots, jeans, and a black T-shirt. Off in the corner, as if someone had tossed it, was a wooden cane with an intricately designed, over-sized gold knob for a handle.

I took my flashlight out of my purse and bent over to take a careful look. As soon as the light hit the knob, I could see there was fresh blood on the ridges and in the crevices.

"Lene, do you happen to know what this is?" It looked similar to the cane Nicholas had said belonged to Derek. I wondered if it was the one he brought for this revue or an odd piece left from a previous play.

She came to my side and peered at the cane. "Oh my, that's Derek's. He uses it in act one, scene four, when he is reprising a speech from his first science fiction movie, *The Emperor of Planet Twenty-Three*. That cane was the prop he carried all throughout the movie. He brought it in here for the first rehearsal along with pictures of his original costume for me to replicate. Oh, you don't think Derek . . ."

I stopped her right there. "Lene, it is far too soon to think anything other than the obvious: Quint is dead and somebody killed him."

"Excuse me, madam. May I ask what makes you so positive that there was a murder committed here tonight?"

As I turned toward the deep voice directly behind me, two paramedics carrying bags and equipment rushed past me and bent over Quint Chabot.

A stocky, balding man wearing a gray pinstriped suit with a purple-and-black tie knotted loosely at the collar of his white shirt held up his identification and introduced himself as Inspector James Radigan of the Edmonton Police Service. "You can surely understand why I have an interest in your certainty that a murder has occurred in my jurisdiction. If you would kindly explain, Ms. . . ."

"Mrs., it's Mrs. Jessica Fletcher," I said as I pointed at the body. "Well, you can plainly see that Quint Chabot has a large wound on the side of his head, which is likely the cause of death and definitely not self-inflicted."

"If I could interrupt for a moment," the inspector said, "I neglected to ask if you knew the victim, but I now know that you did. Sergeant Enook, please take this young lady"—he pointed to Lene Gadue, who was standing silently next to me—"away from this area until I have time to speak privately with her. And have a constable make sure there is no conversation between the other two, ah, witnesses until I have interviewed them."

A trim, thirtyish dark-haired woman wearing a well-tailored police uniform with chevrons on her sleeve asked Lene to please follow her, and they swiftly moved out of sight.

Inspector Radigan immediately returned his attention to me. "Now let's start at the beginning, Mrs. Fletcher. How is it that you are here at the otherwise vacant Northern Alberta Jubilee Auditorium at this time of night with three other people and the corpse of a man you knew?"

I explained that my cousin, Emma Macgill, was performing

in the upcoming Derek Braverman revue and that I'd accompanied her here to meet the costumer, Lene Gadue, for one of Emma's fittings. Spencer Smith, a stagehand at the theater, had been assigned to drive us here from the hotel and then gone off to work on something or other to do with pulleys, while the three of us were in what Emma called the costume shop.

The inspector nodded and stepped toward Quint's body. He suddenly stopped and turned back to me, one hand raised in the air. And when he said, "Just one more thing, Mrs. Fletcher," I nearly giggled. He definitely reminded me of the cigar-smoking Lieutenant Columbo from the television show Frank and I used to watch regularly. "Was there any special reason that you and Ms. Macgill chose Spencer Smith as your driver this evening?"

"We didn't choose Spencer, although we were quite happy to have him drive us. Alan Hughes, the director of the revue, assigned Spencer to bring us here to meet Lene Gadue, probably because Spencer is a stagehand and has keys to the building and all the rooms.

"When my friends and I have gone out to tour the many charms of Edmonton, a hotel employee, Rob Langford—who, fortunately for us, is an expert in local history—has been our driver, until tonight. I don't know why Alan asked Spencer to drive us to the theater other than, perhaps, since this was a work assignment for Emma and not one of our tourist ventures, he may not have considered it to be an assignment suitable for a hotel employee. And, as I mentioned, Spencer has keys to the theater, which Emma does not. When we arrived, Lene Gadue was waiting outside the building, so I presume she also did not have access to the theater keys."

Inspector Radigan's pensive look cleared. He thanked me for my time, and then he told a nearby uniformed constable to escort me to Sergeant Enook. He charged the constable with relaying to the sergeant that I was to stay with her until he gave me permission to leave. I knew that message was intended for me as well.

There was no point in my telling him that Emma, Spencer, and I had all arrived together, which meant that, realistically, I expected it would be quite a while before we would be allowed to leave, since we would be traveling together. I merely smiled my thanks and followed the constable to the costume shop, where Lene was showing the sergeant a pair of antique-looking white lace gloves that were definitely elbow length or longer.

"Today these are called evening gloves, but originally they were known as opera gloves because the ladies wore them as an accompaniment to the elaborate gowns that were considered de rigueur when they attended the opera. Aren't they glamorous? Would you care to try one on?" Lene was passing the delicate gloves to the sergeant as I walked into the room. When she saw me, she changed into questioning mode. "Oh, Jessica, are you finished talking with that inspector? Can we get on with the fitting? Where is Emma? My schedule is really tight. If these costumes are to be ready for opening night, I can't afford to lose precious hours."

Sergeant Enook said gently but firmly, "This theater is a crime scene. Inspector Radigan will make all decisions regarding access to this building. And I am afraid that will include deciding if and when opening night will occur."

The constable who had left me under Sergeant Enook's watchful eye was once again in the doorway. "Excuse me, Sarge. Inspector Radigan would like to see the young lady."

When he pointed to Lene, she hesitated for a moment and then threw back her shoulders and said to me, "I can't tell him anything helpful, Jessica, so I'm sure I'll be back in a few. Feel free to look at some of my costume books on the back table while you wait."

The top of the long wooden table was scarred by years of books, sewing equipment, and assorted costume decorations. I opened one of the books, which happened to contain a dozen pictures of period costumes from what I surmised was the 1930s. I turned a few pages and then casually asked the sergeant if she knew where my cousin Emma was being held.

"Oh, I think 'being held' is too strong a phrase, Mrs. Fletcher," Sergeant Enook corrected me. "It implies that we are forcing you, your cousin, and your acquaintances to remain here against your will, when obviously that is not the case. It appears to me that you all are amenable, if not eager, to cooperate in Inspector Radigan's investigation of the death that occurred on these premises."

I was not surprised by her way of seeing our situation, but I still wished to know exactly what course the interview process was taking and when we might reasonably expect to return to our hotel. "Naturally, we all wish to cooperate in every way possible . . ."

"Mrs. Fletcher," Sergeant Enook interrupted me, "your murder mysteries are quite popular here in Canada, and I have enjoyed reading any number of them, so I know that you are not unfamiliar with police procedure. I am sure you are aware that it is common practice to keep witnesses from hearing one another's statements so that we get each person's version of what they saw and heard without their impression of events being tainted by what they may overhear another witness say."

Her soft smile at the end of her speech made me feel just a tad less chastised than I would have felt if she'd ended by shaking her finger at my thoughtless behavior.

I nodded in acknowledgment that I agreed with her explanation, but nevertheless, I continued to pursue my point. "I understand completely. What I am trying to find out is whether or not they are all right. Spencer Smith was quite shaken when Emma very gently guided him away from Quint's body so that he could unlock the door for you and the medical personnel. Since I haven't seen either of them since, I would like some assurances that they are not in need of medical assistance themselves, particularly Spencer."

"Say no more." Sergeant Enook pulled a radio from her belt and asked who had the male witness.

The radio crackled and a man responded. "Cloutier here. I am providing escort to Spencer Smith."

"Please see that he drinks some water and, when available, have an emergency medical technician examine him for signs of shock," the sergeant said.

The radio went silent after Constable Cloutier replied, "Copy that."

"There you go, Mrs. Fletcher. No further worries. I've worked with Inspector Radigan a long time, and I can assure you he understands that we all have lives and doesn't keep witnesses any longer than necessary," Sergeant Enook said with a profound look of compassion in her eyes.

And she was right. We all have lives. But someone, perhaps someone I'd recently met, had decided to end Quint Chabot's life in an orchestra lift with a theater prop as a weapon. And that was going to cast a dark cloud over the rest of my stay in Edmonton; of that I was certain.

Chapter Twelve

I whiled away the time turning pages in the costume books, but I barely looked at the designs because my brain was busily trying to decipher the small amount of information that I knew about Quint Chabot. I knew he had at least two jobs. He tended bar at the hotel and worked as a stagehand at the theater.

Derek Braverman brought him to the theater to tend bar at our predinner cocktail party after our theater tour. Quint was dressed in his dark pants and white jacket bartender uniform. A few hours later, Spencer Smith found Quint's dead body in the orchestra lift, dressed in what appeared to be work clothes suitable for his job as a stagehand. I wondered if Quint had stayed behind and changed his clothes for a chore of some kind. Did he have a locker somewhere, and if so, what, besides a change of clothes, might he have kept inside it?

I couldn't wait to see Spencer to ask him the many questions spinning around in my mind, although I did realize he might not be in the best condition to answer them.

At long last, Sergeant Enook answered her cell phone, said a few words, and clicked off, then said, "Well, Mrs. Fletcher, Inspector Radigan has asked that I accompany you to the lobby. I suspect the interviews are over and you and your friends will be leaving the theater quite soon."

"Now that is good news." I picked up my purse and followed her out of the costume shop. I noticed she didn't turn off the lights or close the door, probably because the police and forensic analysts would be examining the theater from top to bottom for hours to come.

When we got to the lobby, Emma, who had clearly been crying, ran over to give me a hug. "Oh, Jessie, I wanted this to be a fun get-together, and someone has gone and thrown a major spanner in the works. I am so sorry to have ruined this vacation for you and your friends."

Emma hadn't called me Jessie since we were teenagers, so that was a definite indication that she was far more upset than I was and was going to need some coddling. I drew a tissue from the packet in my purse and handed it to her. "Emma, none of this was your fault. We were merely in the wrong place at the wrong time. If Alan hadn't wanted you and Lene . . ."

I didn't get another word out because Emma turned on a dime, her demeanor leaping from sad to angry.

"Alan Hughes!" The name, dripping with vitriol, exploded from Emma's mouth. "Everyone else is back at the hotel, living the high life and watching the Oilers play their charity match, while I get sent off to work. I should have told him to put a sock in it. If I had, we wouldn't be stuck here with all this going on."

Emma waved her hand imperiously at the cadre of police person-nel moving both in and out of the lobby.

Lene, who, along with her police escort, had been standing by the ticket window, rushed over and grabbed Emma by the hand. "Oh, Emma, don't blame Alan. This is all my fault. I asked Alan to set up costume consultations and try-ons during the evenings because I was extremely fearful that I wouldn't be able to get everyone's costumes ready for final fittings in time for the dress rehearsal."

Before Emma had a chance to respond, I stepped in and said to them both as gently as I could, "The only person responsible for all our turmoil this evening is the person who murdered Quint Chabot."

The look on Inspector Radigan's face said that while we might be in a world-famous theater, he had had quite enough drama from us all. He loudly demanded everyone's attention. "Mrs. Fletcher, Ms. Macgill, one of my constables has already collected your passports from the hotel safe, so I expect that you will be staying in Edmonton for the foreseeable future. Mr. Smith and Ms. Gadue, please provide your home address and any other con-tact information to your police escorts, and then you may leave. I assure you all that my constables will be in touch again in the very near future."

After Lene told us that she had arrived in her own car and was comfortable making her way home alone, Spencer, Emma, and I walked to his Jeep Compass in silence, as though we didn't feel comfortable talking about the traumatic event we had experi-enced. Spencer broke the tension when Emma said that if discov-ering Quint's body had left him too stressed to drive, she would be happy to do so.

"No disrespect meant, Ms. Macgill, but that would make me terribly nervous. You are used to driving in England, so I'd be worried about your forgetting to keep my car on the right side of the road and wind up drifting off to the left," Spencer answered.

"Well, you got me there," Emma said as she opened the back door of the car. "Even as a passenger, I get extremely edgy when I am in any country where the cars are driven on what I always think of as the wrong side of the road. I keep expecting a head-on collision. I will be very comfortable and more than happy to sit back here. Jessica, you can sit up front and be Spencer's copilot."

"Then you are on your own," I said to Spencer. "I'll be of no help since I don't have a driver's license."

Spencer focused his energy on maneuvering around a large swath of the parking lot that was roped off by crime-scene tape. A lone red car in the middle of that section had the undivided attention of multiple crime-scene technicians. Once we were on the main road heading back to the hotel, he spoke. "The police found Quint's bartender uniform and the used trays and glasses from Braverman's lobby party in his car. There was also a half case of champagne in the trunk."

"Really? Why do you suppose . . ."

"That's what they wanted to know. Once I explained that Quint had two jobs, they were curious why he changed his clothes and stayed behind after everyone else left to go back to the hotel."

"I wondered the same thing when you called us and I first saw his body," I said. "Is it possible that he had a job here at the Auditorium that he needed to complete? Did someone have rehearsals scheduled for tomorrow and need scenery finished or updated?"

"Nothing I know of. In fact, Red and I both were at a loss as to why Mr. Hughes decided to add Quint to the team when we had all the stage work well in hand," Spencer replied.

"Alan hired him. Doesn't that beat the cake to fluffy," Emma said. "The purse strings belong to Rosalie, and she watches spending like a hawk. I can't imagine she was happy with a last-minute hire. And he didn't give you a reason for the hire, Spencer? Alan just up and gave Quint a job?"

"Shortly before you all arrived, our third stagehand, a kid named Michel, decided to head off to Calgary, where he thought he might find greener pastures. When Nicholas called Mr. Hughes to relay the information, Hughes told him that the show Braverman envisioned was only a fluff revue and could easily be run with two stagehands. Then in less than a week after he arrived, Mr. Hughes called Nicholas and told him that Quint would be 'helping out' as a part-timer. Made no sense, but that's show people, eh? No offense meant to you, Ms. Macgill," Spencer said as he pulled into the hotel driveway.

Emma laughed. "None taken for anything you've said, I'm sure. I admit I am one hundred percent miffed to hear that Alan has been calling our show a 'fluff revue.' But don't you worry; he'll never know it was you who let that particular cat out of the bag."

We waved as Spencer drove away, but when I began walking to the hotel door, Emma seized my arm to stop me.

"Jess, it really has been that kind of night, hasn't it? What say we take a short walk, just the two of us, before we go inside and are barraged with even more questions than we heard from the police."

I looped my arm through hers, and we strolled toward the hotel garden, breathing in the cool evening air, each of us sorting out our own thoughts about what had happened and what lay ahead.

The garden was peaceful, as quiet as a churchyard at midnight. When we reached the lovely white picket fence that indicated we'd gone as far as we could, we followed the left turn in the path that would lead us back to the hotel. As soon as we did, I picked up the sound of someone crying.

"Do you hear that?" I whispered to Emma, and when she nodded, I said, "Let's see if we can offer some help."

I think we were both surprised when we found Gracelyn Lapointe sitting on a curvy wooden bench with wrought iron trim. Her legs were scrunched up on the bench slats, and she was hugging herself fiercely. Tears were streaming down her face, and she made no attempt to hide them even when she saw us approach.

Emma sat next to her and fished a lace-edged handkerchief from her pocket. She handed it to Gracelyn, who nodded her thanks and blotted her cheeks with the hankie; her tears slowed but didn't stop.

After a few minutes, she hiccupped twice, and then her tears spluttered to a stop. "You ladies are so kind. I'm fine, really. It's just a work problem." Gracelyn tried her best, but a tear began to trickle. I was afraid the torrents would start again, so I asked her to tell us if we could help in any way.

"No one can help me. I am at my wit's end. It's Frederick. I think he is going to fire me." Gracelyn heaved a great sigh.

Emma gasped. "You must be mistaken. Why on earth would Frederick let you go? I've seen your magic act. Your performance is flawless."

"A magic act is all about the props; they are the tools of our trade. And as the magician's assistant, I am responsible for seeing that they are appropriately cared for. But lately some of our most important tools have gone missing. Others are available but not stored properly, when I know I did everything exactly as I am supposed to, precisely as I was trained to do."

"Perhaps the cleaning crew or the stagehands . . ." Emma began, but got no further.

"Exactly my thought—the stagehands, one in particular—and I can guarantee I won't have that problem anymore now that Quint Chabot is dead. Oh, I sound so cruel." Gracelyn began to cry again, which led me to believe she might have undisclosed feelings for Quint that complicated matters between them.

And she also had answered one question that had been floating around my mind. If Gracelyn knew that Quint was dead, I was sure the entire ensemble knew. But I still had to wonder if they knew he was murdered. I sat on the other side of her and patted her hand. "Gracelyn, please tell us why you think Quint would deliberately sabotage any of the apparatus that is critical for Frederick the Great's act."

"It is kind of sordid. Quint and I knew each other a few years ago when we both worked in Vancouver." Gracelyn took a deep breath. "We were involved. Romantically involved. At least we were until he borrowed a couple of thousand dollars from me for an emergency car repair and then, poof! Quint disappeared quicker than the ace of spades in one of Frederick's card tricks."

"Oh, dearie, I am sorry. That's a scoundrel's move if ever there was one," Emma said. "And did you search for him to try to make him return your money? Is that how you found the dodgy bloke here?"

"Glory, no." Gracelyn was adamant. "Once I found out the hard way that he was a user and a thief, I decided it would make no sense to look for him. Two thousand was a small price to pay to be sure he was out of my life forever."

"So you had no idea he was in Edmonton? Your discovering that Quint was here was pure happenstance?" I was sure that, given the site of Quint's murder, Inspector Radigan would soon be here at the hotel, questioning everyone involved with Braverman's revue. Gracelyn was so upset when Emma and I came across her that it would be to her advantage if she could satisfy my curiosity and at the same time organize her thoughts before being formally interviewed, although I was reasonably sure that she had no idea a police interview was on the horizon.

"Absolutely not," Gracelyn insisted. "I never even ran into him here at the hotel because when Frederick and I arrived, we spent most of our time at the Auditorium, sorting through our trunks, checking all our equipment. Unfortunately, the day we arrived, one of the stagehands, a young boy named Michel, up and quit. Although Alan Hughes insisted that there was not enough time to find a qualified stagehand, Frederick was sure that Rosalie was the force behind that idea. She would have been thrilled to have the job line cut from the budget. That left Frederick and me vying with everyone else to get what share of Spencer's or Red's time we could.

"Then, in a complete turnaround, forty-eight hours later, Quint showed up as the third stagehand. Alan had hired him to work part-time. When Red brought him around to meet Frederick, I happened to be in the room. I can assure you Quint was as surprised to see me as I was to see him. We avoided each other as best we could, but it was shortly after he started working as a stagehand that Frederick's props began breaking and/or disappearing. I thought, and still think, that was Quint's way of trying to have me fired." Gracelyn shrugged her shoulders. "I'd like to believe he did have some small bit of conscience left, and having me around made him uncomfortable. He may have felt that if he could have me banished from his sight, any shred of guilt would be gone."

"Gracelyn, do you have any idea why Alan changed his mind and how it was Quint who came to be hired as a stagehand? Did he have a history of doing that kind of work? After all, his primary job as a bartender requires a completely different set of skills," I said.

"I did hear Red say that he thought Eileen McCarthy, Emma's young blond understudy, had recommended Quint to Alan. Red was under the impression that Quint and Eileen were very friendly." Gracelyn emphasized the word "friendly" with finger quotes.

While Gracelyn was speculating about the relationship between Quint and Eileen, I was still thinking about the more perplexing question. Why would Alan Hughes, who had already announced he was not going to hire a stagehand, suddenly decide to hire one based on the recommendation of an understudy? There had to be more to it.

Chapter Thirteen

When Gracelyn felt she was steady enough to go to her room, Emma and I walked her into the hotel through a side door that was close to the elevators. We offered to ride up with her, but she assured us she was feeling much better.

"I can't thank you ladies enough for, well, for listening, and especially for not judging. I think all I need now is a couple of aspirin, a cup of tea, and a good night's sleep. First thing tomorrow, I will start reorganizing all of Frederick's props and explain to him why I think we won't have any more problems," Gracelyn said before she stepped inside the elevator.

When the doors closed, Emma said, "She hasn't so much as a clue of what chaos tomorrow will bring, has she?"

I shook my head. "I'm afraid not. It's likely to be quite some time before any of us are allowed inside the theater again. Now I think we should head into the Beaver Bar and find our friends.

Don't you want to hear how your colleagues are reacting to the word of Quint's death? I know I do. And I'm sure Inspector Radigan isn't far behind us. I am almost surprised that he didn't get here before we did."

We followed the sound of rumbling conversations and raucous cheering to the wide-open doors of the Beaver Bar. Searching for our friends, Emma and I maneuvered our way through those in the standing-room-only crowd, many of whom were continuously jostling for any position that would give them a better view of any one of the numerous wide-screen televisions scattered about the spacious room.

Emma pointed to the only quiet spot in the room, a long table where Seth, Maureen, and Mort looked exceedingly uncomfortable, surrounded as they were by many of Emma's theater associates.

As soon as he saw us, Derek Braverman stood, snapped his fingers for a waiter, and asked for two more chairs. Then he gave Emma a hug and said, "Emma, my sweet darling, and dear Jessica, I am so terribly sorry for everything you both must have endured. What a terrible accident! It is unbelievably inconvenient that it happened right in the middle of our rehearsal schedule."

Emma and I exchanged looks. We were both shocked that Derek would consider someone's death to be an inconvenience, and I was sure we were both wondering how he'd gotten the impression that Quint's death was accidental. I gave a barely there shake of my head to Emma, who winked back that she understood. Inspector Radigan would straighten it all out soon enough. It was not our job.

The waiter took our order for a pot of Earl Grey tea, and as he turned to leave, Rosalie lifted her arm and waved her hand wildly at him. "Hey you, where you goin'? I could use another gin and tonic."

"Rosalie"—Alan yanked her hand down and planted it firmly on the table—"lower your voice, please. I think you have had enough of those."

He pointed to the tall glass with a beaver etching on the front. It was empty save for a limp piece of lime resting on a tiny sliver of ice at the bottom of the glass.

"It's not for you to say when I've had enough. Waiter, bring me a double," she commanded.

The waiter scurried away, probably hoping to avoid witnessing any further scene between Alan and Rosalie. The rest of us were not that lucky, nor were the people at nearby tables.

Obviously trying to change the topic, Jorge Escarra loudly asked Alan Hughes if he had found the script changes that he had been looking for earlier in the evening. Before Alan had a chance to answer, Rosalie stood up, knocked back her chair until it bounced off the wall, and jabbed her finger in the direction of Mort and Seth. "You two Yanks have been nosing around since you got here because you are dying to know a secret. Well, I'll tell you what you want to know. Derek Braverman has been lying to you and everyone else for decades. I am here to set the record straight. His real name is Derek Posh."

The uproar at our table nearly eclipsed the noisy crowds around us.

Alan shrieked, "Rosalie, that is enough. Stop it now. This is neither the time nor the place."

Derek's eyes widened. He banged his fist on the tabletop and glared at Jorge Escarra while tilting his head in Rosalie's direction.

Jorge hastily said, "That's ridiculous, Rosalie. Where did you ever get such an idea? Why, I've known Derek my entire life . . ."

I kept my eyes glued to Derek Braverman, who, clearly enraged, was now scowling at Rosalie. All of a sudden, he was a changed person. Perhaps he slipped into actor mode, because he laughed and said, "Even in London's fancy West End, one would never consider a 'Posh' to be a hero! Let's not forget I was born and got my acting start right here in Edmonton. One thing is for sure: on this side of the Atlantic, heroes need to be brave; hence, the Posh boy became a Braverman."

Everyone at the table laughed and applauded except for Alan Hughes, who wiped his brow with a napkin, looking exceptionally relieved that his wife had not caused nearly the calamity that he feared when she revealed Derek's true name. Unexpectedly, the laughter cut off abruptly, and everyone seemed to be looking directly at Emma.

I turned and saw Sergeant Enook standing behind Emma's chair, notebook in hand, her stance extremely official. Once she had everyone's attention, she introduced herself. "I am sure that by now you have all heard of the unfortunate death of Quinton Chabot at the theater. The manager of this hotel has been kind enough to provide several hospitality rooms here on the main floor for my superior, Inspector Radigan, to proceed with interviews. The inspector felt sure you would be more comfortable if that process took place here rather than at our headquarters."

Derek Braverman was on his feet in a flash and immediately projected his most famous tough-guy title character, one from a movie I remembered well, *Monty Boy-o*. "Why? Why talk to us? We had nothing to do with that stagehand's accident. You can tell your inspector to leave us be."

I was inclined to clap for his spontaneous performance. But there was no time for any response from the audience, as it were, because Sergeant Enook swiftly corrected Braverman.

"For the sake of clarity, I must tell you that we are investigating a murder, not an accident. And while we would like your cooperation to be voluntary, I am afraid we must insist that every person involved in your upcoming production be interviewed during our ongoing inquiries." Sergeant Enook paused, taking time to tuck a long strand of dark hair that had escaped her severe updo back in place. While she was doing so, her eyes moved judiciously from face to face. When she was satisfied that everyone at the table grasped the fact that the Edmonton Police Service would brook no arguments, she ended with, "Please gather your things and follow me. The hotel card room will serve as a waiting area until you are called to speak with Inspector Radigan. Should you need to leave the room for any reason, we have constables assigned who will escort you anywhere within the confines of the hotel. Naturally, anyone who wishes to call a lawyer will be allowed to do so."

Somehow her final remark sounded more like a direct recommendation for the guilty party than a general invitation to us all. We began gathering our things and followed Sergeant Enook out of the bar and down the long hallway that went past the gift shop, where I noticed there was now a large sign—UPCOMING AUTHOR SIGNING—prominent in each window. I would have to find the time to put a stop to that first thing in the morning.

When we followed the sergeant into the room, there could be no doubt it was designed for card playing. A large clock centered on the wall opposite the entrance was a circle of playing cards in order, from the ace of diamonds to the queen of diamonds. The circle appeared to be about two feet in diameter, and in the center, the king of diamonds functioned as the anchor for the clock hands, which were shaped like royal scepters.

A half dozen card tables were scattered around the room, each with four well-padded chairs tucked neatly in place. Two constables stood next to the doorway, as if to deter any attempts at escape, I thought wryly.

In addition to providing a comfortable room for us to bide our time, the hotel staff was extremely thoughtful and had set up a snack table with water bottles, an urn of tea, and a platter of mini pastries. It suddenly dawned on me that since tending bar here was Quint's full-time job, most of the other employees probably knew him, at least casually. Normally, my curiosity would have led me to bring it up casually, but under the watchful eye of the Edmonton Police Service, it was probably not the best of ideas.

When we all filed into the room, Seth had quickly pulled a chair away from a card table that sat in the middle of the room and brought it to a corner table, where Mort and Maureen were already sitting like placeholders, waving for Emma and me to join them.

Emma leaned in and whispered in my ear, "This is just bonkers. Why would anyone have a reason to kill a part-time stagehand? A member of the chorus murdering the star in the hopes of getting the leading role, now, in theater life that is the only killing that might make sense. But a stagehand? Again, I say bonkers."

When I turned to her, she must have seen my shock at her insensitivity; she laughed heartily at me, her blue eyes twinkling.

"I just thought I'd give you an idea or two for your next mystery book, dearie. Now, before we sit down, can I bring you a cuppa?"

"That sounds wonderful," I said. "Especially since we had to leave that delicious pot of Earl Grey in the Beaver Bar."

"And I'm sure a pastry would not be amiss," Emma said, and she hurried off to the hospitality table.

I joined my friends at their table, and Maureen immediately asked if I was all right. "I can't believe that Emma had a costume fitting scheduled at the very same time a man was being killed. I'm glad the body wasn't there when we took our tour. Just to think that we rode on that very same—what did Red call it— orchestra lift." She shuddered.

Mort patted her hand in a comforting gesture. "Don't worry, honey. This Inspector Radigan seems to be a pretty sharp guy. I'm sure he'll have the case wrapped up in no time."

"That's another thing." Maureen looked puzzled. "We are in Canada. Where are the Mounties? Why aren't they here?"

"The Royal Canadian Mounted Police are the national police service of Canada," Mort explained. "If you want to be arrested by a cop wearing those fancy red uniforms, you would have to commit a federal offense or commit a crime in one of the communities where the Mounties have primary jurisdiction." Mort smiled at the idea of his wife committing any sort of crime. "Although they do have peace-officer status throughout the country, so you could get lucky."

Seth nodded as he added, "Ayuh, Sergeant Enook was very explicit. They work for the Edmonton Police Service—a separate entity entirely, I suspect. Well, would you look at this. Nice work, Emma."

Emma had come back to the table carrying a plate of pastries and some napkins in one hand and cradling five water bottles in her other arm.

"Well, back in me hard-luck days, when stage work was not easy to come by, I made ends meet by waitressing in a nice little pub in the West End, just off Leicester Square. The owner, Liam Doyle, a fine old Irish gentleman, was always happy to give me time off when I needed it to audition. When I finally hit the stage regularly and could leave the waitressing behind, Liam and his missus had front-row seats for the rest of his life anytime I was in a West End show. Now let me get Jessica her cuppa. Anyone else?"

Maureen also opted for tea, and Emma was halfway back to the hospitality table when Sergeant Enook returned to the room, causing instant silence. She looked at the paper in her hand. "Mr. Alan Hughes, if you would follow me, please."

And she turned on her heel and began walking away, giving him no choice but to follow.

Alan made a slight detour to our table and asked, practically begged, Emma to sit with Rosalie. "Grateful as I am that the inspector did not allow the hotel to provide alcohol, I am hesitant to leave Rosalie—shall I say, unsupervised?—in her present state. Would you be so kind as to sit with her, keep her amused? You know she does enjoy your company, and quite frankly, there is no one else here I can ask."

While Emma was cheerfully agreeing to her newest assignment, I looked around the room. Alan was definitely correct. I knew where Gracelyn was, but neither Frederick the Great nor Dennis had been in the Beaver Bar, and neither was here now. Eileen McCarthy, the understudy, was also among the missing. I didn't actually expect that Alan Hughes would have invited Red Pompey to the Beaver Bar, but with the exhibition game by the Edmonton Oilers causing such excitement, I would think he might have wanted to be part of the fun with his friends. If so, surely he would have noticed when we were marched out by Sergeant Enook. That parade tore everyone's eyes from the Oilers' game, if only for a few seconds.

It was likely that Inspector Radigan was at this very minute asking Alan Hughes for a complete list of the entertainers and crew associated with the revue. Then Dennis Oliver came through the door, glanced around, and looked immediately crestfallen. Now what?

Chapter Fourteen

He took a few steps toward the table where Emma and Rosalie were sitting, then turned and hurried directly to our table and asked, "Has anyone seen Mary Jo? I am trying to get the hotel staff moving on my request, but no one seems to have the authority to help us.

"We are important guests, paying buckets of money to this establishment, but the desk clerks seem to think that tomorrow is time enough to sort this out. I explained that the police have closed the Jubilee Auditorium for goodness knows how long and we need to confirm a large rehearsal space immediately. That suite upstairs is far from adequate. I am sure Mary Jo could get to the manager and have this organized, if only I could find her."

Seth passed Dennis an unopened bottle of water. "Son, in my professional opinion, what you really need is to sit down and take a few long drinks from this bottle. You are flushed and clammy. Those are signs of stress that shouldn't be so evident in a man your age unless you've been running a marathon or you've just come in from ninety-degree heat."

Maureen took the bottle from Dennis's hand and opened it with a sharp twist. "Here you go. Now follow the doctor's orders and drink up."

Dennis looked around the table, realized he was outnumbered, and took a drink. Surprisingly, his shoulders, which he'd clenched practically to his ears, started to relax. When he took his second drink, Maureen picked up the plate of pastries from the center of the table and insisted he take one.

"Ayuh, good idea, Maureen," Seth said as he reached for a bear claw. "Never know when low blood sugar could strike."

"Dennis, try that one." Mort pointed to a small round cake with a crunchy topping. "It's a butter tart. We ate them the other day on our tea break. Really delicious."

Everyone was so busy fussing over Dennis that no one noticed Emma signaling me to join her at Rosalie's table.

I picked up my teacup, refilled it at the hospitality table, and then sat down with Emma and Rosalie.

"Jessica, seeing Dennis walk in here reminded me of earlier, when we were leaving the theater after the tour. Do you remember when I went back to my dressing room to get my earrings?"

"Of course," I said. "I remember that Derek Braverman was unreasonably disturbed when he realized you'd gone off on your own."

"Well, until this minute, I completely forgot about the argument that Dennis Oliver and Alan Hughes were having when I passed the director's office on my way to the dressing room. But now that a stagehand is dead . . ." She stopped and looked at Rosalie, who nodded for her to continue.

"As long as Rosalie doesn't mind my telling tales." Emma gave a hollow laugh. "They were arguing about the stagehands not doing their jobs or not cooperating, or something like that. I went into my dressing room, and when I came out, I saw Rosalie go into the office, and in a quick minute all was quiet."

"Boys will be boys, bicker, bicker, bicker." Rosalie saluted us with her water bottle and took a sip, then gave the bottle a strange look as if realizing for the first time that it didn't contain alcohol.

When I offered to get her a cup of tea, she groaned. "Noooo, but thank you. As long as we are under house arrest and apparently are not allowed to have cocktails, I suppose this water will have to do. In any event, the death of a part-time stagehand has upturned our entire schedule, and we now have to contend with this." She pointed to Sergeant Enook who was speaking to one of the constables and never missed a beat while still managing to stare Rosalie down.

"Anyway, oh dear, what was my point? Never mind, I recall. So the real issue, if I may be quite blunt . . ." Rosalie gave us a few seconds to object to bluntness, as if either of us would stop her in midstory; then she went on.

"The underlying problem is that, despite his excellent résumé— well, I won't mention any names, but someone does not realize that he is the *assistant* director, so his job is to *assist* my husband, the director, in the artistic creation that will become this fabulous revue. All craft issues, dealing with sets and stagehands, costumers, and the like, are being handled—quite ably I might add—by our excellent stage manager, Nicholas Dufond."

Emma was smiling with such glee that I was quite sure a conversation with Mr. Dufond was not far in our future. Before I could ask Rosalie her opinion of Quint Chabot, Alan Hughes and his escorting constable walked back into the room and Alan headed straight over to his wife.

"Are you all right, darling?" he asked as he took her hand. Then he looked at Emma and said, "I thank you and your cousin for keeping Rosalie company. Now, please, don't let us keep you from your friends a minute longer."

Well, that was a clear dismissal. But before we could rise from our chairs, Derek Braverman rose from his and began shouting, "I demand to see whoever is in charge. You cannot keep us here against our will. I belong in the Beaver Bar celebrating." He held up his cell phone. "The Oilers have just won a charity match, and I am one of the main donors for this event. I demand to return to the Beaver Bar."

Sergeant Enook did not bat an eye. "Mr. Braverman, when I was twelve years old, I decided to become a police officer after watching your performance as the righteous, rule-following detective Thomas Spinelli in your long-running television series. So I know that you are quite aware of exactly what we can and cannot do. Out of respect for your support of Food Banks Canada, I will see if the inspector can accommodate you shortly.

"In the meantime"—the sergeant looked at her sheet of paper—"Mrs. Rosalie Hughes is the next person scheduled to speak with the inspector." She pointed to a constable standing near the doorway. "Constable Alexander will escort you."

Emma and I both turned to Alan, sure that he was going to render some kind of objection, but instead he whispered something to Rosalie. Then he asked Sergeant Enook if he might walk with Rosalie to the interview room. When the sergeant agreed, Alan took Rosalie's arm, helped her from her chair, and guided her out the door directly behind her escort.

Alan came back and, once in his seat, began drumming his fingers on the tabletop in an irregular and annoying beat.

Emma and I returned to our table. And as soon as we sat down, Maureen whispered, "Do you think Derek Braverman is acting whenever he gets up and roars like that?"

I let Emma take that question, and oh, did I love her answer. "Oh no, dearie. I am afraid that over the years, Derek Braverman, or whatever his name really is, has become that posturing bully. So much so that whenever he is challenged, Derek simply revs up whatever character he thinks will shut the conversation down. I'm fairly sure that after all these decades and decades of intimidating people, his fake personalities just pop out as needed."

Seth said, "One thing is for sure: Derek Braverman, the man, is no match for the Derek Braverman we followed on the screen all these years."

"I couldn't agree more," Mort said. "I can't wait to get home and tell Dan Andrews that all of Braverman's bluster and swagger is nauseating when you see it up close and personal."

Seth looked to the ceiling and thought for a second or two before answering. "I almost hate to break Dan's heart, but truth must be told. And speaking of truth telling, I understand why Jess and Emma have to be here. I mean they were right on the scene when the body was discovered . . ."

Mort interrupted. "When isn't Mrs. F. in close proximity to the latest murder victim, no matter who she's with or what country she is in?"

"Be that as it may, can someone explain why you and I are being held all this time for interviews? I was about to ask that very question when Braverman started his tirade. As soon as the sergeant answered, I quickly decided discretion was the better part of valor. But the reality is that we have nothing to do with this revue that they are all working on. The only person we know who has anything to do with the show is Emma. We are merely her guests. Except for accepting a glass of champagne that Mr. Chabot poured after the theater tour, I don't think I've ever seen him before," Seth finished.

"Of course you did, Seth. Don't you remember? Quinton Chabot was the bartender at our welcoming dinner in the Victoria Room." I lowered my voice. "And I noticed Alan Hughes wasn't too pleased about it either. He gave Quint the evil eye more than once."

Emma laughed out loud. "Oh, Jess, you haven't changed a bit since we were girls. You were always the quickest finder when we played hide-and-seek or blindman's bluff. Is there anything that happens in your surroundings that you don't notice?"

"Not a single thing," Mort answered on my behalf. "At least not in all the years I've known her.

"See, Emma, your observations about Mrs. F. are exactly the kind of thing that the inspector is going to want to know about Quint Chabot. While you were in the victim's presence, you may not have thought anything was peculiar about his behavior, but did you happen to consider someone else's behavior around him to be a bit off the mark?" Mort said with authority.

"Oh yes, I quite understand. I was once in a play. It ran for over a year, that one did, and the entire mystery was solved because Anna Belle the maid, she was my character, you understand, she was the sharp-eyed domestic who noticed that there was mud on the master's shoes after she heard him tell the detective that he'd stayed in the house all day due to the unrelenting rain. Anna Belle told the coppers, and it was 'Good-bye, Your Lordship.'"

"That's the kind of thing I am talking about," Mort said. "Now would somebody please pass me that last bear claw?"

Seth harrumphed. "Well, I certainly have nothing to tell the inspector. Except for having a few words about Canadian whisky, I never looked at the bartender, nor did I notice anyone else paying him the slightest bit of attention."

"Well then," I said, "your interview should be extremely brief."

But I had already lost Seth's attention. He was looking over my head toward the middle of the room and murmuring, "Now, what's this about, I wonder?"

I turned to see what had captured his attention. Constable Alexander, who'd left the room as Rosalie Hughes's escort, had returned without her and was conferring with Sergeant Enook.

Seth said, "Do you suppose I should tell them I am a medical doctor? They might think I am a doctor of philosophy or some such. After watching Mrs. Hughes down as many drinks as she did both during and after dinner, I wouldn't be surprised if she needed some medical attention."

He'd begun to stand up when Sergeant Enook walked directly over to Alan Hughes and told him that Constable Alexander would take him to meet his wife and then would escort them both to their hotel suite.

Alan, looking extremely relieved, followed Constable Alexander out of the room without so much as a nod or a good night to anyone else.

Derek Braverman started to move around in his seat, not quite getting up but definitely not sitting still. I was sure he was expecting Sergeant Enook to call him as next to be interviewed, so I was as surprised as he was when the sergeant walked out the door behind Alan Hughes.

Derek leaned across the card table and said something to Jorge Escarra, which I suspected was an irritated complaint. Jorge confirmed my suspicions when he began speaking as if to distract Derek while making a placating motion with his hand. Jorge was likely thinking the same thing I was: *Will this night never end?*

Chapter Fifteen

Sergeant Enook came back within minutes and walked directly over to Derek, with another constable at her side. She introduced them, and then Derek jauntily followed the constable out of the room. He stopped briefly near our table and joked, "If I never come back, remember the show must go on."

We laughed politely, but I was remembering that Emma told me that Derek had refused to have an understudy, so I was sure he had no intention of ever letting any show go on without him.

Emma popped out of her seat and walked over to the table where Braverman had been sitting and Jorge Escarra was now alone. "There is no point in staying here on your own, Jorge. Why don't you and your chair come join us? At the very least, we can all complain about having to spend our evening in this room with nothing to drink but tea and water. And we'll have an appreciative audience—each other."

At first Jorge shrugged his shoulders, but then he nodded,

stood, picked up his chair, and followed her back to our table. Mort and Seth slid their chairs farther apart to make room, and Jorge settled in.

Sergeant Enook came to speak to us again. "The inspector has asked me to extend his apologies for taking up so much of your evening, but under the circumstances, it is important that we get everyone's account of their activities during a specific time period. And the inspector prefers to do so while everything is fresh in the minds of witnesses and potential witnesses."

I thought it was extremely diplomatic of her to refer to us as witnesses rather than as suspects.

She glanced at her sheet of paper, which was starting to appear somewhat wilted, and then she looked at Dennis Oliver. "Mr. Oliver, am I correct in saying that your title is assistant director? And that you work with the director, Mr. Hughes?"

"That is accurate." Dennis gave her a thousand-watt smile, but she seemed not to notice.

"And, just for clarification, what is your professional relationship with Mrs. Hughes, who is listed as the producer of this show you are putting together?"

Dennis looked surprised by the question. "Actually, she and I have very little interaction since I take direction from Alan, and he keeps her informed of the day-to-day because, as producer, she provides the funds."

"Thank you. As a theatergoer, I have always been curious about exactly how those titles interacted." Sergeant Enook opened the notebook she'd been carrying, folded her list in half, and put it inside.

As a naturally curious person myself, I was sure that the sergeant's question was less about her personal curiosity about theater life and more about some suspected relationship to the murder investigation, but I was stymied as to what the connection could be. Still, I assumed that she'd asked her questions at the inspector's direction since she had meticulously avoided publicly asking any of us questions about the play, the rehearsals, or Quint Chabot.

She did have a knack when it came to bringing up people's professions: first my books, then Derek Braverman's television role as a detective, and now asking Dennis about the relationship between the directorial team and the producers. It seemed likely that by pointing out her own familiarity with our professions, Sergeant Enook was implying that she knew more about us as people than she could possibly know. It was an intriguing approach.

"Since we are going to be here for a while longer," the sergeant said, breaking into my reverie, "Inspector Radigan has suggested that I bring in a member of the waitstaff should anyone like to eat something more substantial than pastries."

"How about something to drink besides tea and water?" Jorge didn't sound very hopeful, so I supposed he was thinking an alcoholic beverage would hit the spot.

"Good idea. I will order a variety of pop in a bed of ice," she replied.

I noticed that she used the same word for soft drinks that most Americans in our Midwest used. Jorge looked disappointed, but he nodded his acceptance. I guess he thought any change from tea or water would be welcome.

Sergeant Enook smiled and said she would return shortly. As soon as she moved away from our table, Jorge speculated that we would be here until the wee hours of the morning.

Mort said, "I can't argue with that. Back in Maine, I am a sheriff, and every cop knows that the investigation continues until the crime is solved."

"Don't you people ever sleep?" Jorge asked.

"Yes, he does, and he snores as well." Maureen laughed and then turned serious. "But when he's working a grim case, like, say, a murder, well, no matter how much I hound him, sleep is not a priority."

Just then Derek Braverman and his escort came back into the room, and Derek seemed surprised that Jorge was sitting at our table.

He spread a wide smile around our little group before he said, "I am heading back to the Beaver Bar for the post-hockey-game celebration. Anyone the inspector doesn't arrest is welcome to join me as my guest when their interview is over."

He obviously thought he was uproarious, because he was still laughing at his nonsensical remark as he walked down the hall toward the bar.

"I'll give you all one guess who is showing his prat side for all the world to see. Star of the show or not, he needs must watch his manners when something as serious as a murder befalls an original musical revue that we are trying to put together in his honor." Emma didn't try to hide her annoyance.

"And he is smirking because we are all more or less trapped here while he is free to go to a party." Dennis shook his head slightly as if trying to comprehend what Derek could possibly be thinking.

The turn of the conversation made Jorge look so uncomfortable that rather than being nervous, he seemed to be relieved when Sergeant Enook said it was his turn to meet with the inspector.

Two servers came in. One was pushing a large rolling cart. They replenished the tea-and-water supply and placed a cooler filled with ice and soft drinks on the hospitality table. But the thing that caught everyone's eye was a platter of sandwiches alongside a tray of small dishes, each one filled with piping hot poutine.

Seth was the first to bounce out of his seat. "Ayuh, sitting here all this while, I didn't realize how hungry I'd become, but right about now I sure could use a sandwich. And those look delicious."

Mort was right behind him. "I hope there are some peameal bacon sandwiches. That is quickly becoming my favorite. Yep. Here they are. Anyone want to try one?"

Dennis Oliver raised his hand.

I had to admit that although I didn't often indulge in anything more than a light snack after dinner, the aroma of the gravy that smothered the French fries and cheese curds of the poutine whetted my appetite. I was quite curious about the taste. Maureen opted for poutine as well, while Emma said she wasn't ready to eat.

By the time we'd finished, Jorge's interview had ended, and Dennis Oliver was escorted to meet with the inspector. Maureen kindly asked Jorge if he would like something to eat, but he quickly declined and said good night.

That left Emma, Seth, the Metzgers, and me alone for the first time in what was not really as long as it seemed.

"Well, it's down to us, is it?" Emma said.

"Our interviews can't be long," Maureen said. "After all, we didn't even know the victim, and—getting back to our earlier conversation—I barely noticed him."

"Well, that might be true for the three of you, but don't forget that Emma and I were in the Jubilee Auditorium at the time Spencer found the body. I am sure that, even though he has already spoken to us, our conversations with the inspector will be much longer than yours."

And I was right. Seth and Maureen were in and out in no time at all. Mort was a bit longer, but I assumed that was because he and the inspector had their professions in common.

Each of them came back to sit with Emma and me because, as Seth explained, "I have no idea who is going to be the final interviewee, but I am not going to let that person sit here all by her lonesome."

Naturally, we were all surprised when the inspector decided that he wanted to see Emma and me together.

As we walked to the interview room with Constable Alexander as our escort, Emma asked why I thought he wanted to speak to us at the same time.

Of course, I had no clue, but when Emma offered the idea that he might be tired and wanted to go home to bed, I was certain that wasn't the reason.

Inspector Radigan was in a room that appeared to be one of the hotel offices. He sat behind a desk and had a laptop open. He moved it to one side when we came in, dismissed Constable Alexander, and indicated we should each take a seat.

"So, ladies, I understand that you are cousins. I must admit the resemblance is remarkable." He was using the tactic of trying to make us comfortable, using meaningless chitchat before he began asking the difficult questions. I had the police detectives in my novels use that ploy quite frequently. It was meant to help the person being interviewed relax and possibly feel freer to say things that they might otherwise keep to themselves.

After a few more minutes spent speaking to us in that manner, Radigan asked in the exact same tone of voice that he'd been using since we arrived, "So refresh my memory. You two ladies left the hotel together and arrived at the Jubilee Auditorium to meet Ms. Gadue for a costume fitting. Ms. Macgill, could you explain to me just what that is?"

Emma did so quite succinctly, and then he turned to me.

"And you, Mrs. Fletcher, exactly what was your role in this costume-fitting process?" He smiled as if he suspected he would be amused by my answer.

"My role? Inspector, I had nothing to do with the costume fitting. I simply accepted Emma's invitation to join her so we could spend time together." I was sure the inspector wasn't so dense as to think that Emma, a well-known British actor, had invited her American mystery-writer cousin to come to Edmonton, Alberta, Canada, in order to help her kill a bartender/stagehand, so I was extremely curious as to where his questions were headed.

He swiveled to Emma again. "Ms. Macgill, did you have a specific reason for inviting Mrs. Fletcher to come to the Jubilee Auditorium with you this evening?"

"Well, I don't know if you would call it specific or even a reason. Since Jessica arrived, both she and I have been surrounded by people virtually all the time. When Jessica is sightseeing with her friends, I am working with any number of actors or crew preparing for the revue. Why, Jess's friends and the revue team even share communal meals. So I saw this fitting appointment as an opportunity for the two of us to spend some time alone and catch up."

The inspector furrowed his brow as if he didn't understand a word Emma had said. "But you two weren't alone. You were with Ms. Gadue."

"Of course the three of us were together, but Lene was far more focused on her fabrics and her drawings than on anything Jess and I chose to talk about. Besides, there was the trip from the hotel to the Jubilee Auditorium and back again. Jess and I did get a bit of a gab on during the ride."

"Ah, yes, the car rides to and fro." Inspector Radigan leaned back in his chair, made a steeple with his hands, and stared at a blank wall off to his right as though deep in thought.

I, on the other hand, was certain that he was taking a dramatic pause because, in fact, Emma had brought the conversation exactly to where the inspector wanted it. Although for the life of me I couldn't see why.

Then he folded his hands on the desktop, leaned forward, stared directly into Emma's eyes, and spoke in a very deliberate, less cordial tone. "When we spoke earlier, you mentioned that Mr. Hughes chose Spencer Smith to drive you to the Jubilee Auditorium because, as part of his duties, Mr. Smith had keys to the building."

Emma nodded in agreement.

"Well, here is the thing I don't understand. I had one of my constables go to the hotel and speak with Mr. Hughes, who steadfastly maintained that Spencer Smith somehow learned that you would need a ride to the Jubilee Auditorium. He presented himself to Mr. Hughes and volunteered to be your driver for the evening. Until that moment, Mr. Hughes had planned on giving you, Ms. Macgill, his spare set of Auditorium keys and booking Rob Langford, the hotel's principal limousine driver, to take you there. Mr. Hughes reiterated that same version of events to me just a few minutes ago."

Emma and I looked at each other, totally perplexed.

"Now, just a minute, Inspector. If you are saying—and I think that you are—that Spencer Smith is a suspect in the murder of Quint Chabot, that is just not possible," I said.

Inspector Radigan raised his eyebrows, and his nostrils flared. Then he calmed down and asked in a soft and measured voice, "May I ask how you came to that conclusion, Mrs. Fletcher?"

"Spencer drove Emma and me from the hotel to the theater. He could hardly be a suspect unless you know with certainty that Quint died within the fifteen- or twenty-minute window of time between when Spencer escorted us, along with Lene Gadue, to the costume room and when we heard him desperately calling for help because he had discovered Quint's lifeless body." I crossed my arms, satisfied that I had made my case.

"That's it? If that is your theory in its entirety, Mrs. Fletcher, kindly tell me where Spencer Smith was during the hours before he arrived at the hotel and drove you and Ms. Macgill to the theater."

Chagrined, I had to admit that I had no idea where Spencer had been immediately before he showed up to drive us to the Jubilee Auditorium.

But I knew one thing was certain: I was determined to find out.

Chapter Sixteen

When Constable Alexander escorted Emma and me back to the card room, the waitstaff was removing the food-and-drink supplies from the hospitality table, and the cleaning crew was tidying the room while staying as far away as possible from my Cabot Cove friends.

As soon as we entered the room, Sergeant Enook thanked us all for our cooperation; then she and her colleagues disappeared, presumably to join Inspector Radigan.

Seth stood and stretched his arms over his head and out to the side. "This feels as good as when the drill sergeant finally dismissed us for the day during my time in the army."

"I hear that," Mort said, and he stood up as well.

Maureen practically leaped from her chair and took Mort by the hand. "I suggest we all take a stroll around the lobby. My muscles ache from sitting for such a long time. Oh, unless some of you want to go sit with Derek Braverman in the Beaver Bar?"

"Honey, here's a sentence I never thought I'd say: I've had enough of Derek Braverman. At least for tonight, if not forever. A good stretch of the legs sounds very welcome." Mort kissed his wife's cheek and said, "Ladies, Doc, would you like to join us?"

I looked at Emma, who gave me a thumbs-up, so I said, "Sounds delightful."

Seth was already heading for the door.

I was a bit surprised at how much activity there was in the hotel lobby. A number of people were sitting in small groups, chatting. Others were taking what appeared to be leisurely strolls around the lobby. Maureen opted to walk down the hallway in the hope that the gift shop was still open, and Mort followed along. Seth decided to stop at the desk once again to ask if his pen had been found by the cleaners or turned in by anyone else.

Emma and I tagged along so we could cheer him up should he be disappointed once again.

A man with longish blond hair and an old-fashioned handle-bar mustache was speaking to the desk clerk. "You don't understand. I bought a package of postcards and some stamps in the gift shop. Then I sat on the love seat over there, took out my pen and my address book, and began to write out the cards. I wanted to get them in tomorrow morning's mail so that they would get home before I did."

"And I am happy to oblige," the desk clerk, a portly middle-aged man, said cheerfully as he reached for the cards.

The mustachioed hotel guest repeated, "You don't understand. My pen ran out of ink, so I picked up my address book but left the cards on the table. I zipped up to my room, grabbed a couple of pens from my backpack, and when I came back to the lobby, my postcards were gone."

"But, sir." The desk clerk looked pointedly at the postcards the man was holding.

"Not these cards." The man sounded more frustrated by the minute. "These are the cards I wrote before the pen went dry. I left these on the coffee table as well as the package of cards I still needed to write, and when I came back, these cards were still there, but the still-to-be-written cards had disappeared."

The desk clerk, finally realizing he could provide a solution, smiled and picked up a notepad. "Well, I am so sorry that happened, but let me give you a note to the gift shop, and the hotel will happily supply you with as many postcards as you need to finish sending them to your friends and family."

Mollified, the postcard writer took the note and strode off toward the gift shop.

Seth quickly took his place, and while he was inquiring about his pen, I looked at the grandfather clock that stood behind the reception desk and, happily, it wasn't as late as I thought. I had so many questions rattling around in my head, and I hoped that Emma would help me find some answers.

After the desk clerk disappointed Seth by showing him the only two pens in the lost-and-found drawer, I said, "Excuse me. I was just wondering: Do most items find their way to that drawer, or are they generally lost forever?"

"Strange you should ask. Earlier this evening, a coworker was saying how much she enjoyed the look on a guest's face when we are able to return whatever they lost, be it a pen or, as once happened, a diamond ring." He paused to give me time to acknowledge how happy the owner of the ring must have been, which I did.

"You're right; of course she was thrilled, particularly because the ring had been her grandmother's wedding ring. But lately . . ." He turned his head this way and that as if fearing he would be overheard.

I waited patiently for him to continue.

"Lately, the number of lost objects has increased rather dramatically, while the number of things we are able to return has decreased significantly. I can't tell you how painful it is to have to tell someone like Dr. Hazlitt that his pen is nowhere to be found." He leaned in and whispered, "If this keeps up, I think the hotel will have to keep a much closer eye on the cleaning staff."

"Oh, I hope it doesn't come to that," I said, and followed Seth away from the desk, with Emma right behind me.

When I realized that Seth was headed to the elevators, I asked where he was going.

"I'm sorry, ladies, but it's been a busy day and a hectic evening. I think I will make an early night of it. See you at breakfast." And he took a few more steps and pressed the UP button next to the row of elevators.

Emma and I stood silently by until we waved good night as the doors to elevator two closed with Seth safely inside. Then she turned to me.

"It's about the pen, innit?" Emma said.

"Yes, it is. Poor Seth, that pen means a lot to him. But right now, we have bigger problems to consider," I said.

"Such as—a little hands-on detective work perhaps? Don't worry your head about it, Cuz; I am in for a penny, in for a pound," she said with a glint in her eye. "Oh, here come the Metzgers. Shall I pretend to be knackered and then circle back and meet you once you've evaded them?"

I had to laugh as I waved her off. "Honestly, Emma, there is no need for us to fib; we're not twelve years old anymore. And our mothers aren't standing in front of us, hands on hips, asking difficult questions."

Maureen held up a bag with the hotel logo angled across the front and said, "Wait until you see what we bought."

She pulled two white ball caps out of the bag. Each cap had a dark blue beak and an Edmonton Oilers logo. She perched it on top of her curly red hair and struck a pose. "What do you think?"

Emma clapped her hands. "Well, luv, don't you look smashing. You're a lucky man, Sheriff, you are."

"Don't I know it," Mort said. "Say, where'd Doc Hazlitt go?"

"Seth decided to go to his room, but he said he'd see us at breakfast. Emma and I were just going to take a seat here in the lobby and do some family reminiscing. We'd be happy to have you join us."

I watched as they telepathically communicated as my husband, Frank, and I so often had, and then Maureen answered, "That sounds lovely, but I'm sure those conversations are best left to family members. Besides, I have been dying to watch a few less familiar Canadian television shows, and this seems like the perfect time. Good night."

We watched them walk to the elevators, and then I said, "Let's have a seat and figure out some things. First up, who do you think lied to the inspector? Spencer Smith or Alan Hughes?"

Emma didn't hesitate. "Well, I don't know Spencer Smith all that well, but I've known Alan Hughes for donkey's years, and he would tell you the moon is made of green cheese if he saw some advantage to himself in saying so."

I nodded, as that matched the impression I had of him. "No

matter who is telling the truth, another question is why Alan would assign a stagehand to open the Jubilee Auditorium. Shouldn't Nicholas Dufond be in charge of who is allowed to enter the Auditorium during off-hours? He is the stage manager, after all. Doesn't that make him responsible for all the coming and going regardless of the time of day?"

"Good one, Jess. And why wasn't he here to be interviewed tonight? That's another question that needs to be answered."

"And speaking of those who are among the missing, Dennis Oliver was right. Where has Mary Jo been all evening? With this sort of chaos, you would think she would be hovering over us all. *Derek Braverman's Old Time Revue* is bringing in a great deal of money to this hotel. As I understand it, Mary Jo is our personal concierge. So where is she? And if she happened to be off work for some reason, wouldn't her substitute have checked in on us at dinner as well as kept an eye on the group in the Beaver Bar? And finally, shouldn't a concierge have been holding our hands during that tedious spell in the card room while we all waited to be interviewed? Stay here. I have an idea."

I went to the reception desk and asked the clerk if Mary Jo Simard was scheduled to work this evening. He punched a few keys on his desktop computer and said, "No, madam, I am sorry. Ms. Simard was here earlier, but according to this"—he pointed to his computer screen—"she had to leave due to a personal emergency. Can I help you in some way?"

"Thank you, no. I'm sure I will see her tomorrow," I said, knowing I would make every effort to see her or to find out why not.

I told Emma what the desk clerk said, but her mind had

already jumped to another question that had been bothering us both. "The inspector thinks it is possible that Spencer Smith killed Quint before he picked us up here at the hotel, and then he conveniently discovered the body with us and Lene as witnesses to his very recent arrival at the Auditorium. How are we going to find out where Spencer was before he picked us up?"

"Well," I replied, "first we'll ask him directly, and then we will confirm his story with any witnesses he can provide. Now we may as well head off to bed. Tomorrow is sure to be a busy day."

"Jess, before we call it a night, can you tell me if you have devised our plan for tomorrow?" Emma looked as though she was ready to begin probing at dawn.

I considered for a moment before I answered. "That depends on several things. Dennis Oliver was talking about finding a larger rehearsal space, so we don't know what you will be called on to do. Help Dennis find a space? Report for rehearsal if he has found one? Report to the little rehearsal suite?"

Emma shook her head, red hair bouncing. "I wasn't referring to anything concerning the revue. I was thinking of—"

"I know. The murder investigation. That's where both our minds are focused. The only thing I am sure of is that we'd best avoid getting in Inspector Radigan's way. Other than that, I suppose we will address each of our questions in the order in which we come across the people who can answer them."

Emma gave me a spontaneous hug. "That's a plan I can follow. Now it's off to sleep with the both of us."

As I prepared for bed, I wondered how difficult it might be to find each of the people Emma and I wanted to question. Alan Hughes shouldn't be a problem. We'd likely see him at breakfast. As to the others, well, finding any or all of them shouldn't be too difficult either. With the Jubilee Auditorium off-limits, everyone associated with the show would probably gravitate to the hotel, even those who lived locally.

As I turned off the bedside lamp and began to nod off, my last thought was that Inspector Radigan might be locking up the murderer at that very moment, and I could spend tomorrow as a happy-go-lucky tourist. But things didn't go quite that way.

Chapter Seventeen

The next morning, I awoke nearly an hour before my travel alarm was set to ring. I looked out the window at a clear sky. The leaves on the trees were blowing ever so slightly in a mild breeze. A perfect day to go for a jog.

It was one of those rare nights I hadn't slept well. I woke up several times, tossing and turning with thoughts of Quint's murder scrambling through my brain. Why kill him in the Jubilee Auditorium? He also worked at the hotel, and for any crime, be it petty theft or murder, there would automatically be a much larger pool of suspects at the hotel, when you considered the number of guests and employees. Conversely, the number of people with access to the Auditorium was extremely limited.

I put on my sweat suit, filled my water bottle, and was happy not to have run into anyone I knew before I got out of the hotel and onto a nicely paved road with gorgeous bushes and trees that I could admire along the way.

In about forty minutes or so, I was back at the hotel, feeling more energized than I had since I left Cabot Cove. The desk clerk gave me a cheery good morning and offered me today's newspaper. When I walked to the desk for the paper, I was surprised that through an open door I could see Mary Jo Simard rifling through file folders in the back office.

I called to her, and when she turned to me, she looked—well, the only words for it were "extremely worn out." Her face was pale and drawn. Instead of her usual artfully styled hairdo, she'd tied her hair rather carelessly at the nape of her neck. I signaled her to come closer, and when she hesitated, I pulled the towel from around my neck and wiped it across my forehead, saying that I was so tired from my morning jog, could she possibly come out from behind the counter so that I could sit on one of the comfortable leather chairs and rest while we talked.

Her body language was hesitant, but she was a professional on duty and I was a guest of the hotel, so she acquiesced.

When she came closer, I could see the hollowed rings and red rims that surrounded her normally warm and welcoming brown eyes. Evidently, she'd been crying recently and probably for many hours.

I deliberately chose a love seat so that we would have a measure of privacy while we spoke. Mary Jo came around from behind the desk and sat beside me and said, "How can I help you this morning, Mrs. Fletcher?"

Her voice sounded congested, and she tripped over every second or third syllable.

"We missed you last evening, and when my cousin Emma and I inquired, we were told you'd gone home as the result of some sort of emergency. Are you all right? Is everything better now?" I tried to sound as comforting as I could.

Mary Jo sniffled as she pulled a wad of tissues from her pocket. "Oh, I should never have come to work today. It would probably be best if I signed out for a few days until I am able to get control of myself. I am sorry, Mrs. Fletcher . . ."

Her voice trailed off, and she started to stand up. I leaned across and put an arm around her, which caused her to dissolve into tears.

"Do you want to talk about it?" I asked softly.

"No," she said, although she settled back on the love seat.

"When I am deeply troubled, I sometimes find that unburdening to someone I barely know can help relieve my stress without the long-term consequence of having that person around to remind me of what I might later decide was an indiscretion," I said gently.

I sat quietly during the few minutes it took Mary Jo to decide what to do. Eventually she said, "It's about Quint Chabot."

When she didn't say anything more, I gently nudged. "I can only imagine how distressing it would be to lose a coworker under such horrifying circumstances."

"He wasn't just a coworker," Mary Jo whispered.

"Oh! Oh dear. I understand now. You two were involved romantically." I reached out and patted her hand. "I am so sorry for your very personal loss."

Mary Jo sobbed quietly; then she gained some control, wiped her eyes, and said, "'Were' is the right word. I thought we were in love. I did everything for him. I even got him the bartender job.

Our manager was hesitant because Quint's references were, I guess you'd say, spotty at best. And then Quint dumped me. After he had the job, I suppose he started looking around, because as soon as he met that Eileen McCarthy, I was history. He avoided me at work, stopped taking my calls, and didn't answer my texts. I finally got the message when a friend of mine who works in the kitchen told me that she'd seen Quint and Eileen McCarthy acting quite cozy in the back parking lot a few nights earlier, which jelled with the time he slipped out of my life.

"The worst of it is that, as it turns out, Eileen McCarthy is no better than she should be. I overheard Alan Hughes raging at her. He even threatened to fire her because she told something Mr. Hughes called 'highly confidential' to a man who Mr. Hughes said is now constantly in his face and looking for money. Hughes said he would fire Eileen on the spot, but that would probably cost him more money.

"So there she was, kissing up to Quint while stealing secrets from the theater group for another man—probably a rival producer or writer or someone like that. I only wish Quint had found out what she was really like before he died." Abruptly, Mary Jo stood up with a determined look on her face.

"Thank you, Mrs. Fletcher. You are a wise woman. Saying the worst out loud is so much better than holding it inside. Now if you will excuse me, the desk clerk is signaling for my attention." She leaned down, gave me an unexpected peck on the cheek, and hurried away.

I thought it was interesting that Mary Jo assumed that the man "in Alan Hughes's face" and Quint Chabot were two different people. I needed to talk to Eileen McCarthy to confirm my instinctive belief that they were one and the same. After all, I now knew that he treated both Gracelyn and Mary Jo shabbily. Perhaps Quint's interaction with Eileen also had a few bumps in the road. I hurried to the elevators, eager to get showered and dressed for the day. Unfortunately, when the wide silver doors opened, my unofficial fan club stepped off the elevator.

"Mrs. F., good morning. We were hoping to see you today. Is there any word on the date and time of the book signing?" Iris asked.

Rather than go on and on with the push-pull about the nonexistent signing, I swiftly passed the buck. "You will have to check with the front desk. Now please excuse me. I must get out of these clothes and shower."

I hurried past them and into the elevator. I pressed the CLOSE DOOR button and was relieved when the doors began to shut even as Vivian was telling me something I didn't catch. She and Iris frantically waved good-bye as though I were about to take off on an around-the-world cruise rather than a quick hop to the fifth floor.

I called Emma, gave her a brief update on my conversation with Mary Jo, and arranged to meet by the fifth-floor elevator in half an hour. Then I took a refreshing shower, dabbed on a touch of makeup, and slid into one of my favorite white blouses—it tied in a pretty bow at the neck—and a light blue pantsuit. A quick check in the mirror assured me I was ready for the day.

When Emma and I got off the elevator, I scanned the lobby and was quite happy that Iris and Vivian were nowhere to be seen. Our luck held when we got to the Victoria Room because the only two people having breakfast were Alan Hughes and Dennis Oliver. I was surprised that they were sitting at opposite ends of the table, but that would work in my favor as I wouldn't have to interrupt their conversation when I brought up the myriad of questions I had for each of them.

Emma and I said good morning, but both men replied less cordially than I would have expected, particularly since Emma had a starring role in their project. I was willing to chalk that up to the fact that they were not morning people, but I didn't have time to allow their personalities to interfere with getting the answers I wanted.

I asked Alan if his wife would be joining us, and he replied that she wasn't feeling well, which, after her behavior last night, was not unexpected.

"I was surprised to learn from Inspector Radigan that Spencer Smith contacted you and offered to drive Emma to her costume fitting," I said. "I did wonder how he knew the fitting was scheduled, since Emma herself only found out at the last minute."

Emma picked up on my thread. "And I was surprised to learn he spoke to you and not to Nicholas Dufond. After all, anything to do with the building is generally organized by the stage manager."

Alan raised an eyebrow, briefly looked up from his poached eggs, and mumbled, "I have no idea," and then reached for the newspaper beside his plate. "If you will excuse me, my days are extremely busy, so I'm in the habit of using my breakfast hour to catch up on the day's news."

He opened, folded, and refolded the paper until he found the page he wanted us to think he was looking for, and then hid behind it.

A waitress offered coffee, which Emma and I gratefully accepted; then she took our breakfast orders. Mine was one boiled egg and a piece of plain toast; Emma asked for two eggs, sausage, and a side of toast and jam.

"I wish I had your metabolism. Even with my jogging and biking, I have to watch every bite," I said to Emma as she poured a large dollop of cream into her coffee.

"It's our jobs, luv. They make all the difference. You writers spend every working hour sitting while you are digging up research material or typing away on your manuscripts. We stage actors are on our feet continuously from the very first rehearsal until the final curtain. Isn't that right, Dennis?"

Dennis Oliver looked startled to be included in our conversation but answered more civilly than Alan would have. "Well, I suppose it is true for the actors. I confess that I am glad that, as assistant director, I am able to spend a fair amount of time sitting in the audience, so to speak. My main exercise is walking back and forth from the stage area to the office, which is why I, like you, Mrs. Fletcher, try to spend some of my precious downtime doing cardio."

"Emma, it occurs to me that we have seen very little of—what is her name?—your understudy. Eileen, isn't it? She is rarely at meals, and I am sure she feels particularly fortunate to have been on last night's missing persons list," I said, my voice just a tad louder than normal table conversation.

Alan began rattling his newspaper until Dennis took the hint and immediately changed the topic.

"Mrs. Fletcher, I have been remiss. I want to thank you and your friends for your thoughtfulness last evening. Dr. Hazlitt was especially kind. I had no idea that, with all the running around I did yesterday and not having eaten since lunch, I was due for a meltdown. You and your friends saved the day." Dennis sounded so sincere that I almost hated to ask my follow-up question.

"Now you've aroused my curiosity. What kind of running

around were you doing? Was it work or was it play?" I asked lightly.

"Well, Alan and I spent the day going over script changes until well past lunchtime. Then he had an appointment to go over the changes we'd made with Derek. Alan said I wasn't needed, and he very kindly gave me the rest of the day off." Dennis glanced at Alan's newspaper shield, clearly hoping the man behind it had heard the compliment. "Since this was my first visit to Edmonton, I took advantage of my free time and toured the city. What a terrific town. There was so much to enjoy, I barely knew where to start."

"And if I might ask, where are you from originally?" Emma said. "I am usually good at accents and dialects, but I can't place yours."

"Right now I live in Brooklyn, but I was born and raised in upstate New York near Utica. I know that central New York accent is hard to discern. We have less of an accent than our downstate brothers and sisters, and yet we sound nothing like our neighbors to the north."

I was about to ask if he went touring alone yesterday or traveled with some friends, when we were distracted by Seth, Maureen, and Mort coming into the room.

"Good morning, all," Seth greeted us buoyantly, causing Alan to shake his newspaper as if ordering silence. Seth ignored him and pulled out a chair to sit next to Emma.

Mort and Maureen settled into chairs opposite us; then Maureen said, "We knocked, but you two ladies weren't in your rooms, so we realized you must have come down for breakfast, and here you are."

A server quickly brought coffee for everyone, and as she

poured Seth's, he rubbed his hands together with great energy. "I am starving. I'll have the eggs, back bacon, and sausage platter with a side of potatoes. Jessica, that's the breakfast you tsk-tsked when the waiter mentioned it the other morning, but after last night's tragedy followed by the interminable nonsense of being trapped in the card room, I am going to enjoy my breakfast and then . . . Well, tell us, Emma, what is the plan for today?"

Emma's eyes popped wide as she instantly looked to me for help. Quite unwittingly, Dennis Oliver saved Emma from answering. Of course, his plan was far different from the one Emma and I had discussed last night.

Chapter Eighteen

I'm afraid Emma is going to be busy for a good part of the day," Dennis said. "Last night I finally got one of the assistant managers of the hotel to pay serious attention to my request for a decent-sized room that we can use as a rehearsal space . . . ah, temporarily. It seems that their largest ballroom can be divided into thirds, and this morning Mary Jo Simard, who I might add was among the missing last night, has been authorized to offer me at least one of those sections each day for the next two weeks."

"And how will that work exactly?" Emma demanded. "Opening night at the Jubilee Auditorium is practically on top of us."

Alan Hughes thumped his newspaper on the table, trashing his place setting and knocking his teaspoon off his saucer and straight down to the floor. "Emma, why do you think Rosalie has taken to her bed? All this disturbance is likely to cost us hundreds of thousands of dollars, all because that . . . that policeman insists on closing down the Jubilee for I don't know how long.

How can Dennis answer your question when Radigan won't answer ours?"

He pushed back his chair and stormed out of the room.

Dennis said, "He is upset. He doesn't mean to be rude." And he pushed back his chair and ran out the door calling, "Alan . . . Alan. Wait for me."

Emma reached over and put her arm around me. "Ah, Jessie, me girl, as Granny used to call you, I am sorry that we are in this muddle. I thought we'd have a happy and relaxed time together."

I returned her hug. "Emma, this isn't your fault. And we have been enjoying ourselves tremendously, haven't we?"

I looked at my friends around the table. Seth and both Metzgers rushed to reassure Emma that our trip thus far had been entertaining and educational. They continued to offer comforting words, and we were all being so effusive that we didn't hear Nicholas Dufond come into the room.

"Morning, all," he said as he ran a hand through his graying hair. "Been something of a night, eh?"

"It was for us," Emma said, "but we didn't see you about."

"I was home when I got the call from a sergeant of the Edmonton Police Service. Polite as she tried to be, there was no doubt she was ordering me to the Jubilee Auditorium. Wouldn't tell me a thing until I got there and then . . . well, you all know about Quint Chabot, eh?"

"Why was your presence required at the Auditorium?" I asked. "Most of the people associated with the production were interviewed here at the hotel."

"They didn't want me for an interview, although that did happen early on, a'course. What the EPS was looking for was my assistance. You've all been on the tour. Like most theaters, the

Auditorium building is a tangle of rooms and cubbyholes connected by a staircase here and a ramp there. I became the EPS's expert, like." Despite being obviously tired, Nicholas was equally proud of the role he'd played.

"Anyway, today is another day. I got a message from Alan Hughes that I was to meet him here in the Victoria Room. Has he been in yet?"

"Here and gone," Emma said. "I suggest you have a quick cup of coffee or at least ask for a takeaway before you meet with Alan. He's in a right foul mood."

The server automatically stepped forward. Nicholas gave her a sunny smile and said, "Given the boss's mood, I suppose takeaway is in order. Black, one sugar, please."

"Nicholas, last night before . . . before we knew about Quint, Emma was told to go to the Auditorium for a costume fitting, and I accompanied her," I said.

"Yeah, I heard about that. Bad luck all around, eh?" He shook his head.

"I was wondering if you know how it came to be that Spencer Smith was our driver for the evening," I asked.

"I dunno. No one ran that by me, I can tell you. Spencer had put in a tough, heavy, physical day's work finishing a set that Alan was antsy about, so he'd be the last man I would have asked to come in at night—especially to drive. Ah, here's my coffee. Thank you, miss. Now I better go find Alan before he has my head on a platter." Nicholas moved quickly toward the door, effectively cutting off any further conversation.

Maureen Metzger weaved her way back to our earlier conversation. "Emma, I have to tell you—before going to bed last night, Mort and I had a brief conversation about this trip."

Emma was about to take a sip of her coffee, but she put her cup down and looked directly at Maureen, who was smiling warmly.

"It took the tragedy of a murder to make us appreciate what an absolutely wonderful time we are having visiting this delightful and energetic city, plus we have the opportunity to stay in a hotel that treats us like royalty. None of this would have been possible for us if you hadn't included us in your invitation to Jessica. It's like . . . the honeymoon we never had." Maureen spontaneously jumped up, ran around to our side of the table, and gave Emma a hug, which was joyfully received and returned.

"We had a honeymoon," Mort protested.

"Three days at Moon Lake and then your getting called home because the bank was robbed was not my idea of a honeymoon, as I may have mentioned a time or two," Maureen huffed.

"You are all quite kind, you are. Now, let me find Mary Jo and see if she can't organize a pleasant day for you while I'm hanging around here on standby until Alan summons me," Emma said while brushing a tear from her eye.

I was about to offer to look for Mary Jo so Emma could finish her breakfast, but before I could, Emma's cell phone played a tune I didn't recognize and she answered immediately. Her side of the conversation was brief: "Hello . . . I'll meet you there . . . Cheerio."

"Actually, Jess, it would be a help if you would find Mary Jo; it seems I am wanted elsewhere." And she gave me a side-eyed signal to follow her out of the Victoria Room.

As soon as we were in the lobby, Emma grabbed my arm and whispered, "We've a date in the hotel courtyard. That was Eileen McCarthy on the phone, and she wants to talk to me. With all the chaos, she probably wants me to help solidify her job as understudy. But after your talk with Mary Jo, I think it's best we ask Eileen a question or two."

I left a message with the desk clerk, asking that Mary Jo speak with the guests in the Victoria Room regarding today's event schedule; then I followed Emma to the courtyard.

Eileen McCarthy was sitting in the shade of a green-and-white patio umbrella and sipping on a drink. She stood and greeted us graciously even though she was clearly perplexed to see me arrive with Emma.

Once we were all seated around the table, Eileen picked up a decanter and offered us some iced tea, which we accepted.

The silence at the table was becoming awkward when Emma finally broke it by asking what it was that Eileen wanted to discuss. "I don't mind saying that you sounded a wee bit frazzled on the phone just now. Are you worried about something? Do you think I can help in some way?"

Eileen brightened. "That's it exactly. I am nervous. Well, with all that is going on—I wonder if I will still have a job by nightfall."

Emma said, "Oh, there is nothing to worry about on that score. I think Alan has things well in hand. And, seriously, Derek's ego wouldn't allow him to consider canceling. We might delay a few days until the coppers let us back into the theater. And if Rosalie tightens the money belt that she keeps constantly wrapped around Alan's neck, we might have to take a small pay cut, but there will be a show. You can count on it."

Eileen tried to smile but couldn't quite make it sincere.

"There's more to it for you, isn't there, Eileen? It's not just the fact that there's been a murder in the Auditorium. In some way Quint Chabot was your protector, and without him around, you may well lose your job, or perhaps something even more damaging might happen to you. Am I on the right path?" I tried to sound sympathetic enough to make her feel comfortable in sharing her fears with me. And I believed that having Emma at her side would give her the strength to open up.

Eileen began to cry, but within a minute or two she pulled a hanky from her pocket, and we could see her trying to contain her emotions, although as Emma often said, you can never tell with actors what is real and what is them practicing for their next audition.

It crossed my mind that this was the third young woman to cry because of Quint Chabot's death within the past twenty-four hours. Although I had some idea about Eileen's relationship with him, I wasn't sure if what I'd guessed was all there was to it.

"Quint may have had his faults, but he was good to me," Eileen began. Then she seemed to realize that we might have taken that to be more personal than she meant it to be. "Not that we were romantically involved. I wasn't interested in him that way, and I don't think he had eyes for me.

"We weren't friends, exactly. Okay, I guess you may as well know the whole story. Alan Hughes asked me to come to the rehearsal suite for a run-through of the songs Emma will be doing in the show. He said he wanted to be sure I had the words memorized, and then he would work with me on the movements that go with each song." Eileen stopped and took a sip of her iced tea.

"I sang the first song, and he told me to sing it again from the beginning to the refrain, which I did. Alan stood in front of me and held both my hands in his, waving my arms up and down in beat to the music. All of a sudden, he swooped in and began kissing me."

This wasn't exactly what I expected to hear, but once Eileen started, she became so upset that I knew there was more to come.

Eileen looked at Emma as if searching for courage or confirmation. I wasn't sure which, but she must have found it because she continued.

"I pushed him away, and Alan told me to stop being a baby. He said that the theater is a world for adults, and if I wanted to be in this show, I better grow up. When he reached for me again, I slapped him and ran for the door while he was yelling, 'I take that as your resignation.'

"I took the elevator down and was running across the lobby in need of fresh air when someone grabbed my arm. I was so alarmed. I thought Alan had followed me. I actually flinched at the man's touch and then lifted my hand to slap him again, when I saw that the man wasn't Alan. He did look familiar, and then I saw his uniform. He was a bartender who worked in the hotel."

"Quint Chabot," I said.

"Yes. And he was very kind to me. He walked me outside to the back parking lot, and we stood near my car and talked. It didn't take much for me to pour out the entire story. And then he told me not to worry; he would talk to Alan and make sure I could keep my job. I asked how, and he told me that was his problem, not mine, because from now on he would be my protector. Sure enough, Dennis Oliver called me two days later to find out why I wasn't at rehearsal. I told him I had the flu but was feeling better and would come in that afternoon." Eileen looked relieved that the ordeal of telling her story was finally over, but I knew she wasn't quite finished.

"But Alan did give you some idea about the way Quint had persuaded him to keep you as Emma's understudy, didn't he?"

Eileen looked startled. "How did you—well, I guess it doesn't matter. Yes, one day when Alan was particularly frustrated by the changes Derek had ordered him to make in act two of the revue, Alan lashed out at everyone mercilessly. When he finally dismissed everyone else, he asked me to stay behind. I was nervous, but I couldn't very well refuse. He began by complaining how my boyfriend and I had set him up. He said I got all 'flirty and cutesy,' which, believe me, I didn't. Then he said my boyfriend was all in his face, demanding money or Rosalie would find out what a pig her husband is. I was shocked, but I realized that not just this job but my entire career was at stake, so I told him I'd try to get Quint to tone it down. Alan said it was too late for that and told me to leave. He wouldn't even listen when I tried to tell him that Quint wasn't my boyfriend."

"And that was how he left it?" Emma asked.

Eileen nodded. "I guess he thought it easiest to just pay Quint off and give him a part-time job. Alan and Rosalie would be going back to England after the Braverman revue closed, and he'd never see Quint again. I guess Alan convinced himself that this was a short-term problem that could soon be forgotten."

Still, I wondered if Alan Hughes had decided on a more immediate way to remove himself from under the thumb of a blackmailer.

Chapter Nineteen

There wasn't much more any of us could say. Eileen's story gave me a clear picture of both men—Alan Hughes, dirty old man, and Quint Chabot, blackmailing grifter. I asked Eileen if she had told all this to Inspector Radigan. When she said she had not, I suggested it would be wise for her to call Sergeant Enook and set the record straight.

When we walked back into the hotel lobby, Emma said, "Sad to say, but Alan's despicable behavior is not uncommon in our industry. Do you think Quint's tendency to blackmail had anything to do with his death?"

"We won't know the answer to that until we find out if he is blackmailing anyone else. If so, there could be a long list of suspects," I answered just as I heard someone call our names.

"Mrs. Fletcher, Ms. Macgill, good morning. I hope you had a better night's sleep than I did," said Spencer Smith, who was standing by the bellman's podium with Red Pompey, both of them drinking coffee out of bright red Tim Hortons to-go cups.

Emma stepped up and gave Spencer a kiss on the cheek. "I am so sorry about the ordeal you must have gone through last night. And it was all because I had to meet Lene for a costume-fitting session."

"There's no blame due for anyone but the killer," Red Pompey said quite rightly. "And, given the location of . . . of Quint, once the killer did his work it was bound to be Spencer or me that'd find him. None of the rest a ya would ever have any need to be near the orchestra lift."

"Or Nicholas could have discovered the body, I suppose." I found it odd Red had failed to mention his boss.

"Not likely. He'd always be the last one to come to work in the morning and the first one to leave of an evening, so my money's on us, and as it happens, Spencer won the luck of the draw." Red sounded quite certain.

"Spencer, I thought you mentioned that Alan Hughes called you after hours and asked you to come back to work to drive Emma to her appointment with Lene Gadue. Did I get that right?" I asked.

"Right you are about the one thing—he did call—but as to the other, he didn't *ask* me to come back; he *ordered* me to, just as I was settling in to watch the evening game shows. When my cell phone rang, I should have ignored it. That'll teach me." Spencer laughed just enough to let us know he was trying to put some humor into a very serious situation.

"Would you mind checking your call history so we could see what time he called?" I asked.

Spencer looked perplexed but didn't hesitate. He pulled out

his phone, scrolled a time or two, and turned his screen toward Emma and me. I was ready with my phone in my hand and took a couple of screen shots, which made Spencer question me.

"Why take pictures? What is going on, Mrs. Fletcher?"

"I am not quite sure myself, but I do know that for your own security it is important that you don't delete your call history. Inspector Radigan will need to see it," I said.

"I already spoke to the EPS. I told 'em all I could, which wasn't much, and what does a phone call matter?" Spencer sounded more curious than quarrelsome.

Emma lost patience with my attempt at discretion. "Spencer, Alan Hughes told the inspector that you heard from someone, somewhere, that I had to meet Lene for an evening fitting, and so you volunteered to drive me—and as it turns out, Jessica as well—to the Jubilee Auditorium."

Spencer looked at her in total disbelief. "No, I wanted to watch the game shows and then make an early night of it. I'd had a tough day and was dead tired, truth be told. Mr. Hughes is mistaken."

"Or, more likely, lying through his teeth." Red's opinion was certainly in line with my own.

At that moment, Constable Alexander and another constable I didn't recognize came into the lobby. They were heading toward the front desk until Constable Alexander noticed our little group and made a sharp turn in our direction.

"Good morning, ladies and gents." The constable tipped his hat and introduced his companion, Constable Michaud. "Mr. Smith, Inspector Radigan would like a few moments of your time. He's asked us to drive you to meet him at headquarters."

Spencer was flustered, and rightfully so. "Listen, I have to work. Red and I both got phone calls this morning to report here for work. I can see the inspector after quitting time, if that suits."

"I'm sorry, sir, but the inspector would prefer to speak with you this morning." The constable was polite but firm.

"You better go with them, laddie," Red Pompey said. "I'll explain to his important self, Mr. Hughes. And if these boys can't give you a ride back, give me a call when your little talk is over and I'll come get you."

They shook hands, and then Spencer turned to say good-bye to Emma and me. Along with my good-bye, I reminded him, "And whatever you do, Spencer, don't forget to show the inspector your call list. We'll see you later today."

After Spencer walked out the front door with the constables, Red said, "If that don't beat all. What was Hughes trying to frame Spencer for? Quint Chabot was the kind of guy who made enemies quickly and, to my way of thinking, often."

"What do you mean?" I asked.

"Well, however he got the job as the part-timer we didn't want or need, he didn't seem interested in doing the work. He was only intent on getting to know the actors and the bigwigs, like Mr. and Mrs. Hughes and Dennis Oliver. I would think he'd meet more people with that kind of status here at the hotel, but he seemed happy enough to do a bit of pretend work at the Auditorium. Who knows why? Anyway, thanks for giving Spencer the heads-up about the driving. Now I better let Nicholas know what's going on. Guaranteed he won't be happy to be down to one man for the day." Red gave us a brief wave and headed for the front desk, where, I supposed, he could check on Nicholas Dufond's whereabouts.

"Emma, do you still have those texts from Lene asking you to come to the Auditorium for the fitting?"

"How did I know you were going to ask to see them?" Emma was already scrolling through her texts. "Here you go."

We put our phones side by side and saw that Lene's texts were sent about twenty minutes after Alan Hughes called Spencer.

"That makes sense. Alan called Spencer and told him to pick you up; then he called Lene to tell her you would meet her, and she texted you. The times fit," I said. "The only question is why Alan would lie."

"That's a question only he can answer. Shall we go find him?" Emma asked.

"Hmm, I don't know. I have a feeling that it would be best to let this play out as if we had nothing to do with it. Spencer will tell Inspector Radigan the truth and show him his telephone. I think we should let the inspector be the one to 'catch' Alan in his lie."

Emma linked her arm through mine. "Oh, and wouldn't I like to be a fly on the wall while that conversation takes place. Now let's go find your friends."

"Our friends," I said as we walked across the lobby toward the Victoria Room, where we thought they were still breakfasting.

Maureen Metzger was sitting in a high-back lobby chair near the entrance to the Victoria Room. Seth and Mort were nowhere in sight. When she saw us, she waved the magazine she'd been reading.

"Look at this." She held up a copy of *Nature Alberta Magazine.* "Panuk came along and asked us to watch a local chess tournament going on somewhere in the hotel today. Well, you know Seth jumped at the chance, and Mort decided to go along. When I said I would be quite comfortable sitting here waiting for you ladies to return, Panuk led the men to the tournament and, on his way back, picked up this magazine and brought it to me."

Maureen flipped through the pages.

"As much as we have experienced the flora and fauna of this community, there is so much more we haven't seen. I have already decided that Mort and I should take a long vacation and explore the nature side of Alberta. Look at this picture of Castle Mountain in the Canadian Rockies." And she held up a picture of a multipeaked mountain that looked exactly like a sixteenth-century castle waiting to be stormed by foreign invaders. "Wouldn't that be a romantic climb?"

"Well, it is lovely to look at . . ." I trailed off.

Emma was more direct. "Well, if you can't get the good sheriff to join you on the climb, don't invite me. I'll be busy that day, whatever day it may be."

The three of us were laughing at her bluntness when Mary Jo approached. I was glad to see that she had perked up her hair and put on lipstick. I hoped she was feeling better.

"I am so sorry to disturb you ladies, but Mr. Hughes has requested that Ms. Macgill join him in the temporary rehearsal room that we've arranged in our ballroom area on the second floor. The team is running acoustics testing."

Emma looked disappointed but threw her shoulders back and held her head high. "Well, luv, I thought it would take a while longer for Alan to pull me back in to do whatever he thinks needs to be done, but I guess my free time is over. I should have known when Spencer and Red showed up that there would be some busywork to do today."

"Maybe we could tag along, just for a few minutes. We'd get a look at the new rehearsal area and maybe get an early peek at a performance or two." As soon as the words were out, I could have bitten my tongue when I saw the hopeful expression on Maureen's face and the doubtful expression on Emma's.

Then Emma's face cleared. "Well, we can try. If Alan tosses you out, then I expect you'll get to do something fun, like shopping, while I will have to listen to him whine and complain about every little thing. Never fear; we three will get together later on and talk about what a cad he is."

Even Mary Jo laughed as we headed for the elevator.

On the second floor, Mary Jo led us to a hardwood double door that had a lighted sign above indicating it was the Silver Ballroom.

The name reminded Maureen that the remains of a two-hundred-year-old silver-mining settlement were located quite near to Castle Mountain, and she told us how interesting she thought visiting it would be. I was beginning to realize that Mort was going to have a hard time saying no when Maureen approached the idea of a return trip to Edmonton and its environs.

We opened the door to a large high-ceilinged room with what looked to me like a portable stage across the front. A couple of dozen dining chairs, similar to the cushioned ones in the Victoria Room, were set up in two rows about ten yards from the stage.

Alan Hughes and Dennis Oliver were sitting in the first row. Frederick the Great and Jorge Escarra sat behind them. Red Pompey was leaning against a pile of chairs stacked against the wall. He gave us a wave and a nod.

Nicholas Dufond walked onto the stage from the wings and said, "Okay, Alan, I think I have the microphones set in about the same positions as the ones on the Auditorium stage. Do you want Derek to do his soliloquy? He doesn't have to move around a lot, but, since the hotel won't let us mark the floor with spike tape, this should give you a good idea." And Nicholas asked Red to pass him three chairs, which he scattered in a triangle at center stage.

"I guess so . . . Wait a minute." He turned toward the doorway. "What's that racket? Oh, Emma, it's about time. Did you have to bring an entourage?"

I stopped and stood still, while Maureen half turned to leave, but Emma held her by the arm and answered Alan.

"Matter of fact, I did. What's it to you if my cousin and my friend sit quietly by and watch us rehearse for a while?" Emma crossed her arms as if the matter was closed, and she ushered us to the second row.

Alan shrugged and turned his attention back to the stage.

The stage lights dimmed, and Derek Braverman entered from stage left and stood in the center of the chair triangle. He started a speech that I vaguely recognized from one of his early movies.

Maureen whispered, "I am doubly glad that Mort went with Seth to the chess tournament. He'd be hard-pressed to listen to Braverman after the way he behaved last night."

At that moment, Derek stopped speaking and looked straight out at the audience.

"What now, Derek?" Alan asked impatiently. "Another break? You only started two minutes ago."

Derek pointed over our heads.

The hall door was open, and Spencer Smith was walking gingerly toward where Red was standing, while Constable Alexander and Constable Michaud walked straight to the front of the room and stopped next to Alan Hughes.

"Begging your pardon for the interruption, Mr. Hughes," Alexander said, "but Inspector Radigan would like a few minutes of your time."

Alan looked past the constables, swiveling his head to survey the room. "Well, if he must, he must, but then, where is he? I am very busy here."

"We need you to accompany us to headquarters, sir. To meet with the inspector."

"What? Why, this is outrageous," Alan began to bluster.

"That it may be, but you've little choice," Constable Michaud said quietly. "Arrest is your only other option."

Once that was made clear, Alan stood, turned to Dennis Oliver, and said, "Carry on here."

Then, with his eyes glued to the floor, Alan Hughes walked out of the room, escorted by a constable on either side of him.

Chapter Twenty

As soon as the doors closed behind Alan, Dennis stood, clapped his hands twice, and said, "Okay, everyone, rehearsals continue. Derek, take it from the top, please."

It was as though Derek Braverman was a different actor than the man who'd been performing a few minutes earlier. He stumbled over his words and kept moving around as if trying to escape the triangle Nicholas had set up to such exacting standards.

Finally, Dennis said, "Derek, why don't you take a brief rest? Get back in character."

Then he raised his voice loud enough to be heard backstage. "Nicholas, set up for Frederick, please."

Nicholas came out of the wings carrying a fourth chair. He had taken about three steps when Derek bellowed, "Get back into character? When have I ever been on a stage or in front of a camera and not been in character?"

The battle went on for a few minutes, until Derek relented in the nastiest of ways. "I'll take a rest all right. When Alan comes back, you can tell him that he can find me in my suite. And believe me when I say the only thing that will result in being 'brief' after this conversation will be your career."

Derek jumped off the stage, wobbling as he landed. He recovered his balance and then stormed out the double doors, being sure to slam them behind him.

"Wasn't he more brassed off than I've ever seen?" Emma laughed. "It's too bad he didn't pick an angry scene for his monologue. He wouldn't need to rehearse at all."

I agreed but thought there was more to it. "I do believe he was angrier than the slight interruption should have made him. I mean, Alan's leaving was beyond anyone's control."

Maureen Metzger had a different opinion. "I may have been married to a sheriff for too long, but I think Derek Braverman is really on edge. And I don't think it is because of Quint Chabot's murder, or because the constables took Alan to be interviewed by Inspector Radigan. Even though he laughed it off, I think his nervousness started when Rosalie popped out with his real name."

Reviewing the past twenty-four hours in my mind, I realized Maureen might very well be correct. The more I thought about it, the more eager I was to see if we could find out more about Derek's past. The one person I was sure knew more about it than anyone else was Jorge Escarra, but with rehearsals going full blast, he was sure to be unavailable. Time to go to plan B.

"Emma," I whispered, "I think Maureen and I are going to use our free time to do some sightseeing. Do you mind?"

"Not at all, dearie. If I wasn't trapped here, I'd love to join you, but duty calls." Emma sighed. "Enjoy yourselves."

Maureen and I waited until Dennis asked Frederick to stop for a moment in order for Nicholas to adjust the spatial arrangements, by which, I supposed, he meant the chairs on the stage that marked Frederick's boundaries. That gave us the opportunity to leave the ballroom without causing any disruption.

As soon as we were alone in the elevator, Maureen said, "I feel bad leaving Emma there. Who knew that being a famous actress could have so many boring hours? Now tell me, exactly what kind of sightseeing do you have in mind?"

The elevator door opened, and when I looked cautiously around the lobby, checking for the fandom duo of Vivian Zhang and Iris Crenshaw, thankfully they were nowhere to be seen.

I stepped into a small alcove, with Maureen right next to me. "I think you are absolutely right about Derek Braverman. For a person with his gigantic ego, he is far more upset over the death of a part-time stagehand, someone he barely knew, than you would expect. His type of person would be more likely to say, 'Too bad. So sorry,' and move along as though nothing earth-shattering had happened. But he has been rattled since Rosalie mentioned Derek Posh. So it stands to reason that Derek is concerned that the investigation into Quint's death might accidentally bring to light something that Derek would rather the world not know."

"Agreed," Maureen said. "So what is our plan?"

"I hope that the local library will have some old newspaper files, probably on microfiche, going back to Derek's youth, and perhaps his indiscretion was significant enough to have been reported at the time," I said.

"Oh, Jessica, that's brilliant, but in a strange town, how can we be sure to find the right library?" Maureen fretted.

"I think I know just the person who can help us, but right now we better go find Mort and Seth to let them know that we will be going, ah, shopping."

"Suppose they want to come with us?"

"Do you honestly think that those two would volunteer to come shopping with us? I doubt that will be a problem," I said, remembering how many times Seth had mused about what he called "women's joy versus men's loathing when it comes to shopping."

As it turned out, I was spot-on, although my reasoning was entirely wrong.

We walked down the hallway to the card room, and once again I was irritated to see that the signs advertising my imminent book signing were still being displayed. Obviously, I was going to have to be more forceful in my objection. I planned to follow up with Gloria in the gift shop as soon as Maureen and I came back from our travels.

Maureen saw me grimace at the signs and said, "For now, just don't look."

As we got closer to the card room, we could hear what sounded like dozens of people talking and laughing.

"That sounds awfully noisy for a chess tournament," I said.

"I know. Perhaps the players are on an intermission of some sort," Maureen suggested.

When we walked through the doorway, we had our answer. A huge white banner hanging above the card clock declared CHESS AND CHECKERS FUN DAY in bright green letters at least two feet high.

At a few of the card tables spread around the room, serious chess players were bent over their chessboards as if all the noise around them wasn't happening. I had to laugh when I noticed one player wearing earmuffs. Talk about arriving prepared.

Mort was standing in nearly the same spot where we had sat the night before while waiting to be interviewed by Inspector Radigan. There were two tables pushed together, and Seth was sitting at one of them, looking at the chessboard in front of him. His rook swooped down and took his opponent's knight, which Seth immediately passed to the young man who was playing another chess game on the adjoining table—or perhaps not, because I heard the young man say, "Thanks, partner," and he dropped the knight on a square on his game board.

"What on earth just happened?" I looked at Mort, since the four players were deep into studying the chessboards in front of them.

"It's a chess game called bughouse." Mort was nearly as excited as he'd been when I first mentioned Derek Braverman in Mara's all those weeks ago. "And as it turns out, Doc Hazlitt is darn good at it. This is his third partner, and he hasn't lost a game yet."

At that point Seth turned, looked over the top of his eyeglasses, and said sternly, "Can you please take your chitchat away from here? I get the feeling you are trying to jinx me so we can have that checkers game I promised to play with you."

Mort hurried us to the hospitality table, which was set up where it was last night. "Can I offer you some ginger ale or iced tea?"

"No, thanks, honey. Actually, we just stopped in to let you know that we are going shopping for a few hours. I am eager to see what clothes styles are popular here compared to what we see at Charles Department Store. Girl time, you know?" Maureen smiled. "You have fun with your games."

When we left the card room a few minutes later, I asked Maureen what Mort would think if we came back to the hotel without packages.

"Seriously, Jessica? Was Frank ever unhappy if you came home empty-handed from a shopping trip?"

I grinned. "Well, now that you mention it . . ."

"And just think how pleased everyone will be if we come back with a bona fide clue leading to Quint Chabot's killer."

Maureen was beside herself with glee, and we hadn't even left the building. I hoped she wouldn't be too disappointed if we weren't successful. I approached the same man at the reception desk whom I'd spoken to earlier that morning and asked hopefully, "By any chance is Rob Langford available to drive Mrs. Fletcher and Mrs. Metzger to the library?"

He looked up our registration information, probably to verify that we were entitled to car service. Rather than call Rob so we could get an immediate reply, the desk clerk sent a text and suggested that Maureen and I take a seat until he received an answer.

"How clever, Jessica. If anyone in Edmonton knows where to find information about something that happened a long time ago, be it minor or major, it would be Rob. He is such a history buff, and he knows Edmonton so well."

"Exactly my thought. Now I will do a quick search on my phone to find the year Derek's first movie was released. Then we will know to search from that year backward. My heavens, look who is coming through the door. Emma will regret she missed this."

Alan Hughes was dragging his feet as he approached the front door. He stopped and nodded gratefully when the doorman reached for the handle and opened the door for him. I suspected that was the first time Alan had even noticed that the doorman was a person and not some mechanical convenience.

Emma was going to be sorry that we weren't together to greet him, but that couldn't be helped. I stepped in front of him and said, "It seems that you were able to convince Inspector Radigan that you meant no harm when you lied to the constabulary."

"Are you quite mad, Mrs. Fletcher? I never lied. Why would I?" Alan tried to sound indignant, but by the slump of his shoulders and the downward turn of his mouth, it appeared he felt beaten and defeated.

"That is the question of the day, isn't it? And I am sure the inspector had to ask it multiple times before he got the truth out of you. So, having told the truth once, it should be easier for you to explain a second time. How is it that you thought it was easier to put a spotlight on Spencer Smith than to admit you told him to drive Emma to meet Lene for her costume fitting?"

He looked around to see who might be nearby and then said in a hushed tone, "Mrs. Fletcher, please, it was all a mistake."

"Not a mistake, Mr. Hughes. You were quite deliberate. You told a lie to Edmonton Police Service that encouraged them to focus on Spencer. Unless you murdered Quint Chabot, I cannot see how that lie would benefit you."

"All right." Alan put up his hands in a surrender-like motion. "It was about our arrangement with the Jubilee Auditorium. Had Quint died anywhere else . . . we would have been in the clear. But as luck would have it, there he was, our employee, dead in the orchestra lift. And we would be financially responsible for any financial loss to the theater if the opening is delayed."

"Didn't you have a surety bond?" I asked.

"I was trying to cut as many financial corners as I could. You know Derek aims for the moon. Nothing but the best for Derek Braverman. So to save a bob or two, rather than contracting a surety bond against mishaps, I asked Rosalie to post our surety bond from her own funds. She resisted for a while, but I convinced her that paying for a policy was like throwing money away. And then . . . this. It just seemed easier to deny any knowledge of why *anyone* connected with the show was at the Auditorium last night. It wasn't the constabulary I was lying to . . ."

"It was your wife," I finished his sentence.

He hung his head. "Now I have to tell her the truth. You've seen what she can be like. It wouldn't surprise me if she and her checkbook were on the first plane back to England . . . without me."

"And Spencer Smith?" I asked. "What do you plan to do about him?"

Alan stared at me blankly.

"Apologize, perhaps?" I suggested.

"You mean admit to him that I lied?" Alan seemed shocked at the thought.

"Well, I am sure the inspector will let Spencer know that you have come forward with the truth, but you may wish to direct a show in Edmonton again someday, and Spencer is a career stagehand. Need I say more?"

"No," Alan said somberly. "In any event, I'd rather face Spencer than Rosalie. Now if you will excuse me." He walked slowly toward the elevators.

"That was amazing," Maureen said. "You made him answer you honestly, and I don't think he is used to anyone preventing him from dancing around the truth."

Before I could answer, a bellman asked if I was Mrs. Fletcher and said that Rob Langford was waiting for us in the driveway.

If truth was the word of the day, I was hoping that Rob would be able to help us find whatever ancient truth Derek Braverman was hiding.

Chapter Twenty-One

G ood day, ladies. It's so nice to see you again." Rob tipped his chauffeur cap as he opened the passenger door of the limo for us.

"When we get home, driving around in my beat-up old sedan is going to be quite a letdown," Maureen said as she and I settled into the gray plush seats facing each other.

Rob got into the driver's seat, turned to us, and asked what locations we were planning on visiting today.

"That is entirely up to you, Rob. We are interested in searching through historical records, old newspapers and such. With all your knowledge of history, we were wondering if you knew of a library where those records would be publicly available," I said.

Rob gave us a huge grin. "Well, aren't you two my favorite kind of visitors—wanting to learn about my homeland."

I wasn't sure what Rob would think if we told him the nature of our intended research, so I returned his smile with one of my own and asked, "So, you have a place in mind?"

"Do I ever! The University of Alberta has an extensive collection, and not that I want to deprive myself of the pleasure of your company, but the university has long since made their databases accessible online. You can take a look at any materials they have from the comfort of your hotel room."

"If I were home, I would do exactly that, but as much as I appreciate the hotel providing Wi-Fi, since Maureen and I are planning in-depth research, I'd rather be at the source if at all possible."

"Understood, ma'am. It's off to school we go. I will have you there in a few minutes. Now, would you care for some music on the way?"

When I said no, thank you, Rob shut the privacy window, started the car, and pulled out of the driveway.

"Well, if we can find any gossip at all about Derek, even if it's only his consistent lies about his name, I will have to tell my husband that Derek Braverman isn't who Mort thought he was. I mean, I know 'Sheriff Mort' was irritated by Derek's behavior during and after our interviews, but I have a feeling 'little boy Mort' still holds out hope that his hero doesn't have clay feet," Maureen said.

"I am sure you are correct," I said with a sigh, "but I can't help believing that if Derek Braverman has been hiding his true identity all these years, there has to be a significant reason behind it. I mean, from what we read or see when stars are interviewed, everyone who has a professional identity that is different from their private identity candidly admits it and publicly reveals their given name. I feel certain there is a significant reason Derek

Braverman is so secretive about his name. And let's not forget that at the end of our tour of the Jubilee Auditorium, Derek was loudly adamant in announcing that his real first name was Sebastian, but it was too long to post on a marquee or some such nonsense."

"If he is hiding something," Maureen said, "you can bet we are going to find out what his secret is."

Rob guided the limousine through the main entrance to a large and lovely campus. He drove around buildings and gardens before entering a parking lot. Once he'd parked the limo, Rob volunteered to escort us into the library. When we arrived at the information desk, he handed me his business card. "Call me when you finish your research, and I will bring the car to the front entrance. Have fun, ladies."

A woman with a gray top-knot hairdo, reading glasses hung on a silver chain around her neck, and a decidedly professional demeanor asked how she could help us. Maureen looked at me for guidance, and I immediately decided that "fangirl" would be the least suspicious way to ask for what we needed to see.

"Oh, I hope so; I certainly hope so." I fidgeted slightly so as to appear nervous, but not too nervous. "My name is Jess and this is Maureen. We come from a small town in Maine where, I am proud to say, I am president and Maureen is the secretary of the Derek Braverman fan club. Well, when our members heard we were vacationing in Canada, they wanted us to be sure and come here to Edmonton. It's Derek's hometown, you know."

"I certainly do. He is quite the favorite son here. My name is Mrs. Khan. And since you have come to this particular library, may I ask what kinds of things your club members are interested in learning?"

I began with a fictionalized version of our nonexistent club. "Over the years, our membership has amassed an extensive collection of articles from newspapers and magazines as well as videos of interviews that have been taken throughout his long, illustrious career. Why, if you mention a year, any year at all, one of our founding members, Ideal Molloy, can pull out a manila folder chock-full of clippings and reference numbers to shelves in the cabinet where she stores the videos."

A puzzled look crossed Mrs. Khan's face, so I quickly summed up my request. "So you see, it's the before times that we are interested in discovering. As a young boy, did Derek place third in a spelling bee, or as a teen, did he win a trophy playing hockey? That sort of thing." I smiled appreciatively.

Her puzzled look disappeared, and Mrs. Khan said, "I understand completely, and I am sure, given the right time frame, if any information was published, our newspaper collection will have it. We will, however, need a year to use as a starting point."

Since I had looked up the release date of Derek's first movie appearance, I told her we would use that as a starting point and work backward. She stepped over to her computer for a moment, tapped a few keys, and then printed a page.

Mrs. Khan came around from behind the desk and led us to the far side of the room, where she set us up at a table with two side-by-side computers. She spent a few minutes explaining how we could easily access the databases and then placed the paper she held on the table between us.

"This is a list of the most likely sources of information about Edmonton residents during the time frame you require. Let's look for Mr. Braverman in the first year you mentioned."

She showed us how to search the system. Since we had entered the year Derek filmed his first movie, there were a fair number of "hometown boy is soon to be a star" stories. I suspected Derek Posh would not be quite so famous. Nor would Sebastian Derek Posh.

We thanked her profusely, and she went back to the information desk, where two students were waiting for her attention.

"That was quick thinking, Madam President of the fan club." Maureen laughed.

"Well, I was hard-pressed to come up with any reason why we would be interested in Derek's life before he was a celebrity unless we were groupies. And we had to tell her who we were researching in order to ensure we would get the right materials," I said.

"That makes perfect sense," Maureen answered, and picked up the list Mrs. Khan had printed for us. "Now, how do you want to divide these?"

Mrs. Khan came to check on us periodically during the nearly two hours we spent searching with absolutely no result. We were sure to tell her we were doing fabulously well and would bring home a wealth of information to our club members. I repeatedly pointed to a stack of old sports and graduation articles that we printed out early on and put face down on the table. She kept telling us how pleased she was with our progress, not knowing that all the while Maureen and I were getting more and more dejected.

"I'm beginning to think that whatever Derek's name was in his younger days, it wasn't Posh," Maureen said.

I leaned back in my chair and stretched my arms out to the side and over my head. "I think you are absolutely right. And he could easily have been lying about Sebastian as well. It's time to give up this search and recheck with our source, at least about the Posh name."

"Rosalie? You mean Rosalie Hughes? Are you sure she will even speak to us? She has to be in a fury over Alan's convincing her to post the surety bond, and she must be embarrassed if she learned that he lied about Spencer. And then here we come, questioning something that she announced after she'd had an extra drink or two? Oh, I don't know, Jessica. That woman is not in a pleasant mood at the best of times."

"You're right, of course, but there may be more to it, and we will only be able to find out if we ask. Time to head back to the hotel."

I took out my cell phone and punched in Rob's number. He answered on the first ring and said he would meet us in five minutes.

We discreetly tossed the useless papers we had printed into the recycling bin, and I folded the list of sites Mrs. Khan said would be helpful and put it in my purse. When we got to the information desk, Rob was already there waiting for us, and Mrs. Khan was busy helping a student. I caught her eye, waved, and mouthed *Thank you*, and we were on our way.

The always shiny gray limo was parked right at the front door, and a group of young men was circling it with great admiration.

As Rob held the car door open for Maureen and me, I heard one of the youngsters wonder aloud about horsepower. Rob closed our door but then went over to speak to them before he got into the car. By the time Rob took his seat behind the wheel, the young men were smiling.

"Now, where are we going next?" Rob turned to us, and our faces must have shown exactly how we felt. "Oh. It looks like you didn't find what you were hoping to. I am sorry."

"Thank you," I said. "It may well have been that we were on the wrong path. We will have to reconsider."

I looked at Maureen. "It's probably best that we go back to the hotel for a nice cup of tea and plan our next move."

As soon as Maureen nodded her agreement, Rob asked if we were up for some light classical music, which I thought seemed like the perfect incentive for me to sit back and comfortably re-organize my thoughts. I told him that would be lovely.

"I have just the thing. 'The Tune the Gypsy Played.' It is an ancient melody, but this arrangement was done by Moro in the late 1970s. I guarantee it will help you relax." Rob started the music and closed the privacy window.

As one soft classical piece followed the other, Maureen and I were silent, each wrapped in our own thoughts. We were nearly at the hotel when Maureen said, "I could get used to being driven wherever I need to go while surrounded by comforting music, but seriously, Jessica, is talking to Rosalie our only option?"

I did have something floating in my mind, and Maureen's question crystalized it.

"Rosalie is our best source and we'll have to follow up, but that doesn't mean we can't make inquiries elsewhere," I said, probably sounding more mysterious than I intended.

By the time Rob drove into the hotel's circuitous driveway, I had a fanciful plan in mind. It might not help, but there was no harm in trying.

Chapter Twenty-Two

Rob opened the passenger door, and as Maureen and I eased out of the limo, I asked if he would consider doing us a favor.

"Of course, Mrs. Fletcher. How can I be of assistance?"

"Do you have a few minutes to speak with us in the lobby? I am going to order tea and butter tarts," I added as an incentive. "Would you care to join us?"

"If you add some iced tea to that order, I will be inside as soon as I find an extra-long parking space round back." Rob closed the passenger door and started to get into the driver's seat again, but then he stopped and said, "Whatever it is, I will do my best to help."

Of that I had no doubt.

When we walked inside, I looked around the lobby cautiously, wondering if Inspector Radigan would pop out of nowhere to ask more endless questions or, worse, the fandom duo, as I had come to think of Iris and Vivian, would come along to badger me about a book signing. They were so maddening that I was considering offering to privately sign their personal copies of whichever of my books they might own in order to move them to the "over and done with" column.

But I was pleasantly surprised to find the lobby fairly empty. Maureen and I would definitely be able to talk to Rob with a decent amount of privacy. A table full of tea and pastries would project the illusion that we were merely taking a snack break and that our conversation was mundane.

I stopped at the reception desk and placed an order for tea, iced tea, and butter tarts with service for three. Then I pointed to a quiet corner of the lobby that was furnished with a love seat, two chairs, and a coffee table. "We'll be sitting right there."

A server brought our food just as Rob arrived. He sat down and said, "It's not often I get invited to tea of an afternoon. This makes for a nice pause in my day. Thank you, ladies."

I poured a glass of iced tea and passed it to him along with the plate of butter tarts. Maureen mentioned how much he had contributed to our enjoyment of our time in Edmonton, and Rob responded that he loved showing off his hometown.

That was my cue.

"Rob, you have said, on occasion, that you have lived here all your life, so we were wondering if you would help us solve a small mystery."

Rob set his glass of iced tea on the table and gave me his full attention. "You know I will do my best, Mrs. Fletcher."

"We were fortunate enough to be invited to Edmonton because my cousin Emma is starring in a revue with Derek Braverman to celebrate his retirement. One odd thing that Maureen and I have noticed is that when anyone brings up the possibility that Braverman is not the name Derek was born with—well, the easiest way to describe it is he gets edgy, loud, and nasty. I thought perhaps that, as a lifetime local resident, you might know what the real story is."

Rob chuckled, leaned back in his chair, and thoughtfully ran a finger across his white chinstrap beard. "Don't let the color of my beard fool you; I am not old enough to remember Derek Braverman when he was a young wannabe star living at home here in Edmonton. But"—he waved his hand in a semicircle from Maureen to me and back again as if erasing our disappointment—"I do know a lot of older folks born and bred here, particularly those in any line of work similar to mine, who keep stories about our homegrown celebrities filed in the back of their minds because the tourists always have questions. Let me see what I can find out. And I promise to pass on anything I learn."

When Maureen and I began to thank him, Rob shook his head. "No need to thank me; I haven't done anything yet, and besides, you have gotten my curiosity up to a thousand. If Braverman has a secret past or a hidden name, how is it I've never heard of it?"

Maureen and I both laughed when he pretended to scowl at the very thought.

"There is one more thing," I said. "While we are not sure what his original last name might be, Derek is now claiming that his first name, given at birth, was Sebastian."

"Now, that's a fine name. A strong name. Too fancy for a tough guy like Braverman, I guess?" Rob shook his head. "Ah, these celebrities, always trying to fix what's not broken."

It wasn't long before Rob drained his glass of iced tea, thanked us for the butter tarts, and went on his way, but not before promising that he would stay in touch.

"Well, that's encouraging." Maureen's eyes were bright with anticipation. "I should have realized that people who work with tourists as closely as Rob does would know more about hometown heroes than the entertainment reporter on the town newspaper."

"Don't ever let Dan Andrews hear you say that," I chided lightly. "Now I suppose we'd best find Rosalie Hughes—"

"Mrs. Fletcher, there you are. I have been looking for you all day. I left two messages on the telephone in your room." Mary Jo Simard stood on the other side of the table, wringing her hands.

"I'm sorry, but I have been out of the hotel until a few minutes ago. Is something the matter?" I hoped against hope that whatever had her agitated had nothing to do with signing books, but I knew my chances were slim.

She slid into the chair that Rob Langford had vacated a few minutes before. "I doubt you are aware—most guests aren't—but the hotel recently changed managers and, well, Jane Geeson, our new manager, is desperate to put her stamp on everything. And when Mrs. Crenshaw and Mrs. Zhang cornered her in the ladies' room near the gift shop, well, you can guess the rest. Will you help me, please?"

Mary Jo was no longer wringing her hands. They were now folded together in a prayerful pose. And the look of desperation on her face was truly upsetting. "My job is on the line here, Mrs. Fletcher. Please, if only for an hour, can I go back to Ms. Geeson and tell her we are hosting a book-signing event by the internationally famous author J. B. Fletcher here at the hotel the day after tomorrow?"

I looked at Maureen, whose big blue eyes were now silently pleading with me on Mary Jo's behalf, and I relented. "One hour. That's it. Not a minute more."

Mary Jo flew from her chair and grabbed my hand. For a second I feared she would kiss it, but instead we shook hands briefly and she hurried away, but not before saying, "You won't regret this, Mrs. Fletcher; I promise."

I sincerely hoped that she was right.

I stood up, and Maureen asked, "Rosalie?"

"Yes, we better go now before someone else gets in our way," I said.

We walked to the elevator, and when the doors opened, Alan Hughes stepped out. His face blanched when he saw us. He nodded a greeting and tried to scurry away, but I quickly stepped into his path.

He looked up to the ceiling as if expecting a helpful angel to swoop down and rescue him from Maureen and me, but when that didn't happen, he said, "What is it now, Mrs. Fletcher?"

"We would like to visit with Rosalie for a while. Do you know where we might find her?" I said.

"Visit with my wife? Seriously? Didn't you cause enough trouble when you spoke out of turn regarding Spencer Smith? Whose business is it really whether he volunteered or I asked him to drive Emma to meet Lene? And let's not forget, it was Emma he was supposed to drive, not *you* and Emma. This is the last time I will ever allow cast members to invite family and friends anywhere near a show before opening night."

And he stormed away, still muttering to himself.

"That went well," Maureen said, and burst into laughter. "I suppose we'll have to search for Rosalie on our own."

"I hope she is in a better mood than her husband," I said, although we both knew that was highly unlikely, even on the best of days. "If Alan is wandering around, Dennis Oliver must be in the temporary rehearsal hall. He may know where we can find Rosalie."

We took the elevator to the second floor, and when we entered the Silver Ballroom, Frederick the Great and Gracelyn were on the stage, and Dennis was standing by the row of audience chairs. I was surprised that Emma was nowhere to be seen.

"So you see, Dennis," Frederick was saying in the patient voice of a parent speaking to an overtired two-year-old, "it is impossible for us to practice anything at all without our equipment. And as you know, our equipment is in the basement of the Jubilee Auditorium, which has been declared off-limits by the local police department. We are wasting our time here."

"Frederick, please be reasonable. Alan has asked that we all cooperate." Dennis's efforts to reason with Frederick didn't prevent him from ushering Gracelyn off the stage.

Frederick replied, "Call me when you have our props," and he and Gracelyn continued to walk off stage left and in a few seconds came down a short flight of stairs.

Gracelyn had to struggle to keep up when Frederick increased his pace, and in less than a minute they were out of the room.

I overheard Dennis mutter to himself, "Alan is not going to like this one bit."

Then he raised his voice and yelled for Nick, who came out from backstage. "We have Jorge up next. Can you please call and tell him we are ready for him?"

Nick nodded, pulled his phone from his pocket, and began dialing while Dennis slumped in a chair in the first row and began making notes on his laptop.

Maureen and I walked to where he was sitting and said hello as if this were a casual bumping-into-a-friend kind of encounter.

"Mrs. Fletcher. Mrs. Metzger. How nice to see you. Unfortunately, we don't have any performances on the stage right now. Oh, and if you are looking for Emma, she finished her set earlier and won't be back until later, when she rehearses with Derek. Oh, that reminds me . . ." He picked up his laptop and tapped a few keys.

"We see how busy you are, and we certainly don't want to interrupt. Actually, Maureen and I aren't looking for Emma; we are looking for Rosalie Hughes. Would you happen to know . . ." I said.

"Rosalie rarely leaves her suite, although we could certainly use her assistance since we are overwhelmed by the present confusion, but, sadly, she has little interest." Dennis shrugged.

"Thank you. Do you happen to know her suite number?" I asked, pleased that he hadn't brushed us off.

"It's the penthouse, of course. Where else would Rosalie deign to sleep?" Dennis laughed sourly and began talking to Nick.

We thanked him, and as we walked to the door, Maureen whispered, "I didn't even know the hotel has a penthouse suite, did you?"

I chuckled. "It never entered my head."

When we reached the elevator bank, Maureen wondered aloud, "Do you suppose there is a private elevator, or will the regular elevators take us there?"

"I suggest we climb aboard and find out," I said as I pushed the button marked UP. We stepped into the first elevator that arrived and rode to the highest available floor, the twenty-second. When the doors opened, we got off and were immediately disappointed to see that there were numbered rooms following the same pattern as we had on the fifth floor.

A bellman carrying what looked to be someone's dry cleaning happened to come walking along the hall, and we asked him how we could get to the penthouse. He hesitated until I said we were visiting Mrs. Hughes and had obviously misunderstood her directions. Then he smiled.

"No problem. No problem at all." He led us back to the elevator bank and pointed to the door of the elevator in which we had ridden. "You came up in elevator two. Only elevator one goes to the penthouse." He pushed the UP button by the side of the elevator doors. "When you get in the elevator, there is a blank button right above the button for floor number twenty-two. It is blank for privacy, you know. Push that button and up you go."

Then he tapped the DOWN button, and the doors opened to elevator two. He got in and said good-bye.

Elevator one arrived in a few seconds, and hitting the unnumbered button got us where we wanted to go. The elevator door opened into a lovely tiled foyer with an attractive arrangement of potted plants in one corner and the door to what I presumed was the penthouse straight ahead.

I knocked lightly on the door, but there was no answer.

"Maybe she's not in there or she's napping," Maureen said.

I wasn't willing to give up. If Rosalie was napping, I was quite willing to wake her up. I banged more forcefully on the door, and the next thing we heard was Rosalie shouting, "Whoever you are, go away. Especially if your name is Alan Hughes."

Chapter Twenty-Three

R osalie, it's Jessica Fletcher. Although I hate to disturb you, I have some questions to ask, and your answers may help get the Jubilee Auditorium opened sooner rather than later. I think you'll agree that would be beneficial to all concerned."

It took Rosalie longer than expected to reply, and when she did, her voice sounded weary. "Well, if you must, you must. But you will have to ask your questions through the door. I am not in the mood for company."

Maureen and I looked at each other. Neither of us believed that Rosalie could possibly be serious. Then we heard the elevator doors open behind us. I was afraid it was Alan and a true melee was about to begin, so I was relieved to see a member of the cleaning crew, vacuum cleaner in hand.

The cleaner hesitated when she saw us standing by the penthouse door and asked if we would like her to return at a more convenient time, but I thought her arrival gave us an opportunity that was too good to pass up. I said that would not be necessary. I leaned closer to the door and said, "Rosalie, the cleaning crew is about to start vacuuming the foyer."

"Can't you send them . . . oh, never mind," Rosalie said. We heard the door lock turn, and when she opened it, I was shocked at how disheveled and worn-out she looked.

Her hair was matted as if she'd just woken up, which was possible because when she opened the door, I immediately noticed that she had left the belt of her robe untied. It hung limply from the loops on each side of the robe and did nothing to conceal the once-exquisite set of off-white silk pajamas she was wearing. Sadly, the pajamas were stained and quite wrinkled. And I was not surprised to see a glass of amber liquid in her hand.

"Now that you are here, you may as well have a seat." She waved her arm in the general direction of a yellow floral settee. "Can I offer you ladies a drink? I have some fine Canadian whisky. The hotel provides J. P. Wiser's, but I find that I enjoy Lock Stock & Barrel."

She walked over to a bar next to the sliding glass doors that gave us a view of a lovely terrace surrounded by a tidily kept garden, as well as a spectacular panorama of the city of Edmonton that lay beyond. While refilling her glass, she raised an eyebrow in our direction, and I realized that if we accepted drinks, in Rosalie's mind it might make this seem more like a social visit.

"Actually, if you have any wine . . ." I said.

"As it happens, I do. Believe me, the hotel keeps the penthouse bar well stocked. White or red?"

"Ah, white."

"Wonderful. We have a couple of bottles of Chardonnay. It's

Canadian grown and bottled under the brand Le Clos Jordanne."
Rosalie reached behind the bar and brought out a wine bottle
with a classic-looking white label declaring its name in red print.
She poured more wine than is customary into two water glasses
and handed one to me and one to Maureen.

Rosalie sat down in a white-and-yellow chair opposite us and
asked, "Now, what is so urgent that you felt compelled to seek me
out in the privacy of what at this moment is my own home, so to
speak?"

"You know that my friends and I have traveled all this way
from Cabot Cove, Maine, for a chance to visit with my dear
cousin Emma and most of all to see the fabulous revue that she
is starring in alongside the very popular star of stage and screen,
Derek Braverman. I would guess that you are as upset as we are
that the show is not proceeding on schedule—"

"On that point, you are wrong. I am far more distraught than
you could ever imagine. This venture that Alan assured me would
be a huge financial success is sucking up my money faster than"—
she pointed to the front door—"the vacuum cleaner is picking up
dirt in the foyer. I hate to be blunt. I know it is not considered a
common English trait, but do not keep me in suspense any longer. What is the reason for your visit?"

I had been mentally prepared for this conversation to drag on
and on until I could get Rosalie to focus, so I was overjoyed that
was not to be the case. "When we were together the other evening
and you announced that Derek's last name at birth was Posh, not
Braverman, at first he was quite upset, and then he laughed it off.
But I did begin to wonder, since we are here in Derek's hometown, if it is possible that who Derek *used* to be had some con-

nection to the murder that has put a stop to the show going on as planned."

"What?" Rosalie chortled. "You think Derek killed that stagehand because of some trivial mishap that occurred either last week or decades ago? That is preposterous."

"I am sorry; I haven't been quite clear. Quint Chabot was not even born by the time Derek left Edmonton, so Derek would not have known him. I don't think Derek is a killer, but there is a strong possibility that he was the intended target."

Rosalie set her glass on the end table, got up, and walked across the living room and back again. I was sure she was imagining her large investment as the show's producer disappearing into thin air. Then she stopped and stood directly in front of me. "Derek as the victim. Unthinkable, simply unthinkable. Can you give me any plausible reason to believe your . . . your . . . theory?"

"If we assume that Quint Chabot was merely doing his job, a routine stagehand chore, and he stumbled across the killer, who was examining the theater for an opportunity to commit some sort of crime—if not murder, perhaps blackmail—one thing may have led to another. What we do know is that Quint is dead, he was killed in the Jubilee Auditorium, and the killer is still out there."

"It is possible, I suppose, but I still don't understand why you are questioning me." Rosalie took a large gulp of her whisky and returned to sit in the chair.

"I'd like to know if you told Inspector Radigan that Derek Braverman has, for as long as you have known him, worked diligently to hide the fact that he was born with a different last name," I said, getting to the crux of the matter.

"No, of course not. I didn't see the relevance, and besides, the question was never asked," she said, absolving herself of any responsibility.

"Would it be possible for you to share how you came by that information?"

"It must have been . . . oh, I don't know, thirty-five or forty years ago. Derek was rapidly moving up the ladder to success, and Alan was determined to build a strong director-actor relationship with him before the rest of the industry caught on to what a rising star Derek was destined to be." Rosalie closed her eyes as if reliving the moment and then perked up.

"Derek was staying at our London house for a few days. Alan decided we should have a party, which would be an opportunity to have the West End's most famous and prestigious actors, directors, and, most importantly, producers meet the talented young Canadian actor.

"When the raucous party ended and we were sitting, just the three of us, in the library enjoying a nightcap"—Rosalie absentmindedly swirled the contents of her glass—"Alan declared the party a huge success and said that Derek would soon be the hottest commodity to hit the London stage in ages.

"Then Alan said, 'And when you are signing *Derek Braverman* to every contract put in front of you in the future, remember this night. Remember who gave you your start.'

"I could not see Derek's face, but he must have given something away, because Alan was standing in front of Derek and looking directly at him when Alan asked if Derek Braverman was actually his name.

"Derek hemmed and hawed. He asked for another drink, and then, shamefaced, he said that he had mistakenly signed his first contract with what was then his legal name. He later realized he should change his name legally to prevent confusion, and he hired a solicitor, who guided him in the legal-name-change procedure and went so far as to renegotiate that first contract, where in essence, Derek forfeited some of his payment in order to re-sign a copy of the contract as Derek Braverman, so there would not be so much as a trace of Derek Posh in the industry.

"At least that is what I have always thought he said. What I remember most is laughing hysterically and joking at the thought of an actor with such an outlandish name."

Rosalie lapsed into silence, drained the remains of her glass, and said, "It was late at night; we were all very drunk, and I may well have gotten some of the details wrong, perhaps even Derek's true name."

She stood and headed to the bar for a refill, saying over her shoulder, "Now if you would see yourselves out, I would be most appreciative."

The elevator door had barely closed behind us when Maureen said, "That was some story Rosalie told us. Do you believe her? Or is she just playing a game, like when she needles Derek the way she did in the Beaver Bar because, as the one who holds all the purse strings, she knows she can?"

"I do believe her as far as what she remembers about that long-ago night. Rosalie is so used to the fact that her money—and her role as a producer when Alan needs one—give her extraordinary power in their relationship. But now that they are here in Edmonton and working on a special show starring a world-famous actor who has a secret that she knows, well, don't you think that would increase her power exponentially?"

The elevator doors opened on the eighth floor, and a young

couple entered. The man was carrying a toddler who spent the two minutes to the lobby waving at Maureen or me and then giggling uproariously when we waved back.

Maureen and I followed the young family out of the elevator and gave the child one last giggle-inducing good-bye wave.

Maureen had her cell phone in her hand. "I suppose I should call Mort. He and Seth are probably wondering where we've been all day."

She talked for a few minutes, and when she hung up, she said, "They had a great time at the chess-and-checkers event and right now are taking a walk. Mort did mention that Mary Jo told him dinner would be as usual in the Victoria Room, and she managed to impress both Mort and Seth when she told them that she had talked you into doing the book signing. Apparently, she is planning a major event. Mort said she was prattling on about posters and tea or some such; he really didn't pay much attention."

"Honestly, that woman!" I was close to losing my temper. "You heard what I told her: one hour maximum. How much fuss can she manage to stuff into an hour?"

The elevator doors opened, and who else but Emma and Eileen McCarthy stepped off the elevator.

"And isn't this tickety-boo!" Emma said. "Eileen and I have been rehearsing all day, and we are fine to be finished at last. How did you spend your day?"

With Eileen standing there, I thought it best to say, "Rob took us out for a while, and we had a lovely time." Which was the truth as far as it went.

Then I asked, "I presume that Alan is still insisting Eileen rehearse with you, in case something happens and you can't perform?"

Emma looked at me as if I'd announced a family secret over the hotel intercom, and then said, "Yes, that's it. Eileen has been having a hard time learning the duets that I do with Derek, since he refuses to practice with her. That apparently falls within his 'no understudy' rule. So we have to steal time to rehearse with Jorge playing Derek's part. It is all bonkers."

We chatted for a few more minutes, and then Eileen excused herself.

Emma watched Eileen walk away and said, "She is going to be a major star one day. So, what is on our agenda? I hope dinner is coming soon. I have worked up quite an appetite."

"According to my husband," Maureen said, "dinner is in the Victoria Room at the usual time."

All three of us automatically stretched our necks to look at the grandfather clock behind the reception desk, which indicated we had not quite an hour to freshen up and regroup.

We took a few steps to the elevator bank, and I pressed the UP button. When the doors opened, Dennis Oliver was standing there, and he began grinning from ear to ear at the sight of us, or, as I soon realized, at the sight of Emma. He stepped into the lobby and swaddled Emma in a big hug.

"I just got the call. The police are finished with the Jubilee Auditorium, and we can start rehearsals there beginning at nine o'clock tomorrow morning. The revue will open on time. Have you seen Alan? I can't wait to tell him the news."

I, for one, would be interested in observing how Alan, Derek, Rosalie, Jorge, and everyone else involved in the revue would feel about going back to what was, and would be forevermore, the scene of Quint Chabot's murder.

Chapter Twenty-Four

I invited Emma to my room and told her all about the frustrating time Maureen and I had spent at the University of Alberta Library.

"Aren't you the clever one by half," she replied when I was done. "Asking Rob to help out. That was brilliant. He really knows this town. And you realize there is only one reason why your search was all for naught, don't you, my savvy, insightful cousin?"

"Oh yes. We can be quite sure that whatever Derek Braverman's birth name was, it was definitely not Posh," I said.

Emma clapped her hands. "Brilliant again. And now that we know that for certain, what is our next move?"

I hesitated. "Emma, I will be going home after opening night, but you have to work with these people for the entire time the revue runs, not to mention any future shows where you may wind up being coworkers, so perhaps it's not wise for you to be actively involved in trying to discover Derek's real name and why he is so intent on hiding it. He seems like the vengeful type. And I would hate to see him do anything to hurt you."

"Oh, don't you worry about me, luv. You know I've always been one to take risks, and I am not going to stop now." Emma flexed her muscles like a superhero.

"Well, Rob has offered to ask around among the oldsters in his industry. I expect we'll hear from him again shortly," I said, still not wanting to involve Emma any further.

"Come on, out with it. We both know that our next step is to corner Jorge Escarra and badger him until he tells us the truth about Derek." Emma glowed with excitement at the very thought.

"Emma, I wouldn't exactly use the phrase we two should 'badger him.'"

Emma laughed. "Of course *you* wouldn't. But that won't stop me if given even half the chance. Well, it's getting late. I better go shower and change. Meet you later in the Victoria Room, shall I?"

She opened the door to the hallway and stopped. "Or we could knock to see if Jorge is in his room. He is the one person I am sure can tell us Derek's real last name if it isn't Braverman."

My indecision must have been obvious because Emma continued. "He is more likely to spill a secret in the privacy of his hotel room than in a dining room, a lobby, a rehearsal space, or anywhere else."

I saw the truth in what she was saying, so I asked, "I suppose you know his room number?" as I picked up my purse, determined that Emma not speak with him by herself.

"Across the hall from mine and two doors farther along." Emma's grin was getting more impish by the minute.

We knocked on Jorge Escarra's door, and he opened it without inquiring who was on the other side. If he was surprised to see us, he didn't show it. "To what do I owe the pleasure? Did I miss a rehearsal?"

"Rehearsal! Have you heard the news about our rehearsals?" Emma didn't wait for him to answer. "The police are allowing us back into the Jubilee Auditorium first thing in the morning. I'm sure we'll be given scheduling direction tonight from Dennis if not from Alan himself. I did notice Alan's been a bit disjointed today." She hung her head slightly as if she were seriously concerned.

"You can't possibly find that surprising with all that's going on." Jorge looked from Emma to me and back to Emma; then he said apologetically, "Was there anything else? If not, you must excuse me. I was about to go down to the gift shop for some shaving cream so I can tidy up before dinner."

"Actually, we do have one serious question." I had decided it was less awkward for me to ask rather than Emma, since she would be working with Jorge for a couple of months and, after this trip, I would likely never see him again. "Two things were quite evident when we were all together in the Beaver Bar. The first is that Braverman is not Derek's original last name. The second is that you were the one person present who knows what that last name is."

"Mrs. Fletcher, at the risk of sounding rude, may I ask how the birth name of a member of our assemblage is any concern of yours?" He looked at me pointedly, seemingly certain he'd won the match.

"Yes, well, I do have a concern." I tried to look worried even though I certainly did not have Emma's acting skills. "I am sure the police are looking at all avenues regarding Quint Chabot's murder. My thought is that since he was a new, part-time employee at the theater, it is possible that he may have been in the wrong place at the wrong time. He may have inadvertently come across an outsider who was searching for information. Put that together with the fact that Derek Braverman has returned to Edmonton for the first time in decades, and there are persistent rumors that when he lived here, Derek was known by a different name. It is possible that Quint simply ran into someone who did not belong in the theater but was there looking for information about Derek or even there to try to harm Derek in some way . . . As I said, wrong place, wrong time—and poor Quint."

Jorge eased himself into a nearby armchair. He ran the back of his hand over his forehead as if to clear his brow of nonexistent perspiration but said nothing.

"Jorge, Derek's real name isn't Braverman and it isn't Posh, but I believe you know what it is. Please, for Derek's own safety, tell us," Emma said more gently than I could have imagined.

It took a while, but eventually Jorge nodded. "The other night when Rosalie, drunk as she was, said that she was going to tell your friends, and everyone else within hearing distance, what Derek's last name was, I could tell by the look on Derek's face that he was about to explode. I was helpless to intervene but was greatly relieved when, inexplicably, Rosalie tossed out the name Posh. Here she was, taunting Derek all these years because she was sure she knew his name when, as it turned out, she had the wrong last name. Derek was smart enough to go with it. He made the joke about no one being able to consider a posh boy to be a hero and hoped the entire incident would be forgotten.

"If there is any chance that Quint Chabot was murdered by someone who was looking for information about Derek, I will tell you right now that his last name was Piché. He has kept it quiet all these years because he had what they now call a 'troubled youth,' and he certainly doesn't want any knowledge of that to be revealed to the world at this late date. Not after he has kept it secret for his entire career."

By the time he finished speaking, Jorge had gone completely pale, and his face was glistening. Emma went to the kitchenette and brought back a cloth towel and a glass of water. She handed both to him.

He downed the water in three or four gulps and then handed her the empty glass. "Thank you. I don't know what came over me. I felt lightheaded for a moment."

He wiped his face, and the color gradually returned. Jorge stood. "I suppose I must tell Derek that you both know his true name. It is not going to be a pretty conversation. In all these years, I have never betrayed him—until this very moment."

"If I might," I said. "Wouldn't an easier conversation be for you to explain my theory to Derek, taking it as your own, of course? You could encourage him to speak to Inspector Radigan in confidence and explain that when he lived here in Edmonton, he was known by a different name. If someone—we are not sure who—is trying to link the famous Derek Braverman to a young man named Derek Piché who may have done that person real or imagined harm some fifty or so years ago, well, Derek would be safer if the inspector knew."

Jorge thought for a while. "That might be the best way to approach him. Self-protection has always been one of Derek's primary aims. And as you say, we cannot be sure that Quint's death wasn't an unintended consequence of someone looking for Derek."

Emma said, "Before you speak to Derek, if you need me to go over your lines . . ."

Jorge shook his head. "Thank you, but this is the kind of thing that will be best said after I think about it for an hour or so. It will sound more extemporaneous and probably be more convincing. You know how hard it is to get Derek to change his opinion about anything."

He pushed himself out of his seat and said, "Well, if that is all, ladies, I am off to the gift shop. I will see you at dinner."

He ushered us out the door, and we all walked toward the elevators. Emma looked at me and said, "I guess it is straight to dinner for us."

I checked my watch and nodded. The three of us got in the already occupied elevator and rode down in silence. At the lobby, Jorge reached out his arm to hold the door open, and as we stepped off, he said, "Thank you, ladies, for the sound advice."

He waved good-bye and walked off toward the gift shop. Emma and I were only a few steps from the Victoria Room when I heard, "Yoo-hoo, Mrs. F."

Iris Crenshaw and Vivian Zhang were waving from their perch on a love seat a few feet away. I smiled and dipped my head in their direction, but that was clearly not enough of an acknowledgment. Vivian popped up and hurried toward us, clearly intending to chat.

"I just wanted to tell you that we are so excited about the book signing. Iris spoke to Gloria at the gift shop, and she has promised to set aside two copies of every book of yours that she has in stock so that we don't have to get in line the minute the store opens in the morning. We wouldn't want to miss out on your signing even one book."

"That is quite thoughtful of Gloria. Then I will definitely see you at the signing, books in hand," I said, and had begun to turn toward the Victoria Room when Vivian tugged at my sleeve.

"Iris and I were so sad to learn that the nice bartender who often served our afternoon sherry died so tragically. We wondered, of all the sleuths, professional and amateur, that you have written about in your extraordinary books, who do you think would be most likely to solve the murder?" Vivian smiled as if she were asking a perfectly normal question.

I heard Emma choking back a laugh, which was enough to remind me to be patient in my response. "I am sorry; I hadn't looked at Mr. Chabot's death quite that way. Now if you will excuse me, my cousin and I are late for dinner."

As we walked away, I heard Vivian call after us, "Don't worry, Mrs. F.; Iris and I will be happy to make you a list of suggestions."

"At least when fans approach me, the most they want is my autograph or advance word on my next role. No one has ever asked me to be even remotely involved in solving a murder." Emma was still laughing.

"And yet as I recall . . ." I said, thinking about several instances over the past years when that was exactly what happened.

"I stand by my word. No fan *asked* me. When things happened, I was defending myself from being a victim or taken as a killer." Emma was adamant, and I could not disagree.

I was delighted that Seth and the Metzgers were alone in the dining room.

Seth made a big production of looking at his watch. "We were beginning to wonder if you two had run off to dine somewhere else."

"Not a chance," Emma said as we took our seats. "We stopped

to talk when we ran into Jorge, who was on his way to the gift shop, and then one of those persistent fans of Jessica's waylaid us just a few steps outside this room."

Eager to stop the conversation from even grazing the topic of murder, I said, "Seth, I have been meaning to ask you about that odd chess game you were playing."

"You mean bughouse? Never heard of it myself, but it seems I'm a natural; isn't that right, Mort?"

"Sure is, Doc. I never saw anything like it. Four people, two chessboards, and you were king of the game." Mort was obviously proud of Seth's accomplishments.

"How could that setup possibly work?" Emma wondered aloud.

"Here, I will show you." Seth took the Chess and Checkers Fun Day program out of his pocket, along with a ballpoint pen.

He turned the program over, giving himself a blank paper to draw on, and began boxing out a chessboard, when, less than halfway done, his ballpoint ran out of ink. He threw it on the table in frustration.

"That is one thing I will always remember about this trip. The loss of my medical association pen," Seth grumped.

At that moment, we were distracted by the arrival of Dennis Oliver and Jorge Escarra, and both the chess game and the pen were forgotten by everyone except possibly Seth because Dennis asked for everyone's attention.

"Emma, I hope you shared the good news with your friends. I am delighted to tell you that the Edmonton Police Service has freed up the Jubilee Auditorium for our use beginning tomor-morning. With a few minor adjustments, Derek's revue w
as scheduled."

"That's fine for you," Mort said, "but as a sheriff, I have to ask: What about the murdered man? Is there any new information on that front?"

"How interesting that you should inquire." A voice came from the doorway behind Dennis. "That is exactly why I am here to ask more questions. And since you are standing right in front of me, Mr. Oliver, I will speak to you first."

I recognized the voice as belonging to Sergeant Enook.

Chapter Twenty-Five

The sergeant said that we should proceed with our dinner but asked that we not leave the hotel until she had spoken with us.

Dennis Oliver was back in the Victoria Room in about twenty minutes. He rubbed his hands together and said, "Well, that was smooth and easy. Where is tonight's menu?"

Mort passed the stiff parchment paper that had the available items written on it in fancy black script to Dennis, who glanced at it and said, "Oh, I am going for the steak. It's all cut from local Alberta-grown cattle, and each time I've ordered it, the meat has been extremely tender and delicious."

He detailed his choices to the server and then said, quite casually, "I nearly forgot, Jorge; the sergeant would like to see you next. She is down past the card room in the same office where the interviews were held the other night."

Jorge looked so stricken that I immediately stood and asked if he would mind if I walked along with him. "I am scheduled to do a signing at the gift shop, and I'd like to be sure the notices have been placed in the window. I may have to speak to Gloria if they have not."

Jorge looked at me, gratitude welling in his eyes, and said, "I would be honored."

Emma unobtrusively gave me a thumbs-up just as Jorge hooked his arm and I slipped my arm through his. I am sure we looked as though we were going for a stroll in the garden rather than to a police interview about a recent murder.

We were barely out of the Victoria Room when Jorge said, "What am I going to do, Jessica? I haven't spoken to Derek yet. I can't; I just can't break his confidence after all these years."

"I suggest we walk slowly and think about this. As I see it, Sergeant Enook is focused on the murder victim, Quint Chabot. You are considered a witness because you may have interacted with him in his job as a stagehand. I am sure she will want to re-interview me at some point as well because I was in the Auditorium when his body was found. And unless someone else has brought up questions about Derek's identity, I don't see why you would have to bring it up at this time."

"You want me to lie to the police?" Jorge cringed at the thought.

"No. Not lie. I am suggesting that unless the sergeant asks the direct question, 'Do you know Derek Braverman's original last name,' you simply omit mentioning it until after you have had a conversation with Derek and suggest that, as we discussed earlier, he tell the police himself, removing any clouds."

"And when I am finished talking to the sergeant," Jorge said, "it would be best for me to find Derek, who, since he appears to be avoiding communal dining with us, is likely having dinner in his suite. Once I explain that he could have been the intended target, I am sure he will dredge up everything immoral or criminal he did in his wild days, think of anyone who could possibly be holding a grudge, and, if he is smart, run to tell the sergeant himself." Jorge stood a little straighter.

By the time we reached the hallway leading to the gift shop, Jorge was completely relaxed. I, on the other hand, felt my blood pressure rise as soon as I stopped to look at the signs in the gift shop window.

As far as design, they were lovely. The top right corner had a blown-up picture of me taken from one of my book jackets. The bottom left corner had a fanned-out arrangement of my three most recent novels. There was my name in bold black letters about ten inches high, beneath it the words SIGNING HERE in smaller letters. On the next line, the letters were again large and gave the date and the start time. What infuriated me was that there was no indication that I was not expected to sit there all day long.

"But I told Mary Jo," I mumbled.

Jorge leaned closer and said, "Excuse me. I could not quite hear."

"I am sorry; it's nothing. I was talking to myself," I said, and we continued on down the hall.

The minute Sergeant Enook invited Jorge into the interview room, I marched right back into the lobby and over to the reception desk, only to find that Mary Jo had finished work for the day.

"She is expected to return to duty tomorrow morning. Perhaps I can be of some assistance?" I appreciated that the young lady behind the desk offered, but I knew pressing her would be of no use, so I thanked her and returned to the Victoria Room, where I followed Dennis's suggestion and ordered the steak.

Not only did Jorge come back sooner than I had expected; he was obviously feeling chipper and full of energy, the complete opposite of how he behaved before his interview. My curiosity was bubbling over. I could barely wait to learn what could have happened in his talk with Sergeant Enook that had left him in such an improved mood. But apparently I would have to wait for a chance to find out because Jorge surprised me by saying that Sergeant Enook wanted to see me next. I asked the server to put a hold on my order until I returned. Then I left the Victoria Room, positive that, as I had nothing further to add to my earlier statements, I would return quite soon.

When I passed the gift shop, I resolutely kept my eyes straight ahead, knowing there was no point in aggravating myself over something that could not be addressed until the next morning. The door to what I had come to think of as the interview room was closed, and I heard faint voices inside. I hoped that Jorge had been mistaken and the sergeant was busily questioning someone else. I knocked, and Sergeant Enook immediately opened the door. "Come in, Mrs. Fletcher."

It took only a couple of steps for me to see Inspector Radigan sitting behind the desk. What could that mean? I wondered. A breakthrough in the case? Or, more likely, that I was in for a thorough grilling. I took the seat that was offered and waited for the inspector to speak.

"How are you this evening, Mrs. Fletcher?" he asked pleasantly enough.

"Well, actually, I am moving toward famished. I was just about to sit down to dinner when you summoned me," I said in the hope that he would conclude the interview quickly because, frankly, I could not think of a thing I could say that would help him in any way. Well, there was Derek's identity, but that was not my story to tell, at least not yet. Possibly in the near future, but not until Jorge had a chance to speak to Derek, who would then decide whether or not to reveal it.

"I am sorry to interrupt your dinner hour. Believe me, I will try to keep our meeting brief. First, I wanted to thank you for, ah, reminding Spencer Smith that his cell phone could show us that he most certainly had received calls from Alan Hughes, not the other way around.

"Second, I was wondering, since until you arrived in Edmonton you did not know any of the people associated with Mr. Braverman's musical revue project other than your cousin, Ms. Macgill, would you mind sharing your opinion of some of them with me? Naturally this conversation would be strictly unofficial and completely off the record."

I hesitated, not because I didn't trust the inspector to keep my responses under wraps but because I had to take a minute or two to consider how Emma was going to respond when I told her about this conversation. I decided that since, like me, Emma believed in the truth above all, she would approve.

"All right, Inspector, how can I help?"

"For starters, let's talk about Mrs. Hughes. She is listed as the producer of this project, and yet each time I have spoken to her, she has seemed muddled, distant, and rather confused. Is that an act of some sort? I mean, I know the theater crowd can be quite temperamental, but she is not an actor, although I suppose the temperament can rub off . . ."

"There are two things you need to know about Mrs. Hughes. One is that she is addicted to alcohol, and the other is that she holds the family purse strings, and from what I can discern, she holds them rather tightly." I couldn't possibly describe Rosalie more concisely than that.

"I see, and that would explain why Mr. Hughes has been so skittish each time we've spoken. He was more afraid of upsetting his wife than he was of lying to me. When he tried to explain why he told me that unfounded story about Spencer Smith volunteering to drive Ms. Macgill, he kept going around in circles, and most of the circles involved trying to save money. It made no sense. Now it does."

I was quite sure that Eileen McCarthy had told someone in the police services her story of Quint becoming her "protector" and preventing Alan from making further advances, but since the inspector didn't bring it up, I didn't either.

He made a note on the lined yellow pad on the desktop. Then he looked at me. "And Dennis Oliver? What can you tell me about him?"

"Not much. Not much at all. Truthfully, during the time we have been here, I have seen very little of him. I know he is an American, and he appears to be immersed in his job. His main goal seems to be to keep Alan Hughes happy, and I gather that is no easy task. I suppose he is trying to work his way up the directorial ladder." I stopped there although I wished I had more to say.

"And Nicholas Dufond, the stage manager. What is your opinion of him? And as to the stagehands, you and I have spoken in the past about Spencer Smith, whom you vouched for quite ardently, but tell me, have you ever met Red Pompey?" The inspector began doodling along the margin line of the yellow pad, and I took that as a sign that my answers were boring him.

Well, I thought, this answer should pique his interest. "Actually, I have spoken to all three of them at different times, and there is one consistent thread throughout their conversations. None of them had the slightest clue why Alan Hughes had hired Quint Chabot as a part-time stagehand. In fact, according to Spencer, Nicholas was insistent that they didn't need an extra pair of hands, and Red complained that Quint was not skilled in the profession."

"And doesn't that surprise you, Mrs. Fletcher? Wouldn't you think that men who do such cumbersome and sometimes backbreaking work would be glad of an extra pair of hands, skilled or not?"

I looked directly at him and said, "Well, since I am sure that Eileen McCarthy told you or one of your constables exactly how Quint Chabot wormed his way into the job, isn't it possible that Nicholas and his crew discovered that as well? And wouldn't they resent him because of it?"

"Believe me, Mrs. Fletcher, the same thought has crossed my mind." The inspector stood. "Thank you for your time. When you go back to your private dining room, please ask Ms. Macgill to join me."

To keep my temper, not to mention my blood pressure, under control, I avoided looking at the erroneous signs in the gift shop window as I hurried to the Victoria Room. I was pleased to see that Emma was nearly finished with her dinner because, since Inspector Radigan had only quizzed me about the staff, he was sure to want to interrogate Emma about the actors, and it seemed to me that was a group that might be more difficult to explain, particularly Emma's leading man, Derek Braverman.

Chapter Twenty-Six

Until Emma was finally released from her meeting with Inspector Radigan, Seth, the Metzgers, and I continued to linger over post-dinner coffee as we waited for her return, although it was evident that the servers wished we'd finish so that they could tidy the room.

Bouncy as ever, Emma trooped into the room with a wide grin on her face. "Well, that was a show and a half if I do say so."

When a server stepped forward to say that the remains of Emma's dinner were being kept warm in the kitchen and she would be happy to bring it out, Emma said, "No, that's quite all right. But if you could manage to bring me a cup of tea and a piece of that delicious-looking pie the doctor is eating, I will take this mob out to the lobby and let you get on with your evening."

Then she stood at the head of the table and looked at the four of us with her hands on her hips and her bossy attitude of "the order had been given; the order must be obeyed."

Emma picked up Seth's cup and saucer and said that he should bring along his pie. The servers quickly stepped in to assist, carrying our tableware while also providing additional cutlery and table linens. One of the servers asked if anyone else would like a piece of pie. Mort said he would be interested. She returned with a large tray loaded with pie, a teapot, a coffee decanter, a sugar bowl, and fresh pitchers of cream and milk and led us to the lobby.

In a few minutes, we were settled around a well-dressed coffee table, and the servers wished us a good evening, smiling as they said good night.

Emma poured herself a cup of tea and said, "Jess, you were interviewed first, so while I eat my pie, let's hear how that went."

I glanced around the room until I was satisfied there was no one nearby who would be able to eavesdrop on us. Then I repeated every word of my conversation with Inspector Radigan.

"Interesting that his focus with you was limited to the non-performers associated with the revue," Emma said. "His questions for me not only all centered on the entertainers, but he was also eager to hear my impressions of their interactions with Alan and the rest."

"Oh, I think there was a well-thought-out scheme behind the inspector's plan. In his view, I am an outsider who had access primarily to the Hugheses and Dennis Oliver because we shared meals several times a day. The players rarely showed up in the Victoria Room, so he didn't expect I would have much interaction with them, and when I did, it was bound to be more formal.

The inspector probably thought actors were likely to behave as performers wanting to please an audience in front of people they did not know well," I said. "Emma, over the years, I have heard you say similar things about your colleagues."

"And Nicholas and the stagehands?" Maureen asked. "Why question you about them?"

"Well, let's not forget that Nicholas, with the assistance of Red and Spencer, gave us an exceptionally intimate tour of the theater, so we all had a chance to get to know them at least slightly. Plus, because Emma, Spencer, and I were together on the evening of the murder, the inspector would naturally be interested in determining if there were any prior relationships. I imagine that he was a bit suspicious because I defended Spencer rather vigorously when Alan lied." I thought I had covered everything. "So, Emma, how did your interview go?"

"Quite similar to yours, I'd bet, other than we spoke about far more people, which is why I was gone for such a long while." Emma took a sip of tea. "Although the inspector did seem more focused on which of us had prior relationships with each other before this project. That's what he prefers to call the revue—'a project.'"

"And did you all know one another previously?" I asked.

"Obviously every performer had worked with Derek at one time or another and been in shows directed by Alan, so whether she was producing or not, we knew Rosalie as well. I travel a lot, so I had known and worked with everyone except Jorge. I'd never met Dennis Oliver before, but I certainly knew him by reputation. He is an American and an up-and-coming assistant director, who, I'm sure, will be a full-fledged director before too long."

"That is interesting," I said. "It is hard to imagine a sterling career ahead of Dennis, when he seems completely cowed by Alan."

"No mystery there, luv. As an assistant director, Dennis's job is to fetch and carry. Any unpleasant chore a director needs done always falls to the assistant director. I believe it is considered the most important part of their training." Emma laughed. "And to complete the team, there are Nicholas and his crew, who are locals, so until we began rehearsals they were complete unknowns, at least to me."

The conversation gradually drifted away from our police interviews and moved on to the tourist aspects of our trip. Mort and Seth were still excited by their chess-and-checkers adventure and decided to go to the reception desk to see if there were similar events scheduled over the next few days.

When they came back, each was carrying a tourist guidebook, and Seth had that Cheshire cat grin that was nearly always my advance warning that I was about to be teased.

"Ayuh, there's not much in the way of entertainment in the hotel scheduled for the rest of our stay, unless anyone would be interested in a book-signing event day after tomorrow. Some American writer you may have heard of—J. B. Fletcher."

"Oh, don't remind me, Seth. You are not the least bit amusing. First thing in the morning, I have to hunt down Mary Jo Simard. I agreed to sign for one hour, but nowhere, absolutely nowhere on the posters does it indicate a specific time frame. I am afraid people are going to be wandering in and out of the gift shop all afternoon, and the last thing I want is for readers to be disappointed that I am not available." I was getting more worked up than I intended since I already knew I couldn't change a thing until Mary Jo returned to work.

Emma reached across and patted my shoulder. "Don't you worry. Tomorrow morning we will attack her as a group. She won't stand a chance. But for now, I hear my pillow calling, offering me sweet dreams. Anyone else for the elevator?"

We all agreed it was time to call it a night.

The next morning, I awoke earlier than usual. After one look out the window at the blue sky streaked with occasional white clouds that were in turn dotted by a flock of birds flying toward the horizon, I impulsively put on my gym clothes and took the elevator down, determined to have an outdoor jog before the events of the day demanded all my time. As much as I enjoyed being with Emma and my friends, I always found a solitary bike ride, jog, or even a leisurely walk in the early-morning hours to be my favorite preparation for whatever the day might bring.

I managed to reach the lobby and get to the main door without anyone speaking to me other than a desk clerk who offered me a morning newspaper. I thanked her and said I would pick one up on my way back.

The breeze coming along the driveway assured me that I would have a comfortable run. I zigzagged up and down the blocks surrounding the hotel, always keeping it in sight, mindful that I didn't want to get lost and embarrass myself by having to call the hotel to ask for directions.

Forty-five minutes later, I was back in the lobby, picking up my copy of the *Edmonton Journal* from the front desk when Mary Jo Simard came through the door to the back office. She gave me a wave and a cheery good morning. My response was far less jolly.

"Good morning, Mary Jo. Do you have a minute?" I said without so much as a hint of a smile.

She looked uncertain. "Actually, I am in the process of determining the schedule for you and your friends today."

"And I am far more concerned about tomorrow's schedule, the one you set up especially for me. It needs immediate correction, or there will be no signing event at all." I used my strictest schoolteacher voice in the hope that my message would reach her.

But clearly it hadn't. "Mrs. Fletcher, I don't understand. Gloria and I coordinated everything—the afternoon tea, the arrangement of your books so that they would be easily available, and of course your pens. Gloria took three of the finest pens the gift shop has to offer and set them aside for your use. What could we possibly have forgotten?" Mary Jo looked so confused that for a second I almost felt sorry for her. Almost.

"Listen carefully," I said. "Our agreement was that I would come to the gift shop tomorrow and sign books for an hour. Afternoon tea, fancy pens, and anything else aside, I will not remain for more than one hour. I am on vacation. I am here to visit my cousin Emma and to enjoy some free time with my friends. I am doing you a favor by sharing my time, but I will not have my courtesy abused, do you understand?"

"Yes, Mrs. Fletcher," she replied, hanging her head and speaking in the voice of a student promising never again to enter my classroom without having completed a homework assignment.

I went to my room to shower and change, satisfied that at least one of my problems was solved.

I was nearly finished dressing when my cell phone rang.

"Hello, luv, feeling chipper this morning, are we?" Emma's singsong tone of voice clearly indicated she thought she was privy to a private joke of some sort.

I decided to play along. "I am always tip-top after a lovely jog in beautiful weather."

"Or when you've stood your ground when someone tries to get you to do anything at all that you don't want to do," Emma teased.

"You've spoken to Mary Jo, I see. Did she beg you to talk me into her all-day affair at the gift shop?" I asked, even though I was quite sure I knew the answer.

"She did indeed. And I told her it was a hopeless task to get you to change your mind about anything. You were every bit as determined at age eleven, as I recall." Emma was chuckling.

"Now, Emma, don't start. If I had gone along with your insane plan to take my father's rowboat out onto the river in the pre-dawn hours so we could surprise everyone with a fried-fish breakfast, well, I have to wonder if we'd both be here right now. And you never would admit that we weren't strong enough to control the boat and reel in fish without an adult to guide us."

"I still say that's a load of tosh. We would have been fine, but no, you were always a Goody Two-shoes." Emma still sounded frustrated all these years later.

"And you always weren't." I snickered.

By now the two of us were laughing so hard that if anyone else had been listening, we probably would have sounded like the eleven-year-old girls we were remembering.

"Ah, Jess, I called to see if you were ready for breakfast, but these small trips down memory lane do my heart a world of good. We can't let it be so long between visits next time," Emma said.

"You are right. The years are flying by. We will have to make it a point to get together more often. As for the present moment, I'll meet you in the Victoria Room for breakfast in ten."

When I got off the elevator, I could hear raucous laughter coming from the Victoria Room, and then I heard Emma say, "And that's all you'll get for your preview, lads and lassies; a seat inside for the rest of the show will cost you two shillings three."

There was loud laughter and clapping, and when I entered the room, I saw that her audience consisted of Seth, Mort, Maureen, Dennis Oliver, and two of the servers, who were still laughing as one poured more coffee for Seth while the other cleared Dennis's plate and asked if he would like anything else.

I sat down, ordered a boiled egg with a slice of toast, and gratefully accepted a cup of coffee from the server.

Then I asked what I had missed.

"Oh, not much at all," Emma said. "A two-minute skit I perfected for a charity show in Newcastle upon Tyne ages ago happened to jump from back of mind right to the front completely unbidden, and I had no choice but to let it out. Sorry you missed it, luv, but I'll give you a private curtain call before you go home, and that's a promise."

There was a scraping noise by the doorway. Eileen McCarthy was standing there uncertainly. Emma saw her and said, "Sorry, all; I have to go. I am having trouble with a lyric or two, and Eileen has promised to straighten me out. Enjoy your day."

Dennis Oliver looked as mystified as I felt. I'd never known Emma to have the least problem remembering lyrics, and I suspected that during the rehearsals for this revue, Dennis hadn't either.

I couldn't help but wonder if Emma and Eileen were up to some sort of mischief. Knowing my dear cousin Emma, mischief was never out of the question.

Chapter Twenty-Seven

J ess, before you came down, Mary Jo stopped in to let us know that Rob would be available to take us touring today, and we've been going over this guide." Seth held up a magazine. "After Mort's love affair with that 1919 steam engine in Fort Edmonton Park, I wasn't surprised that he'd like to visit the Alberta Railway Museum. And I have a strong interest in the Telus World of Science."

"Of course you would, Dr. Hazlitt," I said with good humor before I turned to Maureen and asked what she would like to see.

"You may all find it boring, but I would love to spend some time at the John Walter Museum. He came to Canada in the late nineteenth century and built his first cabin by the North Saskatchewan River. He worked at various trades and built his second, more substantial home in the early twentieth century." Maureen seemed doubtful we would enjoy her choice, but I thought it was terrific and said so.

"That sounds exactly like a place that would give us a true feel for how the early settlers lived. Sort of a refresher course for some of what we learned at Fort Edmonton," I said, and then asked, "Did Mary Jo give you some idea when we might be leaving?"

Seth looked at his watch. "Little more than half an hour from now."

I realized that Dennis Oliver was finishing his coffee and listening to our plans, so more out of courtesy than real interest, I asked him, "And how does it feel to be back in the Auditorium? Do you think it will take some time before the cast and the crew will be able to readjust?"

He pursed his lips and looked around as if to be sure we were alone—I suspected he didn't want to be overheard by Alan or possibly Derek—then said, "Well, you know we theater folk have a treasure trove of superstitions, so ghosts are not out of our range, but a dead body in the orchestra lift is a little too realistic for most of us. I would imagine it will take some time for everyone to feel comfortable in the Auditorium." He picked up his napkin and wiped his lips. "Now if you will excuse me, work beckons."

I wanted to take a quick look at the gift shop to be sure that the signs advertising my book signing had been altered to reflect that I was not going to spend the entire day tomorrow sitting, pen in hand, waiting for readers to stop by.

A number of my titles were attractively displayed in both windows of the store, and the signs were nowhere to be seen. As soon as I stepped inside, Gloria hurried over to me, her hands fluttering in the air.

"Oh, Mrs. Fletcher, I am so very sorry. Mary Jo was so upset that I had misrepresented the timing of your event tomorrow. I have taken the signs down, and I assure you that I am going to completely redo them."

"Oh, that's not necessary. Do you still have the original signs?"

She reached behind the counter that held the cash register and a small rack of bookmarks and drew out both signs, which she placed side by side on the countertop.

"Look here"—I pointed—"where it says that the signing starts at noon. Simply write next to that, 'Ends at one o'clock.' Voilà! It is done."

Gloria said, "Stay right here," and went behind the counter again. This time she came up with a rectangular box, and when she opened it, I saw pens, pencils, and markers of every description. She tried first one and then another marker, until she was satisfied she had the one that she had used to write the "start" line. She then wrote in *Ends at one o'clock* and held the sign up for me to examine.

"Thank you, Gloria. That is perfect; really, it is perfect," I said.

"I'll get both signs into the window right away so that people know. And if you wouldn't mind telling Mary Jo how pleased you are, well, I'd be really grateful." Gloria dropped her voice and sounded quite shy.

"I'd be happy to do so. And before I go back to Maine, I promise I will write a thank-you note to Ms. Geeson regarding the hotel employees, and I promise to mention you in a favorable light." I patted her hand. "You deserve the accolade. Now I have to hurry; my friends and I are scheduled to learn more about Edmonton."

As I walked back to the lobby, I was hoping that the history of the city wouldn't be the only thing I would learn from Rob today. But I knew that before he could work his magic, I would have to give him some new information.

"Here she comes." Seth, Mort, and Maureen were standing by the reception desk, and Seth was waving at me to hurry along.

I glanced through the glass doors and saw Rob waiting patiently by the limousine.

"You all go ahead. I will be there in one minute. I just have to stop at the desk," I said.

The clerk gave me the piece of notepaper that I asked for, and I hurriedly wrote, *Braverman's original last name is Piché.*

Then I walked out to the car. Rob greeted me with a cheerful "Good morning" and opened the passenger door. Before I bent to enter the limo, I slipped him the note. He took it with absolutely no sign that anything had transpired between us, although the thought crossed my mind that he may have been enjoying this spot of intrigue. Hopefully his old-timers' brigade would be able to find out whatever secret Derek Braverman had successfully kept hidden all these years, and Inspector Radigan could determine if it had anything at all to do with Quint Chabot's murder.

When he was settled into the driver's seat, Rob turned and asked us what plans we'd made for the day. He listened carefully and added, "I've a few ideas myself, so let's make a day of it."

Our first stop was the Alberta Railway Museum, a wide-open area with historic displays of actual trains, equipment, and railway-associated structures, including a lovely old railroad building known as the St. Albert Station that had been built in 1909 and upgraded a number of times until it was finally transferred to become part of the museum in 1973. It held the museum's gift shop, a library, and a telegraph office.

At one point, Seth got a bit nostalgic when he and I were examining a steam engine built in the early 1900s. "Reminds me of the locomotive you gifted me for Christmas a few years back when I was down in the dumps. It's my favorite holiday decoration."

I was glad that it still brought him joy. Mort Metzger was having the time of his life climbing on the train cars that were open to visitors. Luxury passenger cars, baggage cars, sleepers, and mail cars. His all-time favorite was a car built by the Preston Car Company as a drawing room car that was later used as a sleeper and, much to Mort's delight, became a rule-instruction car. Although it now had seats, the placard said that it was a mobile instruction unit for railway employees and at one time had been outfitted with student desks and a blackboard. In addition, there were living quarters set up for the instructor who traveled on the train from station to station.

"Now that would have been the job for me," Mort said. "Imagine working *and* living on the train. I would be traveling all over the country and bringing my job with me."

"And where, I wonder, would your wife fit into this new lifestyle of yours?" Maureen was only half jesting.

When we'd pretty much seen all there was to see, I texted Rob that we were on our way back to the parking lot, and by the time we arrived, he was parked by the exit gate.

As I was climbing into the passenger compartment, Rob leaned down and whispered, "My sources are working." And, as he straightened up, he gave me a two-finger salute to the brim of his cap.

My earlier impression was not wrong; Rob was enjoying himself immensely. Then he progressed into flawless chauffeur mode and said that he thought visiting the John Walter Museum would be a nice companion piece to the railway museum, especially since at his earliest time, John Walter ran a ferry practically outside his front door, and we all agreed that he knew best.

The John Walter houses were located in Kinsmen Park, and the atmosphere was wonderfully relaxing. We took our time marveling at how people lived more than a hundred years ago. Maureen and I were trying to decide how anyone could survive the winter in Walter's original house, when Seth said, "Speaking of survival, I think I'll need a nice cool drink and some lunch if we are going to make a few more stops this afternoon."

We all agreed that the exploring we had done both at the railway museum and here in Kinsmen Park had certainly sparked our appetites. We walked back to the parking lot and found the limo exactly where Rob had indicated it would be when he dropped us at the main gate. At first I thought Rob might be sitting in the car, but then I noticed he was speaking to a man dressed in an untidy corduroy jacket and jeans who was leaning on a car in the next row. Rob saw us, waved, and ran directly to the limousine.

"I hope you all enjoyed your morning," Rob said as he opened the passenger door for us. "The gentleman I was just speaking to said that the older he gets, the more he enjoys reveling in his memories of the past. Of course, his past doesn't go back nearly as far as John Walter's does."

Maureen and I exchanged a questioning look, both wondering if the man was one of Rob's sources. I guessed we would find out when the time was right.

It was unusual for Rob to leave the privacy window open after he began to drive, but that was exactly what he did. Once we were on the main road, he said, "Our next stop will bring you closer to the present but still in touch with the past. We are about to visit

Yesterday's Auto Gallery, where you will see nearly a hundred classic cars. Some may bring back memories; some you may have only seen in your dreams."

I could see Mort's eyes light up—first trains, then the home of a man who built boats and operated his own ferry across the North Saskatchewan River, and now generations of cars.

"And if you've a mind for lunch, the Retro Diner is decorated like every highway car stop in the 1950s, right down to turquoise plastic chairs and metal tables. My favorite meal is Combo Two: a hot dog, fries, and an old-time double-thick milkshake."

"Ayuh, if everyone else agrees . . ." Seth began.

"Lunch first, cars second," Mort finished, and we all laughed.

We invited Rob to join us, but he said he had something he needed to do. He dropped us off in front of the diner entrance and pointed to the gallery. "Once you've eaten, you can wander through the gallery to your heart's content. I am going to do my best to park right around here, but when you are ready to leave, Mrs. Fletcher has my cell. Just give me a buzz, and I will be by the front door."

Our visit to the Retro Diner was like a trip back in time, and we followed Rob's advice and truly enjoyed our lunch, especially the milkshakes. Maureen said she couldn't remember the last time she had anything so creamy and delicious.

As we walked over to the gallery, Mort was bubbling over.

"Doc, what do you think? What are the odds they'll have a DeSoto Fireflite Sportsman—you know the one—mid-fifties hardtop convertible. Made the cover of every car magazine in the country—I mean, at least in the USA," Mort said. "Only time I saw one up close was in the late eighties. I was on patrol, and when I pulled it over, the poor driver thought he was in for a ticket, but I just wanted to talk about the car. Boy, the tail fins alone, three separate bulbs for the brake lights on each fin. What a look!"

"Well, I am more interested in seeing if they have any Chrysler New Yorkers," Seth answered. "A few years back, I was at the car show in Portland, and they had twin New Yorkers, one red and the other white, and they were the pride of the show. Owning one, well, that was nice enough, but the man—I think his name was Powers—was busting his buttons because he owned two. I'd like to see if there are any here at all."

I did not expect to enjoy the classic car gallery as much as I did. The cars were gorgeous, and the hoods were all raised so the engines were exposed, and there was a sign in front of each car, listing the special details. I found myself taking pictures of several cars and signs. And the author part of my brain thought they might be useful in a future book.

When we had examined every nook and cranny of dozens and dozens of cars as well as several motorcycles, and everyone was ready for the comfort of the limo, I sent Rob a text.

He responded with a thumbs-up emoji. While I knew he meant he'd meet us at the exit, I couldn't help but hope that he was also signaling that his sources were having some success in finding out Derek Braverman's early history in Edmonton.

Chapter Twenty-Eight

I could feel my muscles relax as soon as I settled into the gray plush seats of Rob's limousine, and judging by Seth's long sigh and the contented looks on Maureen's and Mort's faces, I was sure everyone else felt exactly the same.

Rob said, "You've had quite a day. Dr. Hazlitt, are you still interested in walking around the science museum, or might something a little less physical but just as enjoyable suit you?"

Seth said, as I was sure he would, "I'd be interested in hearing what you have in mind."

Rob's grin told us Seth had made the right choice. "As it turned out, all your visits today have been to sites that involve transportation of one sort or another. I'm going to suggest that you go for a ride on an antique streetcar that was built in 1912 and is nearly the same as the streetcar you rode in Fort Edmonton Park. It will take you near the charming Alberta Legislature grounds and past other historic sites, but for me, the main thrill of it is the view you will have in every direction when you cross the North Saskatchewan River on the High Level Bridge. I suggest you take the round trip, which runs just under an hour, and I will be waiting when you return."

The streetcar ride was as glorious as Rob had described, and the view from the High Level Bridge was breathtaking. Much as I tried from every angle, I felt as though I hadn't snapped nearly enough pictures for the scrapbook I wanted to arrange as soon as I got home.

As promised, Rob was waiting when we got off the streetcar, and he was pleased that we were stumbling over one another to tell him how much we enjoyed the ride. Exuberant as we all were, we also agreed that the next stop should be the hotel. Rob closed the privacy window and put on some light classical music that lulled Seth to sleep almost immediately. I, along with the Metzgers, was content to listen to the music punctuated by Seth's occasional light snoring.

As Rob pulled into the hotel driveway, I shook Seth awake. Mort actually rubbed his eyes and said, "Just in the nick of time. I was about to nod off, and I snore much louder than Doc Hazlitt."

We all laughed when Maureen said, "I can attest to that."

As always, Rob held the passenger door open. I happened to be the last one to climb out, and Rob mentioned that he could use some iced tea after the long day. To my mind, that could only mean one thing. He had news about Derek Braverman's long-ago past.

I turned and ducked my head into the limo as if I were looking for something I might have left behind, and when I straightened up, I pretended to fumble. Rob grabbed my arm to steady me. I whispered, "Suite 507." Rob gave me a slight nod.

The moment felt vaguely like the kinds of assignations that spies always have to arrange in some of the thrillers I've read.

When the four of us got off the elevator on the fifth floor, I said to Maureen, "If Mort is ready for a nap, would you like to join me for a cup of tea? We could compare the pictures we took today."

When she replied, "I'm in," I was sure she knew I wasn't talking about comparing pictures.

As soon as we were in my suite, I called room service and ordered a pot of tea and a carafe of iced tea along with three Nanaimo bars and three butter tarts. We sat and made small talk while we waited for Rob or the tea, whichever came first.

It seemed to take forever, but finally we heard a knock on my door. When I opened it, I was flabbergasted to see Mary Jo Simard.

"Oh, Mary Jo, what a surprise. I thought you were room service. What can I do for you?"

"Gloria told me that you were pleased with the way she redid the sign for tomorrow's event. I personally want to thank you for enabling me to save face with the new boss. Believe me, this whole incident taught me to listen before I make commitments on someone else's behalf."

She continued with totally unnecessary platitudes while I tried to hurry her along. When I heard the elevator door open, I prayed it was either total strangers or room service, but, of course, it was Rob.

I suppose dealing as he did with tourists day in and day out, he was prepared for any contingency, but he certainly surprised me when he said, "There you are, Mrs. Fletcher. I hope you aren't looking for this."

He held up a book, which as I could see once he got closer was titled *Best Tales of the Yukon*.

"No one can give the reader the feel of those gold rush days the way Robert Service did. Have you read 'The Shooting of Dan McGrew' yet? A true classic."

"Not yet, but I am looking forward to it. Thank you for, ah, returning my book, Rob," I said.

He gave me the two fingers to his eyebrow salute that I was beginning to take as a special signal between conspirators, and then he turned to Mary Jo. "If you are finished speaking with Mrs. Fletcher, I have some questions about the assignments for tomorrow you left in my inbox." And he deftly guided her back to the elevator.

When I stepped back into the living room, Maureen had her hands over her mouth, choking down her laughter until the door was securely closed. "If Rob ever decided to give up his day job, I am sure he could graduate from acting school with flying colors."

I nodded in agreement. "I only wish Emma had been here to see it."

At that moment, there was a second knock at the door, and this time it was room service.

I was pouring our tea when the third knock came. At long last it was Rob. I invited him in, and when he sat down, I presented him with a glass of iced tea. Then I held up the book by Robert Service. "This was a stroke of genius."

Rob laughed. "In my line of work, you have to be prepared for anything because stuff just seems to happen."

He reached for a Nanaimo bar and said with a twinkle in his eye, "If you open the book to page fifty-seven, you might find an interesting read."

Page fifty-seven was the start of "The Shooting of Dan Mc-Grew," but as soon as I saw a folded piece of paper between the pages, I knew that Rob's true calling was to be the leading character in a John le Carré or Ken Follett novel.

I unfolded the paper and read out loud the message typed in bold:

Derek Sebastian Piché, age eighteen,
and Silas Michael Stanton, age twenty-two,
were brought in for questioning regarding the arson
fire of a grocery store on 104th Avenue.
Although no one was killed, eight people were injured,
two seriously. No arrests were ever made.

"That is the best I could do, Mrs. Fletcher, but the information comes from two men who are long retired from the police service. One had a vague memory of the rumor that Derek Braverman had been involved in an old case. He asked around and was able to send me to a retiree who worked the case. That man identified Derek as the smart-mouth of the two."

"Thank you. This is invaluable to me. If there is anything I can ever do . . ."

"I understand you are signing books at noon tomorrow. I will be out on a job, but if you could manage to set one aside . . ." Rob hesitated, as though he might be asking for too much consideration.

"Rob, that is the least I can do. You have no idea what an enormous help you have been."

"Oh, and I have one more site that I really would like you to see before you go home. We need to go at dusk or a little later. In fact, Mary Jo has already penciled me in to drive you to the Jube for Miss Emma's opening night. That would be the perfect night to see the Neon Sign Museum."

"Won't that be a busy night, getting all gussied up beforehand, and then there is the after-party?" Maureen fretted.

"Not to worry; you won't even have to get out of the car, and you'll see plenty of Edmonton's history in bright bold neon." Rob's phone made a slight noise. He looked at it and said, "Sorry, ladies, duty calls."

I walked to the front door and opened it. Rob stopped, framed in the doorway, and said softly, "I hope that information is of some use to you."

"We will know shortly," I replied. "Thank you again, Rob."

He saluted, as had become his custom, and was gone.

Maureen looked at the paper now sitting on the coffee table next to the teapot. "Now what do we do?"

"Now we find Derek Braverman. He should be at the Jubilee Auditorium rehearsing, but from what I hear, he doesn't think he needs much practice, so perhaps we can find him in his suite here at the hotel," I said.

"Or in the Beaver Bar," Maureen said. "He seemed to really enjoy himself there the other night. He was super cranky that a little thing like a murder investigation interrupted his fun."

"Well, let's see if we can get his suite number from the hotel staff or at least connect to his room on the house phone."

We were heading to the reception desk when we bumped into Red Pompey.

"Mrs. Fletcher, how are you?" He turned to Maureen. "And

don't I remember this bonnie lass from the tour I organized at the Auditorium? Where are you ladies off to, if I might ask?"

"Actually, we were going to check at the desk, but perhaps you can help us. We were hoping to speak with Derek about opening night." I tried to make it sound as though we had become buddies. "And somehow I can't remember his suite number." I sighed. "Such a large hotel."

"He's in 2210, but I wouldn't waste the elevator trip. This time of day, I would wager he is in the Beaver Bar, longing to be surrounded by adoring fans. In any event, we left some sound equipment in the storage lockers behind the Silver Ballroom. I better get it back to the Auditorium before Mr. Hughes takes it out of my hide. Good day to you."

As he walked away, I remembered the clenched-teeth conversation I'd seen him have with Quint Chabot only a few hours before the murder. I never did ask Emma if she'd overheard any of it. I put checking with her on my mental to-do list and said to Maureen, "It looks like Red agrees with you. Can I buy you a glass of wine in the Beaver Bar?"

Without multiple televisions blaring the hockey game, the Beaver Bar seemed extremely quiet. It took my eyes a minute to adjust to the dim lighting, and then I saw Derek sitting at a cocktail table on the far side of the bar. Two men were standing over him, and the topic of conversation was their lifelong admiration of Derek Braverman in all his many roles.

Maureen and I walked directly to his table, and I said, "Derek, what a nice coincidence."

He stood and reached out a hand to welcome us. "Gentlemen, have you met my dear friend, the world-famous mystery writer Jessica Fletcher?"

The men greeted me, but the disappointment in the look they exchanged was clearly because they were sure Maureen and I were about to usurp their time with their idol. And they were right. Derek dismissed them with hardly a thought and invited us to sit down.

The bartender took our order and returned with two glasses of Chablis.

"I was wondering when we'd finally get a chance to get to know each other better, Jessica. I didn't expect you to bring a chaperone." Derek reached out and covered my hand with his. I slipped my hand off the table, opened my purse, and placed the note Rob had given me on the table next to Derek's glass.

"Does any of this seem familiar?" I asked.

He pulled reading glasses from his breast pocket and perched them on his nose. He glanced at the note, and his face contorted. I thought he was going to go into a rage, as I had seen him do before, but he looked around as if realizing that this was neither the time nor the place for such behavior. And he couldn't be sure how Maureen and I would react if he went into one of his tirades.

He flicked the note with his fingers, and it slid back across the table. "That means nothing to me."

I tried another tack. "Did Jorge talk to you about . . . about this?" I pointed to the note.

"Oh, was it you who set him up to tell me some nonsense I should tell Radigan about my personal business from more than fifty years ago because maybe the killer was setting some sort of trap for me based on something that may or may not have happened that far back? Yes, he spoke to me, right up until I told him to shut his mouth and never speak of it again. Now, if that's all you've got . . ." Derek started to get up.

"You can't believe that perhaps someone is after you because they believe you hurt a family member or a loved one badly in that fire? Well, I can believe it," I said.

"And why would they wait all these long years to come after me? There is no logic to it," Derek puffed, as if exhaling the smoke of an expensive cigar.

"How often have you been in Edmonton so publicly that anyone who might want to hurt you would learn that they had a chance? For that matter, you have been gone for so many decades, you are betting there isn't anyone left in Edmonton who would connect Derek Braverman to the young delinquent Derek Sebastian Piché. You have given me no choice. I am going to call the inspector to tell him about this." I picked up the note and took out my cell phone. Derek snatched the note from my hand and quickly tore it into a dozen pieces, which he stuffed into his pocket.

Maureen, who had been sitting quietly by, watching this all unfold, said with more than a hint of amusement in her tone, "Did you forget Jessica writes mysteries for a living? She and I each have several pictures of that message stored in our phones."

"Do as you please." Derek pushed his chair back and stood to get the bartender's attention, and when he had it, he drew an imaginary circle around the table including all our glasses. "Eddie, all on my tab."

Before Derek had left the room, I was dialing the Edmonton Police Service and asking for Inspector Radigan.

Chapter Twenty-Nine

When I walked into the Victoria Room the next morning, Emma was regaling Seth and the Metzgers with a story about an onstage mishap that happened when she was starring in the revival of *Mame* and then took it on tour.

"You remember when I did *Mame*, don't you, Jess? You came to see us in Boston, and we had a rollicking good time," Emma said.

"I certainly do remember. You had four curtain calls the night I was there."

"It was a lovely show. Such a joy for me to play a character that was all vitality and pizzazz."

"You mean a character whose persona is so like your own," I said, and everyone laughed.

I was afraid Emma would continue to reminisce, but I needed her to focus on the present, so I asked her more directly than I had first intended, "Do you remember when we had champagne in the lobby after we toured the Jubilee Auditorium?"

"Are you daft? How could any of us forget, when such a pleasant day turned into such a horrible night?" Emma shuddered.

"Well, I happened to notice that Red Pompey and Quint Chabot had quite a tense conversation at one point. I wasn't close enough to hear, but I think you might have been. Do you remember their having a disagreement of some sort?"

"Oh, that, yes, I do remember. Quint was grumbling about not getting paid enough money for the hours he worked as a stagehand, and Red was telling him to stop whining. At least that is what I remember."

Not much of a motive for Red, even I had to admit as I spread a thin layer of butter on my whole-grain toast.

"So, Jess, how are you prepping for the book-signing extravaganza that I believe starts promptly at noon and lasts for exactly one hour, no more, no less, as I understand it?" Seth teased.

"Oh, Seth, make fun if you like, but I wasn't about to give up an entire vacation day for a signing I never agreed to do. All I need are a couple of pens, which are in my purse, and my smile."

"I would gladly lend you my favorite pen for good luck, but it seems I will never see it again." Seth shook his head.

"Same with Maureen's sunglasses, Doc," Mort said. "I'm not sure how things can just disappear without a trace in such a classy hotel. You would think everything would turn up in the lost and found eventually."

Emma looked at her watch and said, "Well, I have to run. Rehearsals await. Cheerio, everyone. Enjoy your day."

She blew kisses all around and hurried out the door.

Seth looked puzzled. "Emma must be performing a really special act. She has been totally intent on rehearsing, and the closer we get to opening night, the harder she works."

Maureen replied, "That is what makes her a star. She wants every performance to be perfect. Don't you agree, Jess?"

"I certainly do. That has been her way ever since we were children. She strives to be the best." I smiled to myself at the memories.

As I'd been expecting, Mary Jo Simard showed up to remind me to come to the gift shop at least fifteen minutes before the signing was scheduled to begin so that I would be seated and relaxed before the readers would be allowed to enter.

"Oh, and some people who could not attend have asked that you sign books they purchased in advance and will pick up later. I hope you don't mind." And she scurried out of the room without giving me a chance to answer.

I sipped my coffee and decided to go to my room and address the postcards I'd bought at every stop we'd made while sightseeing. The last thing I wanted to do was carry them home in my suitcase.

At eleven thirty I left my room, postcards in hand. Since I was asked to arrive early for the signing, I decided I would use that time to ask Gloria if, as I'd heard, the gift shop also sold postage stamps, so I could get my cards in the mail. Most of the cards were going to my nephew Grady's son Frank, who I was sure would enjoy them. He and I would have fun talking about them on my next visit to New York.

Vivian and Iris, the fandom duo, were sitting in the lobby when I got off the elevator.

"Look, Mrs. F." Vivian waved two small pieces of paper. "We went to the gift shop and stood in line to get our tickets. Unfortunately, we are numbers eight and nine. We hoped to be first and second, but a couple of youngsters apparently sat on the floor outside the door at the crack of dawn, and when Gloria opened this morning, they claimed the premier spots."

Iris chimed in. "I'm afraid our sitting-on-the-floor days are long over. Are you going to start signing now?"

"I am afraid not. At the moment, I am seeking stamps so I can mail some postcards."

"You can get them at the reception desk," Vivian said. "The clerks there are very helpful. Not like that Gloria."

"You will have to forgive Vivian. She is still miffed at Gloria. Yesterday when we found out that there would be 'first come, first signed' numbers handed out this morning, we went to see Gloria and asked if we could have the first two tickets, and she refused to give them to us even after we told her we were your good friends," Iris harrumphed.

"I think she made up the story about the floor sitters," Vivian said. "Wouldn't surprise me if she gave the first two tickets to her own friends."

The two ladies were right about one thing. When I went to reception and asked for stamps, the desk clerk not only provided them but also offered to put my cards in the outgoing mail once I had stamped them.

Glad to have that chore over and done, I headed to the gift shop, where I was surprised to see about a dozen readers waiting for the door to be unlocked.

I smiled and nodded as I walked down the hall and tapped lightly on the gift shop door. Gloria had obviously put a great deal of effort into setting up the room. Three tables had copies of a number of my more recent books artfully arranged around a vase of flowers.

There was a hospitality table against the wall with decanters of iced tea and a few three-tiered cake stands loaded with scones and pastries.

Gloria led me to a desk that had my name as J. B. FLETCHER printed in all capital letters. When I complimented Gloria on the effort she'd put in to make this a hospitable event, she flushed with pride.

"It is a few minutes early, Mrs. Fletcher, but would you mind if I opened the door? The hallway is getting crowded."

How could I say no?

The first two readers came to my desk, wearing MacEwan University sweatshirts. I smiled and said, "You must be the two young ladies Gloria found sitting on the floor when she came to work this morning."

They giggled, and one flipped her dark ponytail over her shoulder and said, "We didn't want to miss out on meeting you. We are communications majors, and I want to write literary fiction."

"And I am going to handle Angie's public relations," her friend said confidently. "We heard you were going to be here and thought you might give us, you know, tips on how to succeed."

"The most important thing any writer can do is read, read, and read some more. It is the way we study our craft. And I would imagine that my public relations person, in addition to reading books in the fields of writers she represents, also reads the press releases and follows the activities of other publicists." I picked up my pen. "Now, how would you like these books signed?"

The next few signings went more quickly, and then Vivian and Iris were in front of me, each with a large stack of books. Vivian took the top book off her pile, opened it to the title page, and turned it toward me. She started to offer me the pen in her hand but then noticed that I had my own. Vivian said, "Silly me, I should have realized you would have a pen handy."

She slipped her pen back into her purse, but not before I recognized that the pen she nearly offered me was Seth's missing medical association pen.

Astounded as I was for the moment, I made an instant decision to continue with my signing and deal with the fandom duo when the event was finished. They left my desk and headed directly to the hospitality table, where I heard Iris say, "These look delicious. Louise Penny didn't have beaver tails at her signing, did she, Vivian?"

I signed for a while longer without any surprises until a striking dark-haired woman in a bright red blouse and blue jeans said, "I was glad to be off from work today so I could come to your signing."

The voice was quite familiar, and when I looked up, it was Sergeant Enook holding a copy of *The Dead Man Sang*.

"I am so flattered that you are here. I suppose you'd rather I inscribe the book to someone other than Sergeant Enook," I said.

She laughed. "That would be a bit pompous. My first name is Ahnah, spelled *A-h-n-a-h*. That is Inuit for 'a wise woman.' When I joined the police services, my mother said she thought maybe I am not so wise after all, but I do love my job."

I looked at the clock over the gift shop entrance and said,

"This signing will be ending in a few minutes. Perhaps we could have lunch, get to know each other as Ahnah and Jessica rather than as sergeant and witness."

"That sounds delightful. Lunch with one of my favorite mystery writers. I will wait for you in the lobby."

I signed books for several more readers, and suddenly the line was gone. I glanced at the clock. Ten after one. Not too far off the mark. I thanked Gloria for setting up such a lovely event, and when she asked me if I wanted her to pack up the leftover pastries for me to take to my room, I immediately suggested that she put them in the employee break room instead. "If I take them, I am bound to eat some, and I am not getting enough exercise on this trip as it is, so I have to watch my eating." Then I said good-bye.

I was halfway along the hall when Gloria called out and came running after me. "I nearly forgot. Mary Jo has some books that someone bought but could not stay to have signed. She told me to call her when you were nearly finished signing and she would bring them around, but she is not answering her phone. I hope I am not in trouble."

"Not at all. When you reach her, simply tell her I am lunching in the Victoria Room with my friend Ahnah. She can feel free to bring the books to me there, and I will be happy to sign them."

Gloria reached over and gave me a spontaneous kiss on the cheek. "You are a true gem, Mrs. Fletcher." And she ran back to the store.

I walked into the lobby, and Ahnah Enook waved to me from a chair where she sat reading while she waited for me. About ten feet away, the fandom duo and petty thieves Vivian Zhang and Iris Crenshaw were sitting with their heads together, chatting and laughing.

I marched directly over to them. "Vivian, I saw that you have Dr. Hazlitt's pen. You must return it immediately and everything else you have stolen. Mrs. Metzger's sunglasses, Margaret Gallagher's compact, everything."

Iris looked shocked. "Mrs. Fletcher, it is not really stealing. It's just a game we play. Vivian and I keep lists, you see, one for me and one for Vivian, or how would we know who is winning?"

"Winning?" I was incredulous. "What part of thievery includes the concept of winning? You make it sound like you are running some sort of contest."

This time Vivian was the one to answer. "Exactly. It is a contest. Iris and I play whenever we travel. It's not like we take anything of value. We each get points for originality, and I admit taking Dr. Hazlitt's pen wouldn't have counted much for originality except for the snakes on the pen clip."

I corrected her immediately. "You mean the caduceus, the symbol of medicine on a pen that means a great deal to my dear friend."

Vivian shrugged. "You don't understand. The contest really is harmless, and we get points for which of us found the first treasure each day. We have a chart in our room if you would like to see it."

I was having difficulty believing that neither Iris nor Vivian understood how serious their misbehavior was. I tried again. "You must return everything you have stolen and stop this 'contest' immediately, or I will have you arrested."

I held out my hand to Vivian. "Now give me Dr. Hazlitt's pen. Then gather up everything, and I mean everything, you have stolen and bring it to the reception desk and ask them to put the items in the lost and found. Explaining how you got the stolen property is entirely up to you, but in one hour, every single missing item must be available to its owner through the lost and found or, I promise, it is off to jail you go."

Iris looked up at me, wide eyed, and said, "You are a detective just like in your books. I had no idea."

"I am not." I pointed to Ahnah Enook, who had closed her book and was listening to our conversation. "The real detective is sitting right there, and unless you return everything you have stolen to its rightful owner or deposit it in the lost and found by the time she and I have finished lunch, I will tell her about the crimes you have committed, and you can imagine the result."

"I don't understand the harm, but if it will make you happy," Vivian said, and handed me Seth's pen, "we may as well do as you ask."

And they walked to the elevator with shoulders slumped as if they were players who'd just lost the championship game of the season.

Ahnah stood and shook my hand. "That was marvelous to watch. I do hope those two old birds have learned their lesson. It would be a shame for them to spend time in court and even possibly in the cells for what they clearly thought was nothing more than a prank."

"I agree. If only murder was as easy to solve as this petty theft." I put Seth's pen in my purse, and I led her to the Victoria Room for lunch.

Chapter Thirty

I was surprised to see Emma sitting by herself at a table. She greeted me cheerfully. "Hello, luv. I am so glad you are here. I didn't fancy a lonely lunch, and no one else seems to be around. I understand that your Cabot Cove buddies are off to visit the zoo, and, well, since the murder, Alan steers clear of everything other than the work he has to do. I believe that he and Derek had such a falling-out that Derek has missed three rehearsals in a row. Temperamental, that one. And Dennis is doing more of the heavy lifting than I would have guessed he could. Of course, it will be helpful on his résumé going forward."

Emma stopped dead and looked at Ahnah, who had taken the seat next to mine. "Now tell me, Jess, whatever have you done to warrant a police escort for something as mundane as lunch?"

"Today I am here as a fan of J. B. Fletcher's books, not as a sergeant. And Jessica was kind enough to invite me to stay for lunch. So please call me Ahnah."

"Only if you call me Emma."

"I am happy to, Emma," Ahnah said, and we all laughed.

We ordered lunch and, chatting about this and that, had begun talking about Ahnah's suggestions for the best stores to shop for women's clothes in Edmonton, when Mary Jo came in carrying a bag that I presumed contained the books she wanted me to sign.

"I am sorry to interrupt your lunch, Mrs. Fletcher, but Gloria said . . ."

"It's perfectly fine." I pointed to the chair on the other side of Ahnah. "I will sign them after lunch and get them back to you."

Our relaxing conversation continued. Emma asked Ahnah a number of questions about the Inuit culture, and I think we were both surprised to learn that many Inuits, including several of Ahnah's relatives, still lived and thrived in the Arctic tundra.

We were enjoying one another's company so much that we decided to move our conversation to the hotel garden so we wouldn't keep the servers any longer.

Ahnah passed me the bag that Mary Jo had left. "Don't forget your books."

I carried them out to the lobby and said, "I better take care of these right away. Let's stop a minute." I sat on the nearest chair and took three books out of the bag. *Ashes, Ashes Fall Down Dead*, *The Killer Called Collect*, and *Stone-Cold Dead on Wall Street*.

"Nice choices. I quite fancied *The Killer Called Collect*. I was afraid to answer my phone for weeks after reading it." Emma laughed; then she must have seen the look on my face, because she said, "Jess, what is it?"

I passed her the note that came with the books. Once she had a chance to read it, I said, "Do you see it?"

"I do. The one person who would never have crossed my mind but . . . you better show the sergeant," Emma said.

I passed the note to Ahnah, who seemed to have gone on high alert as soon as Emma referred to her by title and not by name. She stared at it, then handed it back to me and asked, "So what is our plan?"

"For starters, I am going to sign these books, and then, if you both agree, we three will each have to make some phone calls."

Ahnah said, "That would have been my plan as well. And after we make the calls and compare notes, perhaps we will have solved the petty thefts and the murder both in the same day."

An hour later, I was sitting in the living room of Alan Hughes's rehearsal suite. Emma was marching back and forth between the kitchenette and the windows that overlooked much of Edmonton.

"Honestly, Jessie, I don't see how you can sit there so calmly when a murderer will come through that door in a . . . in a foot-baller's jiffy." Emma pointed to the front door.

"If we have succeeded in luring the person here, it was your telephone call that did it. You were excellent. Your tone of voice was so frantic that I was standing right next to you, and I was convinced that all was lost."

Emma tossed her head. "Well, after all, I am an award-winning actress." Then she lowered her voice. "The door."

We heard a key turn in the lock, and as he opened the door, a man called out, "Emma, darling, how bad is it?"

Dennis Oliver walked into the room and stopped short when he saw me. "Oh, Mrs. Fletcher, so good of you to come and help Emma with her ankle. Has the hotel doctor taken a look?"

Then he realized Emma was standing perfectly straight with no support and no strap around her ankle. "Wait a minute. I thought you were injured and afraid you would have to bow out for the first few days of the revue. I'm here to help you coach Eileen McCarthy. Where is Eileen? What exactly is going on?"

I got up and stood next to Emma. "I came in Eileen's place. And I brought the books you wanted me to sign."

When I held them out to him, Dennis walked cautiously toward me. I could see that he was beginning to get the idea that something was off-kilter, but he wasn't quite sure what it might be.

Once he took the books, I handed him the typewritten note he had given Mary Jo when he asked her to have me sign them. "You might want to take the note as well. It was our initial clue and your fatal mistake."

He looked at what he had typed earlier in the day.

Unfortunately, I have to be at the
theatre today. Please do me the
honour of signing these.
Thank you.
Dennis Oliver

He stared at me, confusion simmering in his eyes.

"Look at each word very carefully," I suggested.

And when he did, he slowly realized what we had seen. "Well, you know, I've been in Canada for a while now working with Alan. We were here long before the actors showed up. I must have picked up the Canadian spelling of 'honour' and 'theatre' from working at the Jubilee."

"Barely two weeks earlier than we actors if Rosalie's emails about staging are to be believed," Emma said. "So that excuse won't work. Try again."

Before Dennis could reply, I said, "I have an American friend married to a Canadian. She has lived in Montreal these past twenty-five years, and when I receive letters from her, she still spells words the American way, just as she did when we were in school together. I suspect if they'd lived in Maine for all that time, her husband would still be spelling words the Canadian way, just as you did here."

"Look. I don't know what is going on here," Dennis practically growled, "but I have work to do. Good day, ladies."

He had taken two steps toward the door when it swung open and Constables Alexander and Michaud stood blocking any chance he had to exit. At the same time, Inspector Radigan, Sergeant Enook, and our own Sheriff Metzger came from the suite's bedroom to join us in the living room.

The inspector gave Sergeant Enook a brief nod, and she walked up to Dennis Oliver and said, "Peter Cross, you are under suspicion regarding the murder of Quinton Chabot."

I was sure she had more to say, but at that point Dennis/Peter went weak in the knees and started to fall. Mort rushed over to help Ahnah get Dennis into a chair while Emma brought him a glass of water. He drank greedily, and the color soon returned to his face.

The room was silent until Dennis said, "How did you know?"

Inspector Radigan looked at me and said, "Mrs. Fletcher, if you would begin."

I nodded. "It's always the little things. I had already noticed that you seemed irritated by Mr. Chabot's presence anytime the two of you were in the same room. And it was very evident that

Mr. Chabot was gleeful to have the unexpected chance to taunt you when you walked into the lobby of the Jubilee Auditorium and found us all at the impromptu champagne party that Derek Braverman had sponsored for 'Emma's friends,' as he calls us.

"After Mr. Chabot was killed, I discovered by chance that he had a habit of blackmailing people for financial gain. Still, I never thought he was blackmailing you, the assistant director. Since he was already blackmailing Alan Hughes, who was the director, what could you possibly have to offer him? I thought you were a foreigner, an American, so what could Quint Chabot have discovered about you that would entice him to extortion?

"But when I opened the package of books and saw your note, your spelling indicated to me that you were not an American. You were either a Brit or a Canadian. If that was true, what else about you was false? It happened I was with Emma and Sergeant Enook when I received the note. We all came to the same conclusion. Emma insisted that your accent was definitely North American, and Sergeant Enook agreed. Inspector Radigan, perhaps you should take it from here."

The inspector said, "Sergeant Enook called me, explained Mrs. Fletcher's quandary, and asked me to examine closely the passports we had taken from all the non-Canadians involved with the revue, particularly your American passport, Mr. Cross.

"Our experts determined that it was an excellent forgery, but a forgery nevertheless. At that point, we ran your fingerprints, which were, of course, all over your passport, and as it turns out, you, Peter Cross, were arrested in Calgary for impaired driving three years ago.

"In the meantime, Mrs. Fletcher was wise enough to call Sheriff Metzger, and he contacted me immediately to offer support. His aid was invaluable. He telephoned one of his former colleagues in the New York City Police Department, who was able to ascertain that Dennis Oliver was still living at home in Brooklyn, New York, while working on an off-Broadway play in Manhattan. Mr. Oliver admitted that he had lent his résumé to his friend Peter Cross so that Peter could apply for a job somewhere in Canada. He thought he was helping a friend who was down on his luck and looking for work. Perhaps, Mr. Cross, you wouldn't mind telling us exactly why you went to so much trouble for this particular job."

The man we'd all known as Dennis Oliver asked for another glass of water, which Ahnah Enook brought to him immediately.

He started rolling the glass between his hands, and then he began to speak in the hollow voice of a man who has lost everything. "My name is Peter Cross. I am an author presently writing a tell-all book about Derek Braverman. When I heard about this revue, I asked my friend Dennis Oliver to share his résumé with me. I bought a forged passport and got the job."

He took a drink of water and then continued. "Everything was fine when I first got here. I knew enough about theater operations to understand just how lowly a job assistant director is. Then one night, I walked into the Beaver Bar, and Quint Chabot happened to be loading fresh bottles of liquor on the back bar. Quint recognized me as Peter Cross.

"Quint had tended bar in Tandy's, a hangout for wannabe writers and artists in Calgary. Worse luck, he recognized me at once. We had a friendly conversation and I explained what I was doing, but I never mentioned my book. I let him think I was just hard up and needed the job.

"My circumstances didn't matter to Quint. He only saw an

opportunity. He had already blackmailed Alan for a close-to-no-show job and additional payoffs on the side. He started by asking me for a few dollars, and then he pestered me for more and more money. He didn't believe me when I told him the well had run dry. So he took to using my real last name as a tease, saying things to me like 'Don't be so cross' whenever my colleagues were around."

He stood up, his water glass crashing to the floor. "Don't you understand? I couldn't let him get in my way. I am writing the quintessential book about Derek Braverman. I was determined to destroy his reputation and make myself famous in the process."

Inspector Radigan signaled his officers and said, "Be that as it may, it is my guess that you will write it under the watchful eye of Correctional Service Canada."

After Sergeant Enook and the constables escorted Peter Cross out of the suite, Inspector Radigan thanked Emma, Mort, and me for what he described as our "superlative" cooperation, and he bid us good day.

"And who do you suppose will assume the joyful task of telling Alan 'Blowhard' Hughes that on the one hand, his blackmailer may be forever gone, but on the other hand, so is his lackey." Emma did a little dance while pointing to herself with both index fingers. "With only six days until opening night, poor Alan is totally on his own. I can't wait to see his face."

Chapter Thirty-One

After Dennis Oliver/Peter Cross had confessed to murdering Quint Chabot, the days flew by. Although I didn't see much of Emma because she was rehearsing nonstop, my Cabot Cove friends and I alternated our time between relaxing and touring.

At long last, the evening we'd all been waiting for arrived, and Rob was weaving the limousine effortlessly through the traffic converging on the Northern Alberta Jubilee Auditorium for the opening night of *Derek Braverman's Old-Time Revue*.

After we left the hotel, Rob made a slight detour so we could drive through the Neon Sign Museum, an amazing exhibit of vintage neon signs that reflected the history of Edmonton. It was such a delight that we asked Rob to circle around and drive through again, which he gladly did.

As we got closer to the Jubilee Auditorium, Maureen was bubbling with excitement. "I have never been to an opening night of a show before unless you count the time I substituted as wardrobe mistress for the Cabot Cove Players when Marion Stipple had to go to Portland because her father had a stroke. And even then, I was in the wings, not in the audience."

"Well, honey," Mort said, "tonight you will be a princess sitting fifth row center. I don't know how Emma managed it, but I will be forever grateful."

"Ayuh, our trip couldn't have a better ending," Seth said. "We have been able to see so much of this glorious city, and now we get to watch Emma doing what she does best up on the stage, singing and dancing and, I hope, a bit of comedy."

"Not to mention we were party to a murder solved, justice served." Maureen gave me a wink, which I returned.

Rob pulled up to the theater's main entrance and came around to open our door. "It will be crowded at show's end, but you just stand your ground and I will meet you right here."

"Oh, Rob, how thoughtless of us. I wish we had gotten a ticket to the show for you," Maureen said.

Rob reached into his breast pocket, pulled out a ticket, and said with a grin, "Not to worry. Ms. Macgill sent me a ticket by messenger this morning. And I won't be too many rows behind you."

"Leave it to Emma," I said to my friends as we walked inside. "She does think of everything. And before she left for the theater, she told me that she was planning a massive surprise for the audience, the players, and especially for Alan Hughes."

"Did she give you a hint?" Mort asked.

"Only that the high point of her part of the show is supposed to be when she reprises her recent smash performance as the star in the London revival of *Mame*, but according to Emma, it won't quite be the peak. She assured me there will be more to it," I said.

*　　*　　*

The entire show was nothing short of stunning. For all the difficulty he presented as a person, as an actor Derek was superb. He excelled in his monologue, and later he got warm and comfy with the audience in a poignant trip down memory lane of his lengthy career. Not to mention his duets with Emma, which brought those in the audience to their feet.

Frederick and Gracelyn performed their magic tricks so expertly that they drew ohhs and ahhs from all corners of the Auditorium. I was especially pleased that Gracelyn appeared poised and self-confident throughout their segment now that she was no longer worried about losing her job.

When Jorge came onstage, I expected that he would sing a few ballads. I had no idea that he had comedic talent as well. He interspersed jokes and humorous stories with showstopping tunes. The audience loved it.

Emma had already been onstage several times, including two sets with Derek, when, dressed in a sizzling red gown, she walked onto the stage. I whispered to Maureen, "This must be it."

When the orchestra began to play, Emma spun around once, turned into Mame, and literally belted out "We Need a Little Christmas," and as she sang the final words, red and green confetti sprinkled down, not only on the stage but on the audience as well.

"There's your surprise," Seth said, brushing the Christmas colors off his shoulder.

Everyone laughed and clapped, while Emma alternated curtsies and bows. Then, instead of the curtain coming down, Emma walked to stage left, held out her hand, and Eileen McCarthy, wearing a matching dress, joined her onstage. Emma signaled the orchestra leader, and as soon as I heard the first few notes, I knew.

Maureen looked at the revue program and murmured, "Eileen isn't mentioned here."

"But it takes two to properly act out the lyrics while they sing 'Bosom Buddies,' or the audience will lose the comedic essence of the song. Now shush," I whispered.

The standing ovation Emma and Eileen received lasted nearly as long as the one the audience gave to the entire ensemble at the end of the show.

Dozens of people, complete strangers to us, filled the Silver Ballroom for the after-party. Seth looked around and said, "Now I understand why we are not in the Victoria Room. Who are all these people?"

"I suppose they are theater people, here to see and be seen. But there is the only person I am interested in." I waved to Emma, who was coming our way.

She planted a solid kiss on Seth's cheek and then squeezed me in a lengthy hug. "So tell me, luv, did you enjoy the show? Was it worth the trip from Cabot Cove?"

"It certainly was. You were spectacular and devious as always. How did you manage to pull off having an additional song, not to mention an additional cast member in the show, without Alan's knowledge?" I was laughing even as I asked the question.

"Well, it helped that the maestro—Raymondo, as he likes to be called—and I had worked together a few times. Twice in London and once in New Zealand. All I had to do was get him to listen to Eileen sing, and he was in on the secret."

"And Alan? How did he react?" I wondered aloud.

"Since two rather prominent Canadian directors have already given Eileen their business cards and asked her to call to schedule auditions, I suspect Alan will be taking full credit for discovering a bright new star."

Chapter Thirty-Two

It didn't take long for me to get back into my normal routine once I was home again in Cabot Cove. One Tuesday morning after breakfast at Mara's with Seth, Mort, and Dan Andrews, I biked over to the Fruit and Veg, took advantage of a sale they were having on salad greens, and pedaled home, my mind totally absorbed by the synopsis I was working through for my next book.

As I walked my bicycle down my front pathway, I noticed that the mail had been delivered. I put the groceries away and went out to the mailbox. The first two envelopes were standards, my power bill and my semiannual water bill. Hidden behind my sub-scription issue of *Alfred Hitchcock Mystery Magazine* was a plain white envelope. I saw the Canadian stamp and thought Emma had taken a few minutes to send me the latest gossip about the revue, which, by the time I'd left Edmonton, was completely sold out for every future performance.

I didn't recognize the return address, but I was tremendously pleased when I read the enclosed letter.

Dear Jessica,

Even though we met under terrible circumstances, I feel as though we've become good friends, and I want to share my news. Inspector Radigan has advised me that I am being promoted to staff sergeant early next month.

While my superiors were impressed with my overall performance since attaining the rank of sergeant, they believe that my ability to work cooperatively with members of the community to solve the murder of Quinton Chabot proved I was ready for more responsibility.

I want you to know that, moving forward in my career, I will always value your wisdom. At each crime scene, I will hear your commonsense voice saying, "It's always the little things."

I am honored to have met you, and I hope our paths cross again someday.

Sincerely,
Ahnah Enook

I read it again and then picked up my phone, hit SPEED DIAL, and left a message on Seth's voicemail. "Hi. It's Jessica. I hope you can stop by for coffee later today. I've received the most wonderful letter. I can't wait for you to read it."

Then I dialed Maureen Metzger.

Ready to find
your next great read?

Let us help.

Visit prh.com/nextread